COMMAND DECISIONS

BOOK THREE OF THE EMPIRE OF BONES SAGA

TERRY MIXON

YOWLING
CAT PRESS

Command Decisions

Copyright © 2015 by Terry Mixon

Published by Yowling Cat Press ®

Digital edition date: 6/21/2023

Print ISBN: 978-1947376113

Large Print ISBN: 978-1947376175

Cover art - image copyrights as follows:

Big Stock Photo/1971yes

Deposit Photos/kevron2002 (Kevin Carden)

DepositPhotos/innovari (Luca Oleastri)

Donna Mixon

Cover design and composition by Donna Mixon

Print edition design and layout by Terry Mixon

Audio edition performed and produced by Veronica Giguere

Reach her at: v@voicesbyveronica.com

ALSO BY TERRY MIXON

You can always find the most up to date listing of Terry's titles on his Amazon Author Page.

Note: the links below (ebook only, obviously) redirect you to my website where you can click a button to go to Amazon. This allows me to participate in Amazon's associates program and earn a little more. Sorry for any inconvenience.

The Last Hunter

The Last Hunter

Bonds of Blood

Alpha Strike

The Enemy Revealed

Command Authority

The Grand Conspiracy

Shield of Humanity

Fog of War

Ships of the Line

Operation Liberty

The Empire of Bones Saga

Empire of Bones

Veil of Shadows

Command Decisions

Ghosts of Empire

Paying the Price

Recon in Force

Box Sets

The Empire of Bones Saga Volume 1

The Empire of Bones Saga Volume 2

The Empire of Bones Saga Volume 3

The Empire of Bones Saga Volume 4

Humanity Unlimited Publisher's Pack 1

Humanity Unlimited Publisher's Pack 2

Want to get updates from Terry about new books and other general nonsense going on in his life? He promises there will be cats. Go to TerryMixon.com/Mailing-List and sign up.

DEDICATION

This book would not be possible without the love and support of my beautiful wife. Donna, I love you more than life itself.

ACKNOWLEDGMENTS

Once again, the people who read my books before you see them have saved me. Thanks to Tracy Bodine, Michael Falkner, Cain Hopwood, Kristopher Neidecker, Bob Noble, Jon Paul Olivier, and Jason Young for making me look good.

I also want to thank my readers for putting up with me. You guys are great.

1

"Behold. Imperial City, the capital of the Terran Empire."

Jared Mertz stepped up to the railing and looked out over the vast city. Monolithic buildings stretched as far as the eye could see in every direction. Sleek grav cars in every imaginable color flitted past at breakneck speeds.

The city wasn't sterile, though. Gardens bloomed in planters on the steep walls where the sun could get to them, and wide green spaces lined the ground far, far below. The scents in the air held a hint of nature.

Pedestrians dominated the ground between the buildings like a swarm of insects. They also filled wide walkways that crossed from one building to another in an endless stream. He'd never seen so many people at one time.

The implant recording fooled his senses. It felt as though he'd gone back in time to stand in the Old Empire at its heyday.

Reginald Bell gazed down with a serene expression. "New York City. The most populous metroplex in the old United States. Two hundred and fifty million people. The first Terran emperor changed its name to Imperial City, but the residents here never accepted it. Even though the United States of America no longer existed as a political entity, New Yorkers never forgot their heritage. Their attitude was legendary."

Jared tilted his head back and looked up. Even though they were on the three hundredth floor, the building still towered over them. "Just how tall is this building?"

"Four hundred and fifty-two floors, counting the penthouse level. It provided homes and businesses for a quarter of a million people. I suspect many of them never left it during their lives. Not even in the end."

A bird landed on the railing about ten meters away. It was a smooth gray and very fat. It stared at them as though it was waiting for them to feed it.

Jared shook his head. "I can't believe how real this looks. I can hear the birds, I can smell the ocean, and I can see everything down to the smallest detail. How is that possible?"

"They brought in special equipment capable of recording in far more detail than any human being can actually sense, even with Princess Kelsey's commando implants. They wanted every Fleet service member to be able to see Imperial City as it was. There are a number of other recordings just like this from across the Empire in *Courageous*'s data banks. Unfortunately, they're made for implant viewing only."

Jared sent a mental command to his implants to terminate the vid. Honestly, the word "vid" felt like the greatest understatement he'd ever made. The incredible view disappeared, leaving him sitting in his quarters aboard the Imperial Fleet battlecruiser *Courageous*. Across the coffee table from him, Bell opened his eyes.

The ice in Jared's drink had almost melted, but he took a deep sip anyway. The alcohol burned going down. "All of that historical detail and only we can see it? That's going to make the historians revolt if we don't capture that freighter and its implant supplies. They'll demand we launch an expedition deeper into the Old Empire immediately."

The old man laughed. "I imagine you're right. Not even the prospect of the Pale Ones would deter them. *Courageous* might be able to display these vids on a monitor, but much of the fine detail is going to be lost."

The Old Empire had designed so many things for people with implants. They hadn't considered unenhanced human beings needing to access them. Yet here in the post-Fall Terran Empire, only the three of them had those implants.

The cataclysmic rebellion and civil war half a millennium ago had wrecked the Old Empire and killed uncounted trillions of people. As of yet, they had no idea how many feral humans survived amid the bones of the Empire. Or how many isolated pockets of civilization like the Kingdom of Pentagar survived.

The Kingdom occupied a single planet. The resurrected Terran Empire added several dozen heavily populated worlds and perhaps twice that number of frontier planets to the count. That left tens of thousands of systems that had once been part of the old Terran Empire to explore.

To do that, they had to deal with the artificial intelligences that had staged the revolt and the poor bastards they'd forcibly implanted.

Bell picked up his glass and sipped his whiskey. "Now that the Pentagarans have their first ships ready, when will you be returning to Erorsi? Have the recordings the AI made changed your plans?"

During the final battle to control the system next door to Pentagar, Kelsey had defeated the controlling AI and salvaged its data banks. In the process of gathering everything they could, the marines had pulled data off the communications systems the AI had used. The news had not been good.

"We're still reviewing the oldest of the transmissions. They go back over five hundred years. I don't think we'll get any deeper shocks than we've already gotten, though. The AI's communications records told us everything we needed to know."

The AI controlling Erorsi received supplies each year about the same time from what certainly appeared to be a ship from the Old Empire. The most recent conversation between a man and the AI had been brief but chilling. The human had looked like a Fleet officer. Definitely not a savage like the Pale Ones.

Unlike this man, the feral humans didn't even seem capable of speech. Once Princess Kelsey and the marines had destroyed the AI that controlled them, the primitives had ceased to be a direct threat. They'd still need to summon them to a central area and overwrite the corrupted implant code. Then the poor bastards could live out their lives in whatever peace they could find.

The man in the recording spoke to the AI in an obsequious tone, declaring that the freighter had all the supplies the AI couldn't build for itself. Including implant hardware. The AI told the man that it had adolescent human beings for them in trade. Children. He shuddered to think of how the others might be using those kids.

Obviously, something of the Old Empire survived. Something twisted and terrible. Jared's problems had become several orders of magnitude more complicated with the revelation.

"Based on the rough schedule of the resupply, it'll be along in another few weeks," Jared said. "We go back to Erorsi tomorrow and set up an ambush. We need that freighter's cargo, and we cannot allow it to raise the alarm.

"Two-thirds of Pentagaran ships will hide behind Erorsi while the rest lie in wait with *Courageous* in the asteroid belt. We'll catch the freighter and its escort, if any, between the hammer and anvil. The marines will clear the freighter before Kelsey boards to work with its computer."

Bell nodded. "You're short on missiles, so will you be able to handle any escort?"

"*Courageous* says the escort is normally a destroyer, so I think so. We have three dozen missiles left. Any battle will leave us critically short, though, so I'm hoping this is one of the years when the freighter doesn't have an escort. It comes alone more than half the time."

Bell took a sip of his drink. "I hope that's how it plays out. My people have enough problems. The kinetic strike might not have directly hurt us, but our facility is dependent on hidden farms for food. The impact sent a tremendous amount of debris into the atmosphere. That means a harsh winter that will last half a decade, if we're lucky. The crops are dead."

"Hopefully all the supplies we brought will tide you through. That won't help the primitive humans out in the wild, though. I'm afraid they're in for a very rough time."

"It's a tragedy," Bell agreed. "One bit of good news. We found where the AI was holding this year's tithe of children. Hundreds of boys and girls between the ages of four and six. We're doing what we can to fit them into our community."

The older man shook his head. "That's a problem we can solve. What if they send someone looking for the missing ships?"

"They might not. The communications logs have several instances when the AI and the humans had discussed the lack of a freighter the previous year. It sounds as though they just shrug when a freighter fails to return and send extra supplies next year. Hopefully by then, we'll be able to deal with them. We don't really have a choice. Once we stop the freighter, we'll do what we can to help your people recover Erorsi."

"We appreciate your assistance, but that's going to take much, much longer than either one of us has left to dedicate to it. Your people will be trying to find your way home soon. Are you taking a Pentagaran embassy with you? Perhaps Crown Princess Elise?" Bell's lips quirked up in a smile.

Jared wished she was coming along, but that wasn't realistic. Their relationship had grown closer over the last several months. They'd taken to dining together almost every night and frequently took sightseeing trips around the Kingdom, enjoying one another's company. They'd become intimate in the last few weeks, but no one could possibly know about that. They'd taken elaborate precautions.

He didn't want to admit he'd fallen in love with her, because that kind of relationship was doomed from the start. One day she'd rule her people in her father's place, while he'd be going far away, perhaps never to return.

Jared sighed. "I'm certain they'll be sending an embassy with us, but I doubt Elise will be coming along."

"Well, I hope for both your sakes that you're wrong."

Jared felt his gaze narrowing. "Pardon me?"

The older man smiled. "Don't frown at me, Captain Mertz. I'm just making an observation. The two of you seem so well suited to one another, and I'd rather not lose the pool."

"Pool? What pool?"

"The pool the crew has on whether she's coming along with us. I'm rather pleased to say that most of us are behind you. The Pentagaran members of the crew think she's not coming. The rest of us are wagering love will win out."

His heart leapt into his throat. "I'm not sure what you mean."

Bell laughed. "Then you're the last one to know, my boy. Everyone can see how the two of you feel about one another. That may well be the worst-kept secret ever."

The news flabbergasted Jared. They'd been so careful!

"Please tell me you're kidding about the pool. Who knows?"

The older man shook his head, his eyes full of laughter. "We go out of our way to spare your dignity and to give you both the privacy you deserve, but we all know. Should I place a bet for you? No, that sounds unethical now that I think about it."

The buzzer to his cabin spared Jared the agony of figuring out how to respond. He rose and walked over to the hatch, still eying Bell. He only remembered that he could've checked the vid feed with his implants after he'd opened the hatch.

His half sister, Princess Kelsey Bandar, breezed past him. Sister, he corrected. She'd insisted they drop the qualifier. He didn't imagine her full brother, Ethan, would feel the same way.

"You wouldn't believe the day I've had," she complained. "Talbot is a slave driver. Tell me you have beer."

Senior Sergeant Talbot, her ever-present Imperial Marine guard, followed her in with an apologetic nod to his commanding officer. "She's exaggerating, Captain. She barely broke a sweat."

Jared closed the hatch with a grin at their repartee and headed for his kitchen. "I have some beer chilled down to the edge of freezing for you. As always. What exactly did the monster have you doing today?"

Not anything she couldn't handle, he was sure. The commando implants the Pale Ones had forced upon his sister made her almost superhuman. Graphene-reinforced bones, artificially enhanced musculature, and sophisticated combat programming in her implants made her improbably formidable.

Kelsey took the beer from him, twisted the cap off, and drank deeply. "Running," she said when she'd finished a long draft. "He made me run up a mountain."

Talbot opened his own beer more sedately. "Pfftt. That was barely a hill. My drill instructor made us sprint up much more difficult terrain than that before breakfast."

"In unpowered combat armor with a pack that weighed more than twice your weight? I doubt that."

"With that exact weight," he shot back. "It's not my fault you're such a little bitty thing."

She smiled wickedly at the burly marine. "That's not what you said when I tossed your ass around the mat yesterday. I seem to recall you saying something more along the lines of 'I think you broke me.' Isn't that right?"

Jared opened his mouth to add his opinion when it hit him. Perhaps it was because Bell had raised the thought in his mind, but now he wondered how he could've missed the way these two were looking at one another. The way they talked to one another.

Their body language spoke volumes. Talbot reached out to touch Kelsey's arm as she sat down, and she wasn't pulling back when their legs pressed together. It spoke of just the same kind of intimacy that he and Elise shared.

They were lovers.

His sister was the daughter of the Terran emperor, second in line to the Imperial Throne. Talbot was a marine noncom charged with guarding and training her. For helping her to adjust to the implants. For them to be involved in a relationship was… none of his damned business, he realized.

She wasn't an officer in his chain of command. She was a civilian. There were no laws or Fleet regulations against them having a relationship.

Kelsey frowned at him. "What's wrong? Did something go down the wrong pipe?"

He nodded. "That's exactly what happened. Sorry. As for running up a mountain, that doesn't sound like much of a challenge for you, Kelsey. I've seen how much you can lift in the weight room. Why was it so stressful?"

"Because he made me do it at a full run for over an hour. I don't care how enhanced you are, your real muscles will complain in half that time."

Jared sat down next to Bell. "I wouldn't last ten minutes. I'm a Fleet officer, not a ground pounder." He gave Talbot an apologetic glance. "No offense."

"None taken."

Jared pinged Bell's implants and asked for a private communications channel, which the other man quickly accepted.

Is there a pool on how long these two are going to be together?

Bell's eyes widened slightly as he looked at the two. *Are you sure? They're always behaving like this.*

I'm pretty sure. Let's find out.

Jared smiled at Kelsey. "Did you know that there's some crazy pool going on with the crew? They think Elise and I are a couple. They're betting on whether or not she comes back to Avalon with us. Isn't that crazy?"

"Really? I hadn't heard." Kelsey looked at Talbot. "You know every gambling table on this ship. Have you heard about this?"

The marine's eyes darted to Jared. "Ah… I might have heard something like that. Purely speculation, I'm sure."

Kelsey slapped Talbot on the shoulder. "There's a betting pool and you didn't tell me? Put me down for whatever you bet on them staying together, because I know that's where the smart money is."

Talbot gave her a flat look.

"Oh, and there's another pool," Jared added. "You might want to get in on it, too."

"What's that?" Kelsey asked.

"It's a wager on how your father reacts when he finds out you're dating a marine. I have my money on him sending Talbot to Thule for the next decade or so."

Kelsey managed to stare blankly at him, but she flushed. That was all Jared needed to know his suspicion was correct. They really were lovers.

His sister sighed. "I knew someone would figure it out eventually, but I never dreamed they'd have a pool."

The marine shook his head as he stared pityingly at her. "There is no pool. I'd have heard. He just baited you out."

She narrowed her eyes at Jared. "That's mean. I didn't bet against you staying with Elise, and I've known about the two of you for months."

"That's only because you didn't know about the pool," Jared said dryly. "We've only been dating for six weeks."

"*You've* only been dating six weeks. Elise started a little sooner. She's subtle like that. Are we going to have a problem about Russ and me?"

It took him a moment to realize she was talking about Talbot. No one called him by his first name. Jared suspected the man's mother called him Talbot.

Jared held his hands up. "No problems from me, though you're going to need a new guard."

She bristled. "That's bull."

Talbot shook his head. "No. The captain is right. Lieutenant Reese needs to appoint a new guard. I'll let him know."

"Are you serious?" The look she gave the marine said that he'd be better off if he weren't.

The man had his work cut out for him, Jared decided. Thank God Elise was much less bossy.

Jared decided to let Talbot off the hook. "Captain's orders. I need your guard to be thinking clearly at all times. I'm not saying you have to go public, as I apparently have, or that your relationship is inappropriate. It's not, and it's no one's business but yours. You'll just have to accept this though, because the change in guards is not subject to negotiation."

Bell, who'd been silent throughout the exchange, ventured a comment. "It's really for the best. Your security team needs to focus on your health and well-being at all times, even when you occasionally disagree with them. Much like the Imperial Guard was with the emperor in my day."

His sister squeezed the bridge of her nose. "I suppose I knew this would eventually come up." She looked at Talbot. "I don't mean that in a negative way. I'm happy that we're together. I just don't want my position to be a negative for you."

Talbot smiled. "We're lucky we had the quiet time we did. If the captain guessed that we're a couple, I'm sure others are wondering. We should beat them to the punch and be up front about it. If you want to."

"Of course I want to." She lifted her chin and stared at Jared. "We have to leave for the surface in the next half hour, but I want to get one thing settled right now. What are the rules about cohabitation? Can he move to my quarters?"

Jared nodded. "There's no rule that says marines need to live in marine country. Relationships with Fleet personnel do happen. He just needs to clear it with his CO. Lieutenant Reese won't say no. How long are the two of you going to be gone? We're flipping to the Courageous system in a few hours to swap the crew on *Athena* and return."

He'd made it a point to rename the system they'd found the battlecruiser in, a move the Pentagarans had heartily endorsed. If nothing else, the system would have a significant mining presence for the foreseeable future. Any name was better than the bland number the Imperial Stellar Catalog had listed for the system.

"Don't wait up," Kelsey said. "I'm meeting Elise for breakfast in a few hours. With the difference between planetary time in the capital and *Courageous*, it's almost dawn down there. Don't worry. I'll let her know you've been outed."

The planetary rotational period was somewhat shorter than Terran Standard Time, so they'd drifted into an almost opposite timeframe over the last few weeks. Which made secretly dating even more challenging.

"Thanks," he said dryly. "She probably already knows. It's me that didn't notice everyone staring at us. I'm surprised it isn't all over the news programs and gossip columns."

"She probably has a deal with them to keep it under wraps. Well, we need to get going. The cutter won't wait." She and Talbot rose to their feet.

Bell rose with them. "I'm afraid I'm going to call it a night as well, Captain. I'm due to transfer to one of the Pentagaran vessels. They're taking me home to oversee the last of the preparations on Erorsi's surface. Good luck and thank you for an enjoyable evening. Highness, Senior Sergeant, my congratulations to you both."

Jared saw them all out before returning to his office to go over a few more pieces of paperwork. It was a never-ending chore, though his implants made faster work of it. When he'd had enough, he took a shower and readied himself for bed.

* * *

HE WOKE SOMETIME LATER when a voice spoke in his head. *This unit is sorry to wake you, Captain,* the ship's computer said through his implants. *There is a priority signal for you from* Athena.

Thanks, Courageous. *I'll take it at my desk.*

They must've already flipped, because his old ship was on station near the weak flip point in the Courageous system. Jared threw his uniform on and sat at his desk. He touched the flashing icon, and the screen cleared to show *Athena*'s bridge. Ensign Danielle Cruz, one of his cutter pilots, sat in the command chair.

Out here in the backend of nowhere, his old ship only needed a skeleton crew. The command experience was good for her and the other junior officers he'd assigned to the ship for the time being.

"Good morning, Captain," Cruz said crisply. "I'm sorry to disturb you so early, but a probe from home just came through the flip point. Fleet has found us."

2

Kelsey enjoyed a leisurely breakfast with Elise. Talbot had declined their offer to join them and gone to bed. She hoped to join him in a few hours.

Elise, it turned out, had been aware that her relationship with Jared was an open secret for some time. She laughed when Kelsey told her how Jared had reacted to the betting pool by clapping her hands and grinning like a fiend.

"That's delightful! He's such a reserved man in public. This will do him a universe of good. When the gossip columns finally find out that the 'rumors' they've been printing for the last two months are true, they'll be out in force. It will be a feeding frenzy."

Kelsey blinked. "Reserved? Jared? You're understating things, don't you think? He's the most serious man I know."

"Then you don't know your brother as well as you believe. He has a wicked sense of humor. He's full of all kinds of surprises when you get him alone."

"Uh huh. I suppose I need to have the official 'what are your intentions toward my brother' talk. I hate to be casting gloom on the moment, but once we take care of the rebel freighter, we're going to be striking out for home. We have to warn them."

Elise nodded, her irreverent mood vanishing into a serious expression. "I've been discussing that with my father over the last few days. As the heir, common wisdom declares that I need to be here, but I believe I'd be serving the Kingdom by accompanying you back to the Empire. I've decided to head the delegation from Pentagar."

Kelsey wasn't sure that was the best idea. "What if something happens to your father while you're gone?"

"My cousin is the next in line to the Throne. He'd assume a caretaker role until I returned. We've already presented this to the Royal Council and Parliament. In secret session, of course. They agreed with me after much arguing. I'm much more concerned about your approval, though."

"You don't need my approval, but I do. Very much. I think he'll be very happy that you're coming with us, and so am I."

"I hope you're right. I see something in him that I haven't seen in any other man I've dated. I think he might be the one. If so, that will bring our people closer still." Elise took a sip of her coffee. "But enough about me. How are things going with Talbot?"

Kelsey smiled more widely. "I figured if anyone knew about the two of us, it would be you. We're doing very well. In fact, Jared figured it out last night. I was worried that he was going to throw a fit, but he didn't. Once the two of us get back to the ship, we're going to make our relationship public. I figure everything will be perfectly fine right up until the point where my father finds out I'm dating a marine. His head will explode, my brother will inherit the Imperial Throne, and he will banish the two of us to Thule for life."

The crown princess of Pentagar laughed. "Oh, I hardly think it'll be that bad. I'm certain that your father will be pleased that you've found someone who makes you happy. Unfortunately, I do worry that your brother's antipathy towards Jared will cause him to take some kind of stand against the alliance between our people."

Kelsey shook her head. "Ethan is many things, but stupid is not one of them. He won't allow his feelings for Jared to color Imperial relations. He'll do what's best for the Empire. In this case, that's a strong alliance with Pentagar."

"But he might not like me very much personally. I understand, but that's unfortunate. How do you think he'll treat Jared when he assumes the Throne? Hopefully, of course, that will be far in the future. Your father is a fit man in his prime, so I expect he'll rule for many years to come."

Kelsey continued to eat while she considered her reply. Feeding her enhanced metabolism was no easy task. She ate like *two* professional sports stars. She'd slowly been getting over her embarrassment at having to gorge at every meal.

"I'm certain you're right. Ethan won't be succeeding my father for another couple of decades, and that won't be because my father is ill. Everyone already knows he plans to retire once he reaches a certain point in his life. By then, hopefully, my brother will have found someone to share his life with and have kids of his own. I, thankfully, will be nowhere near the line of succession at that point."

"You don't miss that?"

"Not one bit," Kelsey said fervently. "I'm not looking to rule the Empire. I'll be more than happy with a husband who loves me and kids of my own. I'll cheerfully dedicate my life to helping other people with this whole implant thing."

Elise nodded. "I'm glad to hear that. Based on how well your people have accepted your condition, I don't think you'll have much difficulty at home. My people seem to have gotten over their initial shock. That's very promising.

"At some point, we're going to start doing implants on a larger scale, and you're setting a tremendous example. We'll literally be following in your footsteps. In fact, if this freighter has replacement parts, I'll be the first in line."

That surprised Kelsey. As much as she tried to put a good face on it, the trauma of the Pale Ones forcibly implanting her colored her reactions. She fought that reflexive reaction every day. "You'd do that? Why?"

Elise's eyes danced devilishly. "Well, I can only imagine what it would be like for two implanted people to be a couple. You know, in the bedroom."

Kelsey paused with her coffee cup halfway to her mouth. "I'd never even considered that. Wow. That's even more intimate than being intimate. It would be like being in the other person's head. I wonder…"

She held up her hand. "Never mind. I don't think I want to think about that. What are your plans for the rest the morning? I'm more wired than I expected, so I'm not going to sleep just yet. For whatever reason, I'm able to get by on a lot less sleep now that I'm implanted. I can take a nap this afternoon, and I'll be good to go."

Elise leaned forward curiously. "How much sleep do you need?"

"If I get five or six hours, I'm good to go. I'll admit that a full night's sleep is a luxury, but it's not something I absolutely need. Talbot will be asleep for long enough for me to get a good rest, if you've got somewhere interesting for us to go."

Elise set her coffee cup down. "As a matter of fact, I do. Repair crews have finally stabilized the Parliament Building, and we're going to remove Master Vestor's carving to be sure the explosion didn't damage it. It was too dangerous to recover before now."

The thought of all the damage the late and unlamented Lord Admiral Shrike had caused trying to kill them made her sad. Priceless art had filled the Pentagaran Parliament Building before the assassination attempt. The explosion must've destroyed so many irreplaceable things.

She hoped Master Vestor's carving had survived unscathed. Based on the incredible level of detail in the carving she was taking back to Avalon, even the slightest damage to the work hanging behind the speaker's podium in the Parliament Building would be disastrous.

"Let's do it."

The two of them made their way to a waiting grav limo. Even though the Pentagarans had crushed Shrike and his rebellion, there were still a large number of Royal Guards escorting them in other vehicles. Several military airships flew high overhead. The crown princess's security detail was taking no chances.

When they arrived at the Parliament Building, Kelsey was dismayed to see how extensive the damage was. The carved reliefs and columns she'd admired along the front of the building were gone. It looked like the explosion had caused the entire façade to collapse.

They'd cleared the debris, and scaffolding showed where repair crews were busy replacing the lost portions of the building.

"My God. I had no idea the destruction was so extensive. We must've only barely escaped being crushed."

"That's not so far from the truth," Elise agreed. "Thankfully, the police had begun clearing the building as soon as the shooting started. Otherwise, so many more people would've been killed or injured."

The thought of it made Kelsey burn with anger. She'd attended the man's execution to show her resolve. It had been awful, but she regretted the gesture much less when she considered how much death and destruction the bastard had caused.

"I still have trouble getting my head around what Shrike hoped to gain," she said, putting the dark memories back away. "He can't possibly have believed your people would accept him after he overthrew the Monarchy. They would've rebelled."

Elise nodded. "I'd like to think so. I'm still shocked at how many Royal Fleet officers he subverted. If he'd managed to take *Courageous*, he'd have beaten us."

"*Courageous* isn't invincible. Far from it. With all the fighting she went through during the rebellion and against the Pale Ones, she's expended most of her missiles. We're going to have to be very careful from here on out."

"It would've been enough," Elise said grimly. "With *Courageous* under his control, Shrike would've taken the Kingdom. I have no doubt of that. We were all incredibly lucky that you defeated him.

"Of course, you and Jared have proved your resourcefulness several times already. I can't wait to see how the historians put that into perspective. Or the vid dramas."

Kelsey frowned. "Vid dramas?"

Elise grinned and opened the limo door after her guards signaled the way was clear. "Hadn't you heard? Several production companies have joined forces to document your triumphant arrival. Money is no object. They've hired only the best and brightest actors and actresses in the Kingdom. Production on several other vids has ceased due to the effort being expended on this one project."

The news actually made Kelsey stop in her tracks. "You're

kidding." She shook her head. "Of course you're not. That's horrifying."

The crown princess took Kelsey's arm and got them moving again. "Surely, you expected that something like this would happen. How many vids do you think have been made about Emperor Lucien's escape to your Avalon?"

Kelsey shrugged. "I don't know. A lot. That's completely different."

"It's precisely the same. You, Jared, and the crew of *Athena* saved the lives of every single person in the Kingdom. Like it or not, you're heroes. Mythic figures, even."

Kelsey had seen that hero worship up close many times in the last few months. It made her deeply uncomfortable. She wasn't worthy of that kind of adulation. Jared and his crew were the true heroes.

Elise continued, unaware of Kelsey's thoughts. "I understand the competition for the leading roles was fierce. Perhaps worthy of an epic story of its own. You should know that Riley Thomas actually challenged several of his competitors to duels for the privilege of playing Jared. Personally, I like Jared much better, but Riley is still dreamy." She sighed theatrically.

With a feeling of growing dread, Kelsey covered her eyes with one hand. "Please, please tell me that I don't have someone ridiculous playing me."

"Oh, no. If anything, the battle to play you was even fiercer. Literally, the role of a lifetime. 'Ridiculous' is certainly not the word I'd use for Eva Griffiths. She's one of the great leading ladies of our time, a true powerhouse on the screen. While she doesn't have your small stature, she makes up for that difference in other ways."

"What kind of ways?" Kelsey asked suspiciously.

"Let's just say that she has a completely different kind of enhancement than you do."

"Perfect. Absolutely perfect. With any luck, I'll be long gone by the time this production is finished."

"Oh, I wouldn't worry about that," Elise said breezily. "I'm sure that we'll have reestablished contact through the Courageous system by then. The vid will most likely be all the rage in the Empire by the time we get there."

"With my luck, that's just about a certainty."

They made their way through the construction area. Sawdust and floating particles of freshly poured plascrete tickled her nose. Her implants tallied the composition of the plascrete and discreetly displayed it in the corner of her vision. The advanced technology of the Old Empire revealed itself to her in the oddest ways.

The workers had parts of the floor roped off to protect the freshly poured flooring. Thick reinforcements held a new ceiling over their heads, but the walls to the main chamber were gone. The speaker's podium remained, as did the carving mounted on the wall behind it. Someone had covered Master Vestor's work with what looked like a thick sheet of transparent plastic.

The marble floor was cracked and crushed. Loose bits crunched under Kelsey's shoes as she walked. The devastation was almost complete. The speaker's podium looked as though something had smashed into it. Perhaps it had saved the carving from damage.

The Royal Guards had already cleared the workers from the room, but Kelsey recognized several of the men standing near the speaker's podium. Master Alec Vestor stood in a huddle with several other men and women in colorful tunics. His apprentices, she assumed.

He turned at their approach and smiled. "Elise, Kelsey, it's so good to see you both."

"Tell me your carving isn't damaged," Kelsey pleaded. "Its loss would make this tragedy even worse."

"I'll have to take it down and return it to my shop to be sure, but I don't think so."

Elise sagged in evident relief. "Thank God."

Master Vestor frowned and shook his head. "It's only wood. If I could save any of the people who lost their lives in this vicious attack, I'd take an ax to it myself. Things, no matter how valuable or treasured, pale in importance to people's lives."

Elise straightened. "You're right, of course, but nothing that we do will change what happened here. I'm just glad that another tragedy wasn't perpetrated by that bastard." She shot Kelsey an apologetic look. "No offense to your brother."

"I don't think he'd be offended," Kelsey said. "Just because he's my father's illegitimate son doesn't make that word something to avoid around him." She gave her attention to Master Vestor. "I second what Elise said. I'd personally destroy this building and everything in it with a plasma cannon if it saved one person from injury, but it won't."

She stepped onto the speaker's podium and eyed the carving through the plastic cover. The material obscured her ability to see the fine detail in the woodwork. She had to admit she was anticipating a much closer look. With her enhanced eyesight, it would be a close look indeed.

That's when she felt it. Something registering on her implants.

Her eyes widened as she turned to Elise. "There's old Imperial technology close by." She stared down at the floor. "There's something down there."

3

Jared stepped onto *Courageous*'s bridge. Charlie Graves, his executive officer, rose from the captain's chair with a grin splitting his face.

"Captain. We're about half an hour from *Athena*. The probe popped back over before *Athena* could send a message to it. Fleet was getting a scan of the system, I suspect."

Jared nodded to Lieutenant Zia Anderson, his tactical officer, and Lieutenant Pasco Ramirez, his helm officer. "We need to send them a message as soon as that probe returns. In fact, let's send one of our probes to make sure that they have our current status. I don't want any problems because of *Courageous*, and they need to know what we found." Jared raised his voice. "Zia, record my response and load it into a probe."

He made certain that his face was professionally neutral as he began speaking. "This is Commander Jared Mertz, captain of the destroyer *Athena*. We're glad to see you, but it's imperative that you *do not* transition to this system. I repeat, you must not use that flip point. It's a one-way trip. There's no way home.

"We're on our way to the flip point now. If you access the high-priority data contained in the probes that we left for you, you'll see a summary of events. The large ship on your scanners is friendly. Again, we're glad to see you, but *do not* come through the flip point. Mertz out. Zia, add a current update of our data and launch the probe."

He turned his attention to Lieutenant Pasco Ramirez, *Courageous*'s helmsman. "Maximum speed to the flip point. We need to be close so we can answer their questions as quickly as possible."

Less than ten minutes later, Zia stiffened. "Multiple transitions at the weak flip point! I'm detecting six vessels."

Jared cursed. Their probe had almost made it. "Record a new message. Fleet vessels, this is Commander Jared Mertz. We are in route to your position. We have medical teams standing by to assist you. Hang on. Mertz out. Zia, can you ID those ships?"

"There's one heavy cruiser, two light cruisers, and three destroyers. I'm comparing them to the databases we brought from *Athena* now." She tapped her console. "Sir, that cruiser is *Spear*."

It took a moment for that to soak in. *Spear*. The ship they'd beaten in the war games before they left on this mission. That meant he was dealing with Captain Wallace Breckenridge. He couldn't think of a worse person to have dropped into his lap. Breckenridge was no fan of Jared's, and the man outranked him.

"Incoming transmission," Zia said.

"Put it on the screen."

Breckenridge looked mussed. Something dark stained the front of his tunic, and his hair stood out in a particularly unflattering manner. "Unknown vessel, this is Captain Wallace Breckenridge of the Imperial Fleet heavy cruiser *Spear*. Stand clear of *Athena*, or my task force will fire on you."

Graves stared at Jared uncomprehendingly. "Does he think we're attacking *Athena*? Didn't he review *any* of the data we left for him? Jesus Christ. Now they're trapped here just like we are."

Jared gave his executive officer a reproving glance. "Belay that. He's a senior Fleet officer, and we will not speak of him in that tone." He sighed. "I can't imagine what he was thinking. We'll find out soon enough."

What *was* apparent to Jared was that Captain Breckenridge hadn't waited to find out what the situation was. If he'd done even a cursory scan of the data, he'd have seen the warning not to use the flip point. A deeper examination of the data would have told him what *Courageous* was.

The implication was that neither of the probes they'd sent deeper into the Empire had made it. Breckenridge and his task force had chanced across the one they'd left at the flip point, and rather than waiting to review the information inside it, they'd flipped across to rescue *Athena*.

The Old Empire battlecruiser must've seemed like an alien vessel. Their probe had picked up *Courageous* closing on the damaged *Athena*. Its appearance must've seemed threatening. It had to have been something like that.

"Open a channel, Zia. Captain Breckenridge, this is Jared Mertz. I'm on board the Fleet battlecruiser *Courageous*, the vessel approaching *Athena*. It's not hostile."

The other man frowned. "Mertz? What the hell is going on? Fleet battlecruiser? Explain yourself at once."

Jared gave Breckenridge a concise report of events while attempting to explain that *Courageous* was a restored Old Empire battlecruiser. The older man didn't seem able to grasp what he was saying.

"You're not making any sense," Breckenridge almost snarled. "You will report to *Spear* and explain it to me in person at once, Commander. Breckenridge out."

Jared tiredly rubbed his eyes as the man's image vanished from the screen. "Wonderful. Zia, load the critical information into a chip, and I'll take it with me. It won't hurt to bring another copy."

"Do you want me to go with you, sir?" Graves asked.

Jared shook his head. "Just to the docking bay. He's angry, and this is going to take a lot of explaining. It's probably best he take his frustration out on me."

He waited for Zia to hand him the chip and then made his way down to the forward docking level with his executive officer. On the way, he summoned Ensign Joyce Enova. The young woman had served on *Spear.*

Jared turned his attention to Graves as the lift arrived at the docking level. "If things go south, you will not intervene. I'm a big boy, and I can handle this. I don't want any ill-considered confrontations. No matter what happens, those are Fleet ships crewed by our brothers and sisters. Got it?"

Charlie nodded. "Yes, sir. Bend over and smile. Crystal clear, sir."

Jared shook his head and clapped his friend on the shoulder. "Your heart is in the right place, but this is why you're not in command of a ship yet. You say exactly what you think."

"Like you're much better." Graves's expression grew more somber. "You need to be careful, Jared. That man hates you, and he's not exactly a free thinker."

"I'll be on my best behavior. See you soon."

Ensign Enova came out of the lift and stiffened to attention as Graves walked past her and returned to the bridge. "Captain."

"Thanks for coming with me, Ensign. Let's not keep Captain Breckenridge waiting."

The cutter pilot looked over his shoulder as Jared peeked into the cockpit. "Captain. We're go to launch as soon as you strap in. Based on their speed, we should be docking in about fifteen minutes."

"Give me five minutes' warning."

"Aye, sir."

He returned to the flight deck and strapped in beside Ensign Enova. "Okay, Joyce. Give me a run down on Captain Breckenridge. Whatever you feel comfortable sharing about his command style and quirks."

The thin woman nodded. "Aye, sir. They didn't allow me on the bridge during my middie cruise, but people talk. He was notoriously strict about following regulations. Sometimes even when they didn't make sense. When things came up that didn't fit his expectations, he wasn't shy about tearing someone up."

That fit with Jared's own experiences with the man. He could only imagine what serving as a midshipman under him would've been like. A nightmare most likely.

When *Athena* had ambushed his ship during the war games, he'd struck out at how he believed *Athena* had violated the rules of engagement. He'd taken out his lapses in preparation on Graves at the after-action briefing. Even when Admiral Yeats had yanked him up short, the man had been inclined to blame circumstances and Jared's actions for his ship's mock destruction.

Which would no doubt make him even more difficult to deal with now.

"Let's see if I can say this delicately," Jared said. "For someone that's so fond of regulations, he doesn't seem to feel bound by them in some situations. Is that accurate?"

"There were rumors, sir. You know people don't feel comfortable talking about the CO in a negative light to the new people, but there were times. Things similar to the war games just before we left on this mission, for example. I read the after-action report. He didn't have his ships at a heightened level of alert during the approach to Avalon. He didn't expect enemy contact without warning. They were still scrambling when we blew them up."

Jared nodded. "Speaking of that, does he hold a grudge?"

The ensign nodded. "Until it dies of old age, and then he has it mounted so he can look at it every morning before breakfast."

"Perfect."

Nothing else they discussed changed Jared's impression of a stiff, vindictive commander bound by rules when things didn't go his way. Which was just about the worst thing that could happen in their situation.

The approach went smoothly enough, and the cutter docked without incident. Jared rose to his feet. "Stay on the flight deck, Ensign. I don't want to take a chance that anyone will recognize you."

"Aye, sir," the woman said in a relieved tone. "Good luck."

"Thanks."

He made his way into *Spear*. Three men awaited him, one a commander by his rank tabs. The other two were marines with sidearms.

The officer extended his hand. "Commander Mertz. I'm Sean

Meyer, *Spear*'s executive officer. The captain is in his office." He didn't offer the names of the marines.

Their presence was a not-so-subtle insult. It implied that Jared wasn't trusted. He had no doubt that the point was intentional.

Commander Meyer's grip was cool and loose, and he didn't smile. His eyes had more than a flicker of disdain. "I'm given to understand that you had something to do with our rather rough transition." He turned toward the lift. The marines fell in behind Jared.

Jared put aside the impression that they'd just taken him into custody. It might be accurate, but it was irrelevant to the situation. "I'm afraid I can't control physics. The scientists tell me that it's part of the way those weak flip points are formed. We included all the data we had on the probe we left for you. Right after the warning not to use the flip point."

A flicker of something showed in the other man's eyes. "Yes, well, we hadn't quite gotten to that part of your data when we saw *Athena*. Due to the circumstances, the captain had no choice but to take action."

The lift deposited them just down the corridor from Breckenridge's office. Two marines stood outside the hatch at attention in their dress uniforms. Somehow, Jared guessed they weren't there just to impress him. Their presence seemed in line with Breckenridge's personality.

Meyer ignored them and rapped on the hatch. It slid open, and he stepped inside. Jared followed. The marines accompanying them came in and took up positions on either side of the hatch.

The office was somewhat larger than Jared's had been on *Athena* and rather more expensively decorated. Breckenridge had replaced the regulation desk and furnishings with pricy civilian ones. There was no chair in front of the desk.

Jared took the pointed hint and centered himself in front of the desk before snapping to attention. "Commander Mertz, reporting as ordered, sir."

Breckenridge looked up from the screen on his desk, leaned back in his chair, and scowled at Jared. "I've skimmed the data your tactical officer just sent, Commander. I'm only now beginning to grasp the mess you've landed us in. Let me see if I can sum things up before we get into the details. You've led us into a dangerous section of space, involved the Empire in a war it had no business being in, crippled your ship, and left us trapped with no way home. Did I miss anything important?"

Oh, yes, this meeting was going to be a pleasure.

4

————————

Kelsey walked around the speaker's podium, focusing on her implants. The trace vanished when she stepped more than five meters away. That probably meant whatever she was sensing was right under the dais. No more than ten meters down, probably less. Her implants didn't have the range to interface with anything at longer distances. She needed a headset for that.

Elise looked at Kelsey curiously. "What are you seeing? Ah, feeling? Sensing?"

"Sensing is a good word. I'm not quite sure what it is. It's not responding when I attempt to connect. It doesn't feel like a switch. It's not transmitting anything other than its own signature. How old is this building?"

"Older than the Kingdom. It was the Planetary Parliament Building back before the Fall. The representatives worked here and sent select members to Terra to serve in the Imperial Parliament on our behalf."

"Then it could be something left over from back then. Implants like mine were restricted to the military, but I'd imagine that civilians had something similar. Perhaps that's why the device won't respond to me. I assume there's a level below us. How do we get down there?"

One of the guards cleared his throat. "I took the liberty of summoning the foreman. He has the full plans to the building."

A few minutes later, a portly man in dusty denim pants and a sweat-stained work shirt came in. He carried rolls of paper and bowed low to his princess. "Highness. Joshua Powell, at your service. I have the plans you requested."

Elise gave him a bright smile. "Thank you, Mister Powel. We appreciate your promptness. Have you looked at the level below us? Specifically the area under the speaker's podium?"

The man nodded. "I've been over every meter of this building, checking for damage. There are several levels under this one, but nothing directly under this chamber. It's one solid block. I assumed that was so no one had access to plant a bomb. There aren't any maintenance panels or conduits."

Kelsey took the plans from him and spread them out on the speaker's podium. They showed an area somewhat larger than the parliament chamber as a significant blank space going down three levels.

She handed the plans back to the man. "It's possible that whatever I'm sensing is only attached to the speaker's podium. Or whatever was here back then. However, I can't imagine how an isolated device could still have power after all that time. I think there's something more significant down there. Does the original speaker's podium still exist?"

Elise nodded. "Of course. It's in the Royal Museum."

"Then unless you'd like to start cutting holes in things, it might be best to bring it back for a return performance. Perhaps it interfaces with whatever is underneath us."

It took the workers an hour to disassemble the current speaker's podium, so Elise and Kelsey broke for lunch. Or Kelsey did, anyway. Her new world had about six meals in it, when she timed them correctly.

Her appetite reminded her of an Old Empire vid she'd found in *Courageous*'s archives. A primitive 3D production with small people in a fantasy setting that ate all the time. Thankfully, she didn't have hairy feet.

Kelsey had discovered a taste for entertainment vids from

prespaceflight Terra. She had plenty of time to peruse *Courageous*'s library in the dead of night. The combination of requiring less sleep than before and high throughput via her implants meant she'd seen thousands of them. They had an exuberance that she enjoyed.

The two women made it back to the parliament chamber just before the workers were ready to begin putting the original podium in place. Kelsey examined the newly revealed floor carefully. There were power connections, which should've raised a question in someone's mind when they removed it. Where did the lines go? A check would've shown they didn't go elsewhere in the building.

She'd half expected to find a hatch, but there wasn't one. The floor was one solid piece. How did people get into the area below? What purpose did the old podium serve?

It took half an hour to assemble the podium and install it. It looked very much like the one that had replaced it, but there were Old Empire electronics deep inside it. Unlike the device below, it responded to her mental touch.

Kelsey found an interface in the podium and connected to it. It needed no authorization and behaved as a terminal. An access point.

She'd been practicing under Reginald Bell's instruction and had gotten the hang of this sort of thing. He'd been using his implants to do things like this for hundreds of years, and it was second nature to him. She was almost able to do it without marveling. Almost.

The interface opened into a series of systems much like a library. Exactly like a library, really. One dedicated to politics and law making. She found she was looking through a listing of the laws of the Empire at both the Imperial and planetary levels.

It seemed that each world of the Old Empire was able to make laws at the local level, so long as they did not exceed the boundaries set at the Imperial level. Murder was murder everywhere, yet in some localities, there were exceptions for dueling. Including on Pentagar, at least back then. Elise had mentioned something about those actors almost getting into a duel, so perhaps the tradition still lived on here.

There was also an interface for tallying votes cast by members. It was almost completely offline. Only the receptor here on the speaker's podium still functioned. The other members of parliament must've cast their votes at their own desks, which were long gone.

There was also a projection system built into the ceiling. There were dozens of separate units mounted among the lights. A few were offline, probably due to damage from the explosion, but the system declared itself functional. She wondered what the people that maintained the lights thought they were.

The system had a record of things it had played. Kelsey scanned down the list and came to one of the last: a message marked high priority and routed to members of the Imperial Parliament and all Fleet vessels. She instructed the system to play it just to see if it would.

An image of the bridge of a ship appeared, hovering in the air just above them. The center seat sat higher than those around it, and it had a wraparound console.

The man staring down at them was instantly recognizable to her. Emperor Marcus the Fifteenth. The last emperor of the old Terran Empire. Father to Lucien. Her great-grand-something-father.

Or at least he would've been if she'd really been of the blood. True, no one but Doctor Stone and she knew that her mother had had an affair, but it still counted. Oh, and her mother might know, too, or at least suspect.

Emperor Marcus was a handsome man, with an almost spooky resemblance to Kelsey's father. The two could've been brothers. Marcus looked like her father had when she was a girl. No grey colored his hair, and he seemed to be a vital young man in the prime of his life.

She noted that she was receiving the transmission on her implants and switched to that feed. This version was significantly clearer and much more personal. It was like when she wore her commando armor. The outside world vanished as her implants overwrote her senses.

"People of the Empire," Marcus said. "I bring you devastating news. Terra has fallen."

The sadness and horror in his expression were just as clear as if she'd been standing directly in front of him. Kelsey glanced around and found she could see more of the ship than what was in the purely visual transmission. It focused on the emperor to the exclusion of all else. Her view encompassed the other consoles spread out around the circular compartment, manned by men and women in Fleet uniforms. Those long-dead people watched the emperor speak with tears openly flowing down their faces.

There was also a tall—very tall—dark-haired woman in commando armor standing beside the lift. She seemed to be about half a meter taller than Kelsey was, so two meters. Huge for a woman.

The raven-haired woman's eyes were dry, her expression grim and determined. Her most unusual feature was a tattoo on her forehead. It started between her eyebrows and covered her forehead in a pattern that was reminiscent of eyes with a horned helmet above them. It looked sinister. Hints of smaller tattoos on her cheekbones peeked out from under her long hair.

Kelsey had never heard of anyone tattooing their face like that, though with modern medical techniques, it was possible to do so and remove it at any time. No one else on the bridge had anything like it.

An older man in a Fleet admiral's uniform stood beside the woman, dwarfed by her height. Frankly, he seemed too old to be still serving, but who was Kelsey to judge? He looked every day as old as Reginald Bell. Come to think of it, Bell might be able to identify these people for the historical record.

She grasped all that in the pause after the emperor had spoken. He nodded gravely. "Indeed, the core worlds of the Empire have all fallen. Even now, rebel forces push us back on every axis, yet hope is not lost.

"We've gathered what remains of Fleet together to force them back. We will retake every world. We will crush them under our heels. The rebels have gravely wounded our beloved Empire, but she will survive. We will win this war."

How wrong he'd been.

"I've sent my son, Lucien, to a place far away. He has everything he needs to return in due time if we fail. The Empire will live."

He leaned forward and gave the camera a stern look. "I command you to continue the fight. Protect the people of the Empire. If you lose contact with the rest of the Empire, take your orders from your Imperial Representatives, nobles, and above all those appointed by the Throne. We will not surrender. The Imperial edict codifying my orders is attached to this transmission and will remain in force until we win this war and I or my successor rescinds it."

Emperor Marcus rose to his feet. "Take this message to heart, my people. The rebellion will be undone. Have faith in me and those of my blood. Have faith in Fleet. Have faith in the key. Have faith in yourselves." He saluted the screen with a closed fist on his chest, and the image faded.

The transmission released her implants, allowing her to see those around her. The message had left them all thunderstruck.

Elise turned to Kelsey, her eyes wide in wonder. "Was that Emperor Marcus? It was, wasn't it? Ah, what a message of hope for his people in such a dark time."

"A message that was doomed. He failed, and everyone died. Or worse."

The crown princess nodded, but she didn't seem deterred. "I'm not sure that matters. The people needed every glimmer of hope to keep fighting. He told them what they needed to hear. Obviously, they fought back well enough for humanity to survive. That counts for something. Lucien survived. The Imperial line is unbroken."

Kelsey sighed. That again. The line broke with her and her brother. The emperor's blood would carry on in Jared's line, and perhaps the line of Pentagaran kings, if their relationship prospered.

"I hope we can set up a camera and you can play that again," Elise said. "Do you have any idea what this key is? Or what is under our feet?"

"Not a clue. I've never heard of a key. Perhaps it's the code to undo the virus in a compromised person. The rebels vaporized the task force protecting Lucien. It could've been lost in that battle. We'll probably never know what it was for sure."

Elise stared up at the ceiling. "The image seemed to be focused on me. When I walked around the room a little, the image moved with me. That's quite amazing. I hope we can duplicate the technology."

Other than library access, the dais failed to respond to Kelsey. It had to be connecting with the device below, but it wasn't granting her any insights.

"I'm not getting anywhere. We know there isn't direct access from up here, so there must be some other way to get into that area. Let's examine every inch of this place."

Elise nodded her agreement. "We should start with the speaker's chamber. If there was any secret access, it would be there."

Kelsey followed Elise into the sumptuous chambers reserved for the speaker. It obviously served as an office as well, because it rode the line between luxurious and functional. This was the kind of room where powerful men and women made secret deals.

The artwork here was very similar to what she'd seem in the halls outside. Statues and paintings, mostly. Including, ironically, one of Emperor Marcus.

Feeling nothing out of the ordinary, Kelsey wandered the room, her senses attuned to anything her implants could detect. Nothing.

Actually, there was too much nothing. She felt an area behind the office that didn't register at all. Just like the shielded chamber she'd discovered on the asteroid in the Erorsi system, it was a blank spot in her senses.

"There's something back here." Kelsey glanced at Elise. "Do you know what's back there?"

"I'm not sure." Elise walked over to the only door in that wall, opened it, and peered inside. "It's a storage room."

One without a lot of space, it turned out. Some packrat had stuffed it full of furnishings and boxes. Dust covered everything in a fine gray sheen, and it smelled musty. There was barely enough room for Kelsey to push in after Elise. One of the Royal Guards seemed to consider pushing inside with them but probably decided that would be getting a little too personal.

"It's a storage room now," Kelsey said, "but at some point in the past, it was probably something else. It's shielded."

She probed the area with her implants. Perhaps now that she was inside, she could sense something else.

In fact, she could. The area of wall directly beside the door had a switch, just like the kind that secured her quarters on *Courageous*. That probably meant this shielded room used to be for secure storage. A mental push of the switch likely controlled the shielding field.

She triggered the switch.

An unseen hatch slid out of the wall and locked the guards outside. The piles of furniture shifted as the floor lurched and the entire room began sinking lower.

Kelsey kept the sofa beside them from falling on Elise and grinned. They were in a hidden lift dropping into a previously unexplored section of the Pentagaran Parliament Building. The only negative she could see was that Talbot was going to be pissed he'd slept through the adventure.

5

The debriefing was every bit as painful as Jared had imagined it would be. Breckenridge wouldn't let him finish one subject before he interrupted with a different criticism. He sniped from behind his desk, using hindsight to his full advantage. Commander Meyer stood to the side, faintly smirking, until Jared finished.

Breckenridge shook his head, not bothering to hide his disgusted expression. "You've had a remarkable run of poor decision making, Commander. Even for someone with your background. Thankfully for the Empire, a more experienced commander is at hand to take charge. I am assuming command of this mission as of this moment."

As much as Jared hated the idea, he'd known this was coming. "Aye, sir."

"You will report to *Spear*'s medical center for an exam. Then you will accompany me back to the derelict. Dismissed."

Jared saluted and spun on his heel. The two marines fell in behind him as Meyer directed him toward the lift. Jared stood beside *Spear*'s executive officer as the man sent the lift toward the medical center. "I hope you'll read the briefing material in more detail, Commander

Meyer. This situation is serious. The rebels will be coming to Erorsi in a matter of weeks. They are nothing to sneer at."

The other man gave Jared a dismissive flip of his hand. "Your destroyer might not have been up to the task, but Captain Breckenridge and this task force will handle the situation."

"Like he did the war games?" Jared regretted the question as soon as he'd asked it, but it was true. "No matter what you think of me, I beg of you, don't underestimate these things. They took out the Old Empire. It doesn't get more serious than that."

Meyer's expression softened a little. "Point taken. I will read every word and advise Captain Breckenridge accordingly."

Spear's medical center was significantly larger than *Athena*'s was, though smaller than *Courageous*'s. Someone had called ahead, because an older black man with a shaved head stood waiting for them. His commander's tabs indicated he was the ship's chief medical officer.

He held out his hand. "Commander Mertz, I'm Justin Guzman. Captain Breckenridge has asked that I give you a complete examination." He turned to Meyer. "I'll let you know when I have my report ready, Sean."

"We need it as quickly as possible, please. Time is of the essence."

Once Meyer left, Guzman turned his attention to the marines. "You can wait outside." His tone made it clear he wasn't making a request.

The two marines glanced at one another and went outside.

Guzman shook his head. "Let's move over to the examination table, Commander Mertz. I took the liberty of requesting your file from Doctor Stone. I have to say that what I've read shocks me deeply. You shouldn't be walking. Or breathing. If you don't mind my asking, what in the world possessed you to put those things in your head?"

Jared lay back on the exam table and spoke as the doctor scanned him. "If you could see how the Old Empire equipment interfaces with these implants, you wouldn't need to ask. Imagine being able to have these scan results fed right from the table into your brain. Being able to grasp the information as fast as it comes in. Being able to control the equipment in an operation with such exactitude that you always knew precisely what was happening.

"Imagine that as a ship's commander. I can directly interface with *Courageous*'s scanners and control systems. I can communicate with the ship's computer in real time. The ship's records are available to me at a thought. This morning, I stood on a tower in the center of Imperial City on Terra herself before the Fall. It wasn't like a vid. It was exactly as if I'd been standing there myself."

Guzman looked impressed. "That certainly sounds compelling. You can sit up. My God." He stared at the readout on the wall. "It goes all through your brain. How the hell did they get that in there without killing you?"

"Perhaps Doctor Stone can answer that. All I can say for certain is that I was walking and talking within minutes of the procedure. While you might see this as radical, every Fleet officer in the Old Empire had this exact equipment. Every one. Frankly, it wasn't nearly as invasive as what happened to Princess Kelsey, and she's fine."

The other man frowned. "Princess Kelsey? What was done to her?"

He'd mentioned that the Pale Ones had implanted Kelsey to Breckenridge, but it occurred to him that he hadn't elaborated. "Didn't Stone send you her file?"

He consulted a tablet. "No. So, she has a similar set of implants?"

"She had a little bit more done than I did. You should talk with Commander Stone."

"I'm going to want to examine her, too."

"I'm sure she'd be happy to let you, but she's in the next system over. Pentagar."

Happy was something of an overstatement. His sister had grown downright hostile to medical procedures since she'd been forcibly implanted.

"I'm certain Captain Breckenridge will insist on it," Guzman said. "Let's finish your workup."

The doctor put Jared through an exhaustive set of tests, looking closely at the results as they went along. He peppered Jared with questions about *Courageous* and the task force's new situation as he worked. The exam took two hours.

When they were through, he clapped Jared on the back. "Well, to my shock, you show no signs of impairment. I'll endorse Commander Stone's duty certification. You're fit to command."

"Somehow, I don't think that's what your captain is expecting to hear," Jared said dryly.

"Perhaps not, but that's what he's getting. For what it's worth, I think you've done an astounding job, Commander. You've done Fleet proud."

"Thank you. Now all we have to do is stop the rebels and get back home."

Guzman called Commander Meyer and handed him a printed report. The other officer scanned it and looked up sharply. "This can't be right. How can someone with unauthorized equipment in his head be fit for duty?"

"By being fit for duty," the doctor said acerbically. "He's not impaired at all. In fact, his memory and ability to correlate information are off the charts. I'd sign up for something like these implants in a second."

Meyer looked like he'd bitten into something sour. "The captain will not be pleased."

"As senior medical officer in this task force, this is my decision to make, and I've made it." Guzman's tone brooked no argument.

The thin man harrumphed. "Very well. We don't have time to deal with this in any case." He turned to Jared. "The captain is ready to see this Old Empire battlecruiser for himself. We are to accompany him in your cutter. Let's go."

The man's tone grated on Jared's nerves, but he kept his peace. He'd faced hostility like this before, and he'd no doubt do it again. Being the Imperial Bastard gave him some experience in that. After Ethan, Meyer was a lightweight.

Ensign Enova wisely remained out of sight on the flight deck when they boarded the cutter. Unlike Jared, Breckenridge didn't seem inclined to poke his nose up there.

The older officer seemed to be in an even worse mood than earlier, if possible. "So Guzman cleared you for duty? Unbelievable. Don't think for one moment that this changes anything. You will not be allowed to escape the consequences of your actions so lightly."

Jared ground his teeth. "Perhaps the captain would educate me on what actions he would've taken under the same circumstances?"

Breckenridge looked down his nose at Jared. "The first thing I would've avoided was rushing through an untested flip point."

Jared said nothing and kept his face neutral.

The other man scowled anyway. "Do not try to equalize our circumstances, Commander. Your ship appeared to be under attack and severely damaged. Coming after you was the right choice."

Deciding he had little to lose, Jared pressed the subject. "We left a drone with all the data we'd gathered. The warning not to use the flip point was right up front. If you'd taken a few minutes to read it."

"You will keep a civil tongue in your head, Commander, or I'll see you in the brig. Your second error was revealing yourself to the Pentagarans. The third was involving yourself and, by extension, the Empire in a war that we have no business in."

Jared resisted the urge to shake his head. That wouldn't be helpful. "Those events are inextricably linked, sir. If you can jump in to save my ship, how could we do any less for helpless civilians? We already knew we had to go through that system to get home. If we'd stood by, many thousands of people would've been killed, and the Empire's reputation would've been ruined."

"Not if they didn't know you were there to witness the fight. The prudent action would be to observe and determine whom to aid. You were lucky you didn't help the wrong people."

Jared felt shamed he'd even considered that course of action. Hearing Breckenridge say it made him feel dirty. "Luckily for me, I had the princess along to advise me."

"We'll call that mistake number four. You should never have listened to an untrained neophyte, with all due respect to Princess Kelsey and the Imperial Family. She virtually gave away the technology you'd discovered. And for what? The gratitude of people who turned around and almost killed you and your crew.

"Mistake five, trusting these people any further than you can throw them. Mistake six, getting almost a hundred of your crew killed and your ship wrecked. Perhaps you'd care to point out even one thing that you did right. That might take less time."

Jared took a deep breath and let it out slowly. How had this idiot ever achieved a Fleet command?

"We've made mistakes, sir. No doubt. That said, we've done a few things right. We saved millions of people from almost certain death. If we'd stood aside, we'd have been complicit in an atrocity. Second, we've made a firm ally of the first advanced civilization the Empire has discovered since the Fall. Third, we've recovered a priceless artifact, an Old Empire battlecruiser filled with technology we're still trying to grasp. Not just as defunct equipment, but as a working ship. Fourth, we've recovered a treasure in data and cultural information in her computers."

He leaned forward. "Fifth, and most important, we've given the rebels a bloody nose and discovered their threat before they could attack the Empire. A surprise attack by the Pale Ones could've ended us. These new people might be even worse. Now we can prepare and take the fight to them."

Breckenridge shook his head with obvious disbelief. "You've lost your mind, Commander. I thank the gods that I arrived when I did. You have delusions."

The cutter docked with a slight bounce. Breckenridge stood, turned his back on Jared, and exited as soon as Meyer opened the hatch.

Graves stood waiting outside the docking hatch. He looked a little startled when Breckenridge and Meyer came aboard without asking permission, but he didn't let it put him off his game. "Commodore Breckenridge, Commander Meyer, welcome aboard *Courageous*. I'm Lieutenant Commander Charlie Graves, Captain Mertz's executive officer."

The courtesy promotion was Fleet tradition. There could only be one captain on a ship.

"You may refer to me as captain on this ship, Commander," Breckenridge said. "Whatever this derelict might once have been, it's no longer a Fleet vessel."

"Incorrect," *Courageous* said from the overhead speakers. "*Courageous* has not been decommissioned and is in active service."

Breckenridge's head jerked back. "Who the hell is that? If you want to speak to me, you can come down here and do it to my face. Don't you dare tell me the facts of the matter. I'll tell you."

"This unit is the AI controlling *Courageous*. It is customary to refer to a ship's AI by the same name as the ship on which it resides. Much as it is customary to request permission to come aboard a ship not your own, Commodore Breckenridge."

For a moment, Jared thought Breckenridge would have a stroke. "How dare you?" He whirled on Jared. "Are you telling me that you've allowed an unknown computer to control this derelict? Absolutely unacceptable."

"*Courageous* is just as much a part of this ship as the hull, sir," Jared said. "You aren't aware of just how intimately it is woven into all the ship's systems."

He sent a second command mentally to the computer. *Don't press him,* Courageous. *Now is* not *the time.*

"You've obviously lost all sense, Commander," Breckenridge snarled. "Allow me to clear up a few things. This is not an Imperial vessel. It's salvage. You are not its commanding officer. You are the jumped-up commanding officer of a destroyer and a bastard that Fleet should have dismissed years ago. You will report to *Athena* and remain there until further notice. Commander Meyer will lead a prize crew and bring this wreck home."

"Unacceptable," *Courageous* said. "This unit has a lawfully appointed commanding officer, Jared Mertz. Attempting to seize control of this vessel without authority will not be allowed."

Meyer cleared his throat. "Perhaps that course of action is somewhat premature, Captain."

Breckenridge looked at his exec as though the man had grown two heads. "Explain yourself."

"Whatever his flaws and failures, Commander Mertz is intimately familiar with this ship and the computer controlling it. He has the only direct method of accessing its records. He's correct in that this is a tremendous find for the Empire and a great stroke of luck that he could restore it to any level of functionality. We should take advantage of that."

"What are you suggesting? Leaving him in command of this ship? After everything he's done?" He sounded incredulous.

Meyer shrugged. "He's been in command of it in every way that mattered for months. What are a few more days? I suggest you make it clear to Commander Mertz that I am here acting with your authority. Then it doesn't matter that the ship's computer won't recognize me as being in command. If he doesn't do so, you have clear grounds to place him under arrest."

Breckenridge turned his attention to Mertz. "I dislike playing games, but so be it. Commander Meyer speaks with my authority. You will obey his orders as though they come from me. Is that clear enough, Commander Mertz?"

Jared kept his face blank. "Crystal clear, sir."

The old man grunted. "Then let's finish this tour so I can get back to my ship. We need to be in Pentagaran space as soon as possible so that I can undo what damage I can. The princess no doubt needs my support and advice. Frankly, I'm certain that she'll be glad to see you replaced. Move this along, Commander. The clock is ticking."

6

"My guards aren't going to be very happy," Elise said as the lift descended into the Parliament Building. "Why would the Old Empire need to hide this so effectively?"

Kelsey shrugged and drew a flechette pistol from a concealment holster at the small of her back. It wasn't very comfortable because it was large and she was small, but she liked having something to hand if trouble came looking for her. As it had done all too often of late.

She didn't expect to find anything living down here, but it paid to be cautious. Not that Talbot was going to see this as anything but reckless.

Kelsey smiled a little. "In my defense, I didn't expect the room to move."

The lift jerked to a halt and the hatch slid open, revealing darkness that slowly began brightening. Kelsey stepped out and scanned the area. It was a corridor similar to those aboard *Courageous*.

Elise tried her communications unit. "I'm not getting a signal. Shouldn't we go right back up? They're going to be going wild about now."

One glance showed Kelsey that she didn't have a connection either. "The area is screened. We *could* go back up, but I'd rather see what's down here first. Admit it. You're curious. Are they going to be any more upset if we spend a few minutes checking things out?"

"Probably not," the noblewoman admitted. "Lead on."

The corridor led to a single armored hatch, not unlike the one protecting *Courageous*'s computer center. It slid open at their approach. The room beyond was cloaked in darkness. Kelsey sensed a light control near the doorway and commanded the lights on.

The bright lights made her blink for a moment but revealed a command center that made the bridge on *Courageous* feel small. It had to take up almost the entire shielded area.

At least this level. Perhaps there was more underneath it. An even larger hatch occupied the far side of the control center, and smaller ones sat on the right and left sides.

Elise gaped. "My God. What is this place?"

All of the consoles were dark. Kelsey walked to the central dais and powered it on. The system went through a boot sequence and came to life. Once it felt online, she attempted to connect with it. It promptly rejected her.

This system is restricted. Authenticate.

Kelsey felt it probe her implants and, to her surprise, they responded with a complicated authentication code.

Authentication accepted. Standing by.

She probed her implants but couldn't figure out why they had responded at all, much less with some kind of code.

Identify this system, she instructed it.

This unit is the primary planetary defense center for the Pentagaran system.

Kelsey turned toward Elise and holstered her weapon. "We're not in any danger. This is the Old Empire planetary defense center. I guess they controlled the fight against the rebels from here."

Elise put her hands on the back of a chair in the center of the room. "I always knew there had to have been one, but I thought it long destroyed. The rebels pounded us from orbit. They destroyed the spaceport and two other cities."

"Hang on while I try to figure out something." Kelsey cocked her head. *What was the thing you did with my implants?*

This unit authenticated your clearance level and diplomatic codes. Everything is in order.

What diplomatic codes? What clearance level?

Your diplomatic codes, Ambassador Kelsey Bandar. This unit acknowledges your authority over it. As an heir to the Imperial Throne and ambassador plenipotentiary of the Terran Empire, you have clearance to communicate and instruct this unit. What are your orders?

How the hell could it know all that? How could her implants have codes like that? The Pale Ones certainly hadn't known or cared.

Then the answer occurred to her. It had to be *Courageous*. Nothing else explained it. It had to have put the codes into her implants. Probably in the same way a captain controlled his ship. The computers knew who people were and what they could control based on the codes in their implants and their serial numbers.

She remembered *Courageous* had updated her implants for her. It must've added the codes then. Why hadn't it told her? She'd have to ask it.

The question of why it had done so was a little murkier. It might have accepted Jared as its commanding officer, but why would it grant her diplomatic codes? How did it have them to begin with? Well, perhaps it knew them because a computer had to have them to know they were valid, right?

She looked at Elise. "It seems that *Courageous* gave me diplomatic codes. At least that's my guess at where they came from. The computer accepts my authority as an ambassador of the Terran Empire. Which is somewhat awkward, since Pentagar isn't part of said Empire."

"I'm not going to quibble right now." Elise walked around the room and peered at the consoles. "I can hardly imagine even being in here. This is part of our history. The baron, my great-great-and-so-forth-grandfather probably stood in this room. Of course, that begs the question of why he never mentioned it."

"Without weapons systems, it may not have seemed relevant after the rebels failed to return."

Computer, can you respond verbally?

"Affirmative."

Elise jerked at the voice from the hidden speakers. It sounded female and soothing.

"What is your status?" Kelsey asked.

"This unit is online. Scanner net degraded to twenty-three percent. Weapon systems offline."

"Amazing," Elise said softly. "Computer, do you have records of the attack on Pentagar?"

"Voice not recognized. Implant authorization required to divulge classified information."

Fortunately, Kelsey had dealt with this situation before. "Computer, I authorize you to respond to Crown Princess Elise Orison."

"Authorization not accepted. Implant codes required for each individual accessing this system."

Kelsey frowned. "So, you're saying you recognize my authority as an ambassador of the Terran Empire, but I can't authorize someone to access you?"

"Incorrect. Access to the system can be granted once the appropriate authorizations are entered into an individual's implants. This task may be accomplished at any computer that possesses the appropriate diplomatic security databases."

"Well, that's not very helpful," Kelsey grumbled. "I can see this is going to be a recurring theme. You can do whatever you like, as long as you have the appropriate authorization. Oh, and by the way, you can't get the appropriate authorization, because there's no one left to give it to you. Or the people you want to authorize won't have implants."

Elise put her hand on Kelsey's shoulder. "Now, now. Let's not be so negative. You received the appropriate authorization for diplomatic purposes, didn't you? Surely, that means that other computer systems can do something similar. What is it that you're not able to do?"

"The first thing I'd like to do is give you the appropriate authority to access this computer. It's on your planet, so you should be in control of it, not some visitor from another world. Then I'd like to get more specifications on my implants. I have to cobble together little bits and pieces of information to figure out their functionality. I should be able to find a help manual somewhere."

"*Courageous* doesn't have something like that?"

"Apparently not. Though it must have a diplomatic security database."

Elise walked around the control room slowly. "So, what was it you were detecting from the speaker's podium?"

Kelsey located the access point she'd detected earlier. "Computer, what is this?" She forwarded the signature of the device to the computer.

"That is a closed-circuit data repeater. It interfaces with the podium in the parliamentary chamber. Through it, the podium computer can access authorized material in this unit."

Kelsey nodded. That made sense. "What restricts access to the podium? Is it only due to the fact that I had diplomatic codes in my implants that I can access it?"

"Correct. The podium computer is designed to interface with all authorized personnel and their designees."

"What are the criteria for you to designate someone?" Elise asked.

Kelsey repeated the question to the computer.

"Authorized users may designate other individuals to access the podium controls through implant or verbal access."

"Finally. I designate Crown Princess Elise Orison as my designee. She has complete access to any files that I would have access to through the podium."

"Please state your name and position for the record, Crown Princess Elise Orison."

Elise stood a little straighter. "My name is Elise Patricia Orison. My position is crown princess and heir to the throne of Pentagar."

"Access granted to console systems on podium, Crown Princess Elise Patricia Orison."

"Please call me Elise."

"Preference acknowledged."

The tall noblewoman rubbed her hands together. "I cannot wait to dig into the contents of this computer. However, we really should head back up before they find a drill to come after us. I figure just about enough time has passed that Talbot will be there."

Kelsey snorted. "I'll bet you're right. He's probably ready to dig his way down with his bare hands. First, let me get a little bit more information."

She accessed the system and requested plans for the hidden facility. As she'd expected, there were other levels below this one, probably filled with computers and control systems. The hatch directly across from where they'd entered supposedly led to the known areas of the Parliament Building, but the corridor read as sealed. She imagined someone had filled it in with plascrete to hide the facility. Why, she wasn't sure. The other two led to various rooms and lifts connected to the areas below.

That mystery was one Elise could figure out on her own. "Okay. There used to be another entrance, but I think someone filled it in. You'll need to dig it out to get access. I'll give you the maps as soon as I can. Let's go back up. This is enough excitement for one day."

They retraced their steps, and Kelsey sent the command to the switch as soon as they were safely inside the storage room. The hatch closed, and the lift lurched upward. A minute later, the hatch opened to bedlam.

It seemed they had indeed found a drill, a very large one, and a determined crew of men and women. Everyone stepped back to allow the two women to exit.

The Royal Guards surrounded Elise as their leader examined her anxiously for signs of injury. "Are you harmed, Your Highness? What happened?"

Elise held her hands up. "It's okay. We discovered a lift leading down into the sealed section. We were never in any danger."

In comparison to the Royal Guards, the female marine assigned to guard Kelsey took her disappearance in stride. Except for the eye roll and head shake.

Talbot rushed in at that moment. He slowed when he saw Kelsey standing there, but she could see the worried expression on his face. "What's with you? I can't take a nap without you sneaking off to find some secret facility. I thought we had an agreement?"

Kelsey put on her best innocent face. "It wasn't my fault. I thought I was turning off a stealth field. I had no idea that it was a lift, and I'm perfectly fine. See?" She held up her arms and turned in a circle.

He pulled her into a hug. She knew it was a sign of just how worried he was that he did so with everyone around. He had an exaggerated opinion of how to protect her dignity.

She sighed and melted into him. "This is more like it. Next time I promise to wait for you to come protect me before I explore some strange, possibly dangerous place."

He squeezed her tight for a moment and then released her. "Okay. I'll let this go, this one time." He grinned. "Like I have any control over what you do. So what'd you find down there?"

"It seems that the planetary defense center for Pentagar is still operational. There are no weapons, of course, but the databases are intact. In fact, it seems that *Courageous* gave me some kind of diplomatic codes. The computer recognized me and gave me full access."

She looked over at Elise. "Come on. Let's go see if you can access the console on the podium."

Talbot stepped beside her as they walked out. "I hear you played something back in the main chamber. Some kind of message from the old emperor?"

Kelsey nodded. "Emperor Marcus's final message to the Terran Empire. His order to fight. It was pretty moving."

"We'll need to make a copy for the historians. I can almost hear them drooling from here."

"You can hear somebody drool? And here I thought my hearing was good."

He laughed. "You know what I mean."

She stepped onto the dais. "See if you could play the vid again, Elise. I think Talbot would enjoy it."

"'Enjoy' might be the wrong word," he said. "I know how that story turns out."

Elise stepped up to the console. "Computer, this is Elise Orison. Please replay the last message from Emperor Marcus."

Once more, the holo of the emperor from the bridge of his

unknown ship played out, and again, Kelsey tapped into a view that wasn't visible to anyone else. She spent her time examining the strange woman. Not just her but her armor. It was definitely commando armor. Kelsey had seen images of the bulkier marine version.

One thing was immediately obvious. This armor had seen plenty of combat. Unless she'd borrowed the armor, that was. Kelsey decided she'd go with the assumption that the woman was a combat veteran. It looked as though it had been through hell.

The woman's expression hardly faltered during the speech. It seemed to Kelsey that the woman had already decided that their chances were slim. She looked like she was determined to fight it out to the bitter end, even though she knew that death most likely awaited her. Or worse.

Kelsey wondered what had happened to her. Had she died well? Had the rebels captured her and turned her into one of them? She would probably never know.

Even as the vid was playing, the computer interrupted her with an implant transmission. *Ambassador Kelsey Bandar, this unit has detected a number of vessels entering the system.*

Let me see.

A schematic of the system appeared in her mind's eye. The unknown vessels had transitioned through the flip point leading to the Courageous system. There were eight vessels.

A jolt of excitement ran through her. They had to be ships from home. Someone had come to rescue them.

Then the reality hit her. Those ships had made a one-way trip. Now the weak flip point had trapped them, too.

As soon as the vid stopped playing, Kelsey leaned close to Elise and tugged Talbot with her. "We have visitors from home. They just transitioned through the flip point to the Courageous system."

Both of them looked suitably surprised, but Elise recovered first. She smiled. "Then we'd best get ready to welcome more of our allies to Pentagar."

Kelsey nodded. "I'm not sure what the protocol is, but I think

Talbot and I should go out to meet them. I'm certain that Jared explained everything, but it doesn't pay to take chances."

"Then you'd best get ready to travel. I look forward to meeting more of your people. Their presence will make capturing the freighter, and possibly dealing with any escort, easier."

Kelsey nodded again, but she couldn't escape the feeling that something just wasn't right. For once, she hoped her instincts were wrong.

7

Jared watched the approach of the Pentagaran fast courier *Lance* from *Courageous*'s bridge. Commander Meyer hadn't insisted on taking the command console but instead watched events unfold from one of the observation seats. The one Princess Kelsey normally used, in fact.

Once *Lance* launched from Pentagar, Jared assumed that Princess Kelsey was aboard her. He'd sent a brief message on tight beam giving her the basic situation and warning her that Breckenridge was in control. His implants allowed him to do so unobserved right under Meyer's nose.

Half an hour later, long after he should've opened communications, Breckenridge sent a message of greeting to *Lance*. He asked if Princess Kelsey was aboard and requested that she come to *Spear*.

His "request" sounded like an order, though. Not the smartest approach in dealing with Kelsey, as Jared well knew.

The courier pilot—Jared recognized him as Lieutenant Parker—politely responded that Princess Kelsey was aboard and was looking forward to meeting Captain Breckenridge. He passed along her request that he gather all his commanding officers aboard *Courageous* for a briefing so that she could bring them up to speed on the current situation.

Breckenridge declined, instead reiterating that Kelsey come to him.

Jared was unsurprised when her cutter undocked from *Lance* and arrowed directly toward *Courageous*. Breckenridge immediately ordered her to divert to *Spear*. The princess didn't respond.

Meyer stalked up to Jared. "What does she think she's doing?"

He looked up at the other officer blandly. "It seems that she thinks she's coming aboard *Courageous*."

"Stop her."

Jared allowed himself a wry smile. "Princess Kelsey is second in line to the Imperial Throne. My ability to direct her in any way was limited to my position in command of this mission. I no longer have that lever. Captain Breckenridge does."

"You know her," Meyer snarled. "Find a way."

"Short of firing on her cutter—which I of course will not do—I see no way of stopping her from coming here. If you want to redirect her, you'll need to do it face to face."

The unspoken subtext was that she was his problem now. Jared was looking forward to watching her roll over the other man.

Meyer looked as though he'd bitten into something sour. "I see. Then we'd best go down to meet her. Perhaps I can convince her to follow Captain Breckenridge's lawful instructions in person. She is not a member of the Imperial line for purposes of this mission. She is subordinate to the military commander."

Good luck with that, Jared thought as he followed the man to the lift. A glance back at his crew showed that they shared his opinion.

They arrived just as the princess's cutter docked. The hatch slid aside with a puff of cold, misty air, and the marines assigned to watch over Princess Kelsey came out. They stood beside the hatch and braced to attention. He noted Talbot was standing with them. A good choice on his part. The less these outsiders knew about the man's relationship with the princess, the better.

Kelsey came out next, her head held regally high. Obvious

posturing to someone that knew her as well as Jared did, but not so much for Meyer.

Even after saying that she had no Imperial place other than diplomat, Meyer bowed his head. "Highness. I'm Commander Sean Meyer, at your service."

For once, Jared couldn't blame him. Respect for the Crown wasn't easy to put aside. The other officer's deference actually did him credit. Of course, at this point, almost anything he did right would do the same.

"Commander Meyer, Captain Mertz," Kelsey said as she strode right past the two of them. "We'll wait in the main conference room."

"But—"

Obviously ready for an objection, she whirled on Meyer. "You will not argue with me, Commander. Your captain's tone has left me in no mood for it. You will accompany me to the conference room, where we shall await the arrival of Captain Breckenridge and the other officers in your task force."

The tall officer bowed his head again, probably deciding that it was easier to let Breckenridge fight that fight.

They proceeded to the lift as a group. It was just large enough to hold them all. Expecting it, Jared accepted Kelsey's communication request. Meyer had no idea the two of them could communicate around him, an advantage Jared intended to take full advantage of.

You're putting on quite the show, Jared thought with some amusement.

A small twitch of her lips was her only physical response. *I've had years of practice. Is this Breckenridge as much of an ass as he seems?*

Unfortunately for us, I think he's worse. Everything I've seen tells me he's an opinionated man incapable of thinking outside his narrow worldview. One who thinks highly of his power. Frankly, his arrival is probably the worst possible outcome of sending a probe home. If I'd had a clue this might happen, I'd have avoided leaving any information at all.

The lift opened, and they all trooped toward the main conference room. Jared tapped into *Courageous*'s scanners and noted that a cutter was on its way from *Spear*. Breckenridge obviously wasn't taking Kelsey's request to gather his senior officers seriously.

This was going to be an entertaining meeting. He wondered if they'd all end up in the brig.

Kelsey was obviously tapping into the scanner feed herself, because when she sat—at the head of the conference table—she gave Meyer a cold stare. "Your captain is ignoring my instruction to gather your ships' commanders. He's choosing to come over alone. This is not an auspicious beginning to our relationship. I suggest you contact him and correct this deficiency."

Her words surprised Meyer. "How could you possibly know what he's doing, Highness?" He shook his head. "You have those implant things. Of course. I'd forgotten. It's Captain Breckenridge's opinion that those devices leave a person's competency in doubt. Perhaps he only intends to see that you receive the medical care that you deserve."

The chill rolling off her became arctic. "Questioning my competency is an unwise course of action. I assure you that I have received the very best medical care possible. I understand and accept that you are following orders, but do not make yourself my enemy in your support of his policies. Do you understand me?"

"I will obey my orders and do what I think best for the Empire, Highness," he said stiffly.

Meyer took a seat near the other end of the table. Jared sat on Kelsey's right. The marines arrayed themselves behind the princess.

Jared knew the moment Breckenridge docked and even watched the vid feed as he made his way toward the conference room. He looked supremely pissed, and he wasn't alone. He'd brought half a dozen marines in light body armor. He obviously expected trouble.

If he tried to take Kelsey, he'd get it, too.

Courageous, *pass a message to Lieutenant Reese. I want an armed response team with neural disruptors ready to respond at my call. If this situation gets physical, I want it stopped without loss of life.*

Acknowledged. Should this unit instruct the bridge to bring the ship to battle stations? This vessel's screens and beam weapons give it a decisive advantage at this close range.

Negative.

Breckenridge strode into the conference room as though he owned it, his marines at his back. He hesitated when he saw the marines arrayed against the bulkhead. "You marines are dismissed."

"You overstep yourself, Captain," Kelsey said, holding up a hand to stop her marines from moving. "These men are acting as my guards. They stay."

Jared was proud to see how she didn't back down one centimeter.

Breckenridge scowled. "You are out of line, Highness. You are only authorized to act as the backup diplomatic presence on this mission."

"Wrong. When Carlo Vega died, I assumed the mantle of Imperial ambassador. You are being insubordinate, and it will stop now."

The Fleet officer looked flabbergasted. He'd probably hadn't had anyone speak to him with that tone in years.

He finally found his voice. "With all due respect to your father, you've been through a terrible ordeal. I have assumed command of this exploratory mission. Your position is subordinate to mine. You *will* submit to an examination on board my ship, and I will see that the Empire's interests are represented appropriately."

Kelsey smiled without the least bit of humor. "I absolutely will not *submit* to anything. I will *allow* your medical personnel to examine me, but only under the circumstances that I dictate."

She paused a moment to allow her words to hang in the air between them. "The Empire is at war. As the voice of the emperor, I decide what response is appropriate. The exploratory mission ended when we discovered the fight against the rebels wasn't over. You, sir, are under my orders until such time as the emperor appoints someone else to speak in his voice."

"That's preposterous," Breckenridge sneered. "You don't have the authority to make any of those declarations. We don't go to war at your say-so."

"You don't need my say-so. Emperor Marcus issued an Imperial edict for all Imperial forces to continue the fight. None of the emperors since has rescinded it. The fact that we didn't know about it means nothing. The Empire remains in a state of war, even though we thought ourselves at peace. Allow me to play those orders for you."

The screen on the wall came to life, and Jared found himself mesmerized as the vid feed played directly into his implants. He found himself rising to his feet without thought as Emperor Marcus began to speak. He heard the words, but his attention focused on the flag bridge, for obviously that was what it was. It dwarfed even *Courageous*'s control center.

Courageous, *can you identify that ship or its class?*

This unit does not know the particular ship, but the flag bridge belongs to a P.G. Holyfield–class superdreadnought, the most modern and powerful warship in Fleet service.

Basic schematics presented themselves in the corner of his vision. Holy God, that ship dwarfed *Courageous*. It had enough firepower to take on half a dozen battlecruisers head to head and win. It might be a wreck afterward, but it would take them down. It could singlehandedly destroy the present-day Terran Fleet in one engagement.

The vid ended, and Breckenridge waved his hand. "Irrelevant. He and everyone with him died with the Old Empire. Until and unless your father declares war, the Empire is at peace." He shot a glare at Jared. "Or we would be if someone hadn't started shooting when they should've stayed hidden. A flaw that he has displayed more than once."

Kelsey shook her head slowly. "So we finally get down to the reason you're pushing this. You dislike Captain Mertz because he defeated you. Humiliated you, from what I hear. Understandable enough, I suppose, but not relevant to this situation. You speak of the Old Empire and the Terran Empire as if they are two separate entities. They are not. The rule of the emperors is unbroken."

"Enough of this preposterous fantasy," Breckenridge snapped. "Senior Sergeant Jones, please escort Princess Kelsey to my cutter so that she may be examined by our chief medical officer."

"Stop," Jared said. "You heard the Imperial edict. Unless the emperor countermands it, Princess Kelsey is the most senior Imperial official in this system, and she's given us our orders. Stand fast, Senior Sergeant."

"Senior Sergeant, take Her Highness into medical custody,"

Breckenridge snarled. "Arrest Commander Mertz. He'll face charges for insubordination and disobeying a direct order. His blood won't save him now."

The man looked torn, but he moved when Breckenridge snapped his fingers. One of his men followed closely behind him. Two others started toward Jared.

Kelsey held up her hand one last time. "Captain Breckenridge, you're about to make a career-limiting error in judgment. As an ambassador plenipotentiary of the Terran Empire, I order you to stand down and submit to my lawful authority."

Senior Sergeant Jones took Kelsey by the arm and looked suitably shocked when she stood and slammed him face down onto the conference table without the slightest effort.

Jared opened his mouth to say something, but Meyer beat him to it. "Captain, we need to take a step back. The princess may have a point. Legally speaking. We should withdraw to consider the situation before we make the wrong choice."

Breckenridge looked as though he wanted to lash out, but he stepped back from the abyss after a very long moment of silence. Very reluctantly. "Commander Mertz, you will come with us."

"He will not," Kelsey said firmly. "*Courageous* says you don't believe she is an active Fleet vessel. Fine. I hereby declare her my diplomatic ship and transfer Captain Mertz and his crew from the disabled *Athena* to *Courageous* to act as my crew on detached duty. You may be the senior Fleet commander in this area, but they are no longer under your authority."

Breckenridge's expression was apoplectic. He backed out into the corridor. "This isn't over. We're leaving."

Kelsey released the marine, and he backed out with his fellows. Meyer inclined his head and strode out.

Once they were all gone, she slumped back into her seat. "Well, that could've gone better."

Jared agreed, but he wasn't sure how they could have gone about salvaging the situation once Breckenridge attempted to assert dominance. "*Courageous*, without sounding an alarm that Captain Breckenridge or his people can see or hear, go to general quarters. No battle screens unless they fire on us. Block all transmissions from inside this ship, and signal *Lance* that she is to withdraw at once. This isn't the Pentagarans' fight, and I don't want Breckenridge to think she's a threat."

He rubbed his face as Lieutenant Reese looked into the conference room questioningly. "Take your men and follow them to the docking level, Lieutenant. I want them off my ship without force, if possible. Be gentle. They are Fleet personnel."

"Aye, sir."

"Well," he said to Kelsey, "this certainly makes things harder. What do we do now?"

She sat down and buried her face in her hands. "I haven't got the faintest idea, but we need to get this settled as soon as possible. That freighter could pop up at any time now. If we're still bickering, it'll bring the wrath of the rebels down on us."

8

Kelsey listened closely as Jared finished detailing his interactions with Breckenridge. "The man sounds like a real ass. How does someone that lacking in talent become a senior captain in Fleet? I ask only because I intend to make sure it never happens again."

Her brother stalked around his office. "Good luck with that. You'll have to get his uncle thrown out of the Imperial Senate first."

He sighed. "While that's a worthy goal, we need to worry about our current situation first. The freighter and its escort will be along shortly. I'd intended to make our way over there today, just in case they came early. We have to stop them, or we're completely screwed."

She took a breath and forced herself to focus. "We will. It's been three hours. If Breckenridge was going to reject my authority, he'd already have done so."

"Or he's trying to figure out how to take *Courageous* out," her brother said grimly.

"Let's hope not. Even his uncle wouldn't be able to save his ass if he attacked the daughter of the emperor or other Fleet personnel."

They'd separated from the Fleet task force and entered into orbit around Pentagar. A probe kept an eye on the other ships as they sat out in space a short distance away.

Talbot sat beside Kelsey. "And if you can't work it out?"

"We'll work it out," she said firmly. "Even if we don't, they don't have enough military force to do anything terminally stupid in Pentagar space. The Pentagaran Navy would chew them up, and the interdiction zone fortresses would keep them bottled up in this system. They're not going to make that mistake. That's the reason I know that we'll work it out. Because they have no choice."

Jared shook his head. "Life's taught me that you can't count on someone else doing the smart thing. Sometimes you can't even count on yourself for that. Bright people make terrible mistakes every day. Once you factor in stupidity, well, all bets are off."

"Pardon the interruption, Captain," *Courageous* said. "There is a cutter departing the Fleet task force. *Spear* is also signaling, asking for Princess Kelsey."

She rose to her feet. "Thank you, *Courageous*. Jared, may I borrow your desk?"

He gave her a lopsided smile. "It's your ship."

"It was the best I could come up with on short notice. Tell me you'd rather be over there with him right now. In the brig."

"I'll take our current circumstances. Thank you."

Kelsey sat at the desk and activated the console. An image of Captain Wallace Breckenridge appeared.

"Princess Kelsey."

"Captain. Have you reached a conclusion on my position?"

The man looked as though he smelled something bad. "Those familiar with legal matters have advised me to accept your claims for the moment. Rest assured that I will dispatch a probe for home to get this situation clarified at once. In the meantime, I recognize that this situation requires some compromise. My ships and I are yours to command.

"However, I insist that my chief medical officer examine you in your medical center. I also insist that one of my officers be present on your staff."

She didn't like the idea of his people on board *Courageous* at all, but even if he'd stuffed that cutter full of people, they could handle it. "I accept those conditions. Once I have satisfied your doctor, we need to have the meeting I originally called for. There is very little time before the rebels arrive to discover that we've taken the other system from them. We can't afford to allow them to escape."

"I feel confident that I will be able to formulate a plan of attack to stop a freighter and its escort."

"Captain Mertz and his team have been working on a plan for months. I'm certain that he will be able to execute it successfully."

Breckenridge shook his head. "Unacceptable. I am the senior Fleet officer and task force commander. You have given me the order, and I will determine the best method to carry it out. Commander Mertz is on detached duty and solely responsible for you and your ship."

She sighed, recognizing a futile situation in his intransigence. "I'll contact you as soon as we're done here."

"I look forward to your call." His tone indicated otherwise. "Good day, Highness." The transmission terminated.

"Isn't he just a joy to work with?" she asked rhetorically. "It shames me to ask this, but how do we know that cutter isn't loaded with a missile warhead?"

"*Courageous*, was that transmission via tight beam?" Jared asked.

"Negative."

"Then all his people heard him acknowledge your authority and identity. Would he try to kill the second in line to the Throne with that many witnesses?"

"I certainly hope not."

Talbot stood. "You two wait for them in the medical center. Commander Graves and I can meet the cutter."

She glared at him. "Getting yourself blown up makes this better how, exactly?"

"It's better than you and the captain going up in smoke."

Jared nodded. "That's the best plan. We'll go with it."

She felt her eyes narrow. "Isn't this my choice?"

"Not when it comes to your safety. Come on. There's just enough time for Talbot to arrange everything."

She and Jared went to the medical center. She filled Doctor Stone in while they waited.

The doctor smiled. "I've worked with Doctor Guzman before. He's not inclined to be anyone's yes man. If he gave the captain a clean bill of health, he'll do the same for you."

"Cutter docking," *Courageous* said from the overheads.

"I don't know if I'll ever get used to that," Stone said.

Kelsey chuckled. "Wait until he can say something in your head without warning. While you're in the shower."

She brought up the vid feed to the docking area and saw Commander Meyer and several others come onto the ship. It only took them a few minutes to arrive in the medical center. One of the men, a massive black man with a shaved head, smiled at Stone. "Lily, it's so good to see you again."

"Justin." Lily took his hand into hers. "Welcome aboard. I can't wait to show you around my medical center."

"I can't wait to see it. First, though, I need to examine Princess Kelsey." He bowed his head apologetically. "I'm Doctor Justin Guzman, Highness. I'll be as quick as I can."

She smiled even though she'd rather go through an armed combat drop than a medical examination. "Shall we start with a full body scan?"

"That sounds fine. I'm given to understand you received implants similar to Captain Mertz's?"

"Why don't I let you see for yourself?"

Kelsey reclined on the examination table and let Lily take over. She knew the exact moment when the other doctor grasped the scale of her modifications, because he gaped at the display.

"My God," he muttered. "What the hell did they do to you?"

Kelsey smiled up at him sardonically. "As hard as it is to believe, they gave me Imperial Commando implants. That's like a marine on steroids. A lot of steroids."

"Look here," Lily said, pointing to the screen beside the table. "You'll note she has the same cranial implants as Captain Mertz. In addition, her bones now have a graphene coating. She has artificial musculature in all her major muscle groups, as well. I've seen her lift a weight machine. Not the maximum weight. The entire machine."

She'd been wearing her combat armor at the time, but Kelsey saw no reason to elaborate.

Doctor Guzman looked down at her with ill-concealed shock. "That's hard to believe."

The marine from *Spear*—Senior Sergeant Jones—spoke up. "Believe it, Doc. She slammed me onto a table without any problem at all."

The older man shook his head as though clearing out the cobwebs. "I'll accept it, hypothetically. What is this?"

Lily smiled. "You'll love this. That's her pharmacology unit. I've been working on deciphering what the drugs are, but some of them are still a mystery to me. I know they can do something to speed up the reactivity of her nerves, as well as accelerating her brain functions. There are some powerful painkillers and just about anything that would be useful in combat."

Chemical data scrolled up the screen. The doctor examined it. "That's astonishing. Some of these have the potential to revolutionize pharmacology."

"She also had enhancements to her eyes, ears, and sense of smell. Finally, she has medical nanites, as does the captain. There are millions of small machines throughout her body that can repair a tremendous amount of damage. Do you see any signs of surgery?"

The older man examined the readouts closely. "None at all. The cuts must've been incredibly fine to leave no traces."

Kelsey knew what was coming, but it still made her stomach roil when Lily put up the image of her just after they'd rescued her. She lay flat on the table as the medical team prepped her for the regenerator. Terrible scars, red and raw, covered her skull and arms. They couldn't see under the sheet, but the scars had covered her entire body.

Everyone from *Spear* sucked in horrified gasps. Even Commander Meyer looked ill, his glance toward her filled with pity. Pity she didn't want or need.

"The scars covered every part of her body, and the surgery was done without any anesthesia at all," Stone said dispassionately. "The regenerator did what it could and would probably have fixed everything well enough that the scars wouldn't be visible, but the nanites fixed the damage right down to the cellular level. They also corrected other damage from childhood injuries.

"From speaking to someone knowledgeable with these kinds of nanites, she can also expect an extended life span. Approximately three hundred years, from what I've been able to determine. Though I've begun to suspect that her nanites are even more effective than those used by a normal Fleet officer or marine. She might live half again longer. Or forever. We just don't know."

Guzman shook his head again. "That's... well, I was going to say preposterous, but I think I might need to move the marker for that word out a little bit. Difficult to believe, then. I'll want to see all your medical records for the princess, please. Highness, you can sit up. We two sawbones will adjourn to Doctor Stone's office to hash this out."

Senior Sergeant Jones stepped over after the doctors had left and she'd sat up. "Highness, I want to apologize for putting my hands on your person. I deeply regret doing so."

She considered being snippy with him but rejected the thought almost at once. He was Talbot's fellow marine. "You were following what you thought to be the lawful orders of your commanding officer, Senior Sergeant. I won't hold that against you. Besides, I might have caused you some embarrassment. I'm sorry about that."

His face took on a wry expression. "It *has* been mentioned a few times. I'm sure I'll be able to live it down in a few years."

"I bet I can help with that," Talbot said. "There's a Pentagaran vid of some assassins ambushing a group of us. It's very... educational."

Kelsey wanted to tell him not to play it, but she knew she'd have to live with that recording for the rest of her life. At least she hadn't shared the recordings of the ambush on the asteroid and in the sunken battlecruiser housing the Pale Ones' AI. They were still safely isolated in her implant memory.

She'd watched the vid several times, and it still shocked her. It hadn't felt like she was moving that quickly during the attack, but she was. Her implants had taken control of her and moved her through the attackers like a ghost. Yes, they'd grazed her arm with one shot, but she'd been empty-handed against half a dozen armed men. She'd killed most of them before their bodies had hit the floor.

The men from *Spear* were quiet as the vid played out. Afterward, they stared at her with an expression much different from pity. Shock and awe, Talbot had called it.

"That was her on autopilot," Talbot said to the hushed gathering. "Less than a week after the Pale Ones ripped her apart and rebuilt her. In the last two months, she's been training and has much better control of her enhancements. She's significantly more deadly now, especially with weapons. Her implants link right into them, and she can outshoot me.

"We don't have recordings, but she interrupted a Pale Ones ambush. She was in powered Imperial commando armor with a high-powered flechette railgun and a plasma rifle. Armed like that, she'd have a better-than-even chance of taking out the entire marine compliment on *Spear* while they were in an entrenched defensive position."

Kelsey took a deep breath and let it out slowly. "It's not something I ever saw myself as, Senior Sergeant, but there is no shame in losing out to me physically. I'm not the little girl I look like. I'm a killing machine, and every single Pale One is just like me. Underestimating them means death or worse." Her voice turned grim as she told him how outclassed they were.

She shifted her gaze to Commander Meyer. "On a different level, I can interface with *Courageous*. I watched you when you boarded this ship through my implant feed. I can access the ship's scanners right now and tell you exactly how far away *Spear* is from us. I know her weapons status. I know her precise course.

"I'm so in tune with my armor that I forget I'm wearing it. Jared is just the same way with this ship. He could take *Courageous* to battle stations, fire her weapons, and anything else he would normally do on the bridge from his shower. Imagine what this ship could do if every officer and crewperson were implanted. At this moment, she's not nearly as efficient as she will be one day. Even in this reduced state, she could take all of your ships from a standing start."

"It seems I may have underestimated the threat that these Pale Ones pose and the benefits of enhancement," Meyer said, sounding a bit overwhelmed. "You envision all Fleet personnel having these one day?"

She nodded. "I don't see how we can avoid it, Commander. Honestly, the Fleet implant surgery isn't that hard to recover from. Jared was on light duty the same day and fully recovered the next. A commando should have the work done in a series of procedures with recovery and training time between them. Regular marines would have less work than me. I've fully recovered, even though I'm still learning what I need to know about using them. This is nothing to be afraid of."

The door to Lily's office opened, and the two physicians came out. Guzman bowed his head. "I've been over every aspect of your enhancement, Highness. You have my full medical approval."

She smiled. "Thank you, Doctor. Gentlemen, if you have no further objections, we need to have that briefing. I want all ships' captains brought aboard *Courageous* tomorrow morning. I've been up all night, and they need time to examine all the data we've gathered. Come ready to plan our next moves in a hurry. The rebels will be back in less than a week, and we must be ready for them. That means we leave for Erorsi as soon as we finish."

9

Breckenridge came spoiling for a fight. He and his officers arrived in a phalanx and sat across the table from Jared, Kelsey, and Graves. Other than introducing the others briefly, the captain sat silent and hostile. Jared hoped the other ship commanders would be more open-minded than the senior captain.

Thankfully, he had ported *Athena*'s files over to *Courageous* and had access to their dossiers. Those told him a little more about the men and women arrayed against him—the people he had to convince to follow his battle plan if they were to have any chance of success.

The commanding officers of the two light cruisers flanked Breckenridge: Captain Justin Macumber of *Titan* on the right and Captain Paul Cooley of *Shadow* on the left. The destroyer commanders flanked them: Commander Scott Roche of *Ginnie Dare* and Commander Ryan Stevenson of *One Bullet* on the right and Commander Eliyanna Kaiser of *New York* to the left. There should've been one more destroyer to make for an even set, but it had been detached to escort one of the other exploratory expeditions.

Based on the maps he now had of the Old Empire, the other three expeditions were probably safe from running into anything dangerous —unless they found an unexpected path deeper into the Old Empire like *Athena* had. For all the distance a flip point could traverse in a moment, they shepherded the direction of travel to a greater or lesser degree. The other expeditions were moving away from the Old Empire.

Jared cleared his throat. "Thank you all for coming. Let me start with the basic rundown of our situation. The next system over, the Erorsi system, was under the control of the Pale Ones until two months ago. We've defeated them and destroyed the artificial intelligence controlling the system. We blew up one orbital and captured two shipyards, one of them completely intact. The other one is repairable. The planet took a major kinetic strike, though. The damage to the ecosystem is extreme."

He brought up a diagram of the Erorsi system. "The green diamond is the flip point leading to Pentagar. The red diamond is the flip point leading deeper into the Old Empire. The yellow diamond is a weak flip point leading to areas unknown. As you can see, any vessels coming through from the Old Empire will need to go quite some distance into the system before they will be able to detect anything about the planet or the orbitals around it. In fact, they will need to pass directly through the system's asteroid belt.

"After consultation with the Pentagaran Navy officers, we decided the best course of action was to place one force behind Erorsi and another in the asteroid belt. Once the freighter and any possible escorts are between the forces, we can strike and hold them from escaping. Because that's the key factor in this engagement. We want the contents of the freighter, but under no circumstances can we allow any information about our presence to get back to the rebels."

Macumber raised his hand, earning a sharp glance from Breckenridge. He continued in spite of the warning. "What kind of firepower are we looking at? A ship like this one? Something bigger? Or perhaps only a destroyer?"

"We don't know," Jared said. "Communications logs we recovered only indicate that this yearly resupply mission sometimes has an escort. If this were a Fleet mission, it would probably be a destroyer. We can't count on that, though. If they send a battlecruiser like *Courageous*, this is going to be an exceptionally deadly fight."

Breckenridge sniffed. "Let's say that we do capture this freighter. What's its cargo? Better yet, how do we access the computer on board it to get the information we need to make better choices going forward? In other words, *Captain*, what is your long-term plan?"

The subtle emphasis he placed on Jared's title made his repugnance clear. Jared ignored it. They needed to bury their problems, or they'd never get home. "Without information on what lies further into the Old Empire, it's not easy to develop a long-term plan. There are several possible routes leading back to Avalon. Once we have an idea of what we face, we'll be able to pick the appropriate direction to go."

Captain Cooley earned a glance of his own from his commander when he spoke. "If these artificial intelligences are that advanced, how do we intend to get access to the records at all? As the commodore asked, what exactly is the cargo on board this freighter?"

Kelsey spoke up for the first time in the briefing. "The computers on board the ships are accessible through our implants. Based on what I've seen, we'll probably have to have physical access as well. And by that, I mean someone with implants will need to be on board the freighter to gain access to its systems. Either Captain Mertz or myself will need to be included in the boarding party sent to secure it."

Breckenridge shook his head. "Unacceptable. Under no circumstances will I risk the life of a member of the Imperial Family like that. Neither of you will be allowed into the other system until we have secured it. My task force is quite capable of handling any problems that come our way. Once we have secured the freighter, we will send word, and *Captain* Mertz can come do whatever he thinks necessary."

Kelsey leaned forward. "That is unacceptable as well. I cannot stress how important it is that no word of our incursion filters back to the rebels. Whatever plan you decide to go forward with, Commodore Breckenridge, it needs to include *Courageous*. This vessel is faster than any of your ships, and her scanning gear is infinitely better. As are her weapons.

"I understand that you have no desire to cooperate with us on this matter. You're going to need to modify that attitude. Allow me to stress that you have no idea how deadly Old Empire technology can be. This ship is quite capable of exterminating your entire task force. If one like her accompanies that freighter, it's entirely possible that it would leave the system as the sole survivor. Whether or not you include *Courageous* in the initial attack, she needs to be present so that she can deal with any threats that you cannot."

They glared at one another. Breckenridge relented. "If that is the case, then I insist that you not be present on board this vessel, Highness."

"Agreed," Jared said before Kelsey could argue.

Kelsey frowned at him. "Excuse me?"

Just play along, he sent to her implants.

Once she sat back, Jared continued aloud. "Commodore Breckenridge is correct. If *Courageous* is going to fight, we can't risk losing both of the people with implants. In any case, you're the less expendable of the two of us. You're in command of the Imperial forces in this sector."

Breckenridge grunted. "Now that we've settled that, we need to discuss the possible contingencies in this battle."

The way that Breckenridge assumed that Kelsey would do what they decided amused Jared. His real plan for Kelsey might give the older man a stroke. Once the Imperial task force deployed in the Erorsi system, he'd make certain that Princess Kelsey was available in a marine pinnace. If the ship had to fight, his sister would be safe in the asteroid belt, undetectable at low speed but able to get to the freighter quickly if needed.

Once they got into the details of planning the ambush, some of the tenseness in the air bled away. Aside from Breckenridge, Jared found the Fleet officers competent and knowledgeable. They examined the Erorsi system layout as a group and suggested refinements to the attack plan, as well as contingencies based on certain possible reactions by the other side.

After about an hour, they had what Jared believed to be a workable plan that wasn't too different from the one he'd already settled on with the Pentagarans.

Commander Kaiser pointed at the weak flip point in the Erorsi system. "What about that thing? Should we send a probe through just to be certain that nothing is going to be coming after us while we're fighting?"

Jared shook his head. "Nothing has come out in the last two months, and I'd rather not provoke something on the other side that we're not aware of. The Pentagaran forces are already in orbit around Erorsi. We've moved the probe that we had monitoring the rebel flip point to a safe distance so that any ship coming through won't spot it.

"It's in range to detect any incursion and signal the forces around the planet, as well as the probe waiting here at the flip point to Pentagar. We need to proceed to the Erorsi system as soon as possible and take up our positions. Every minute we delay leads to a higher possibility that the enemy will arrive before we're ready for them."

"Status change," *Courageous* said from the overhead speakers. "Transition detected in the Erorsi system at the enemy flip point. Two vessels are currently proceeding toward Erorsi prime. ETA five point seven hours."

"Dammit," Jared muttered. "This couldn't have come at a worse time. We need to get over to the other system as soon as possible."

"Wait," Roche said. "At that speed, they won't be into scanner range of the planet to see the damage for most of the trip, unless their scanners work completely differently than ours. How long did the AI wait to signal them before?"

"We have no idea."

Roche nodded. "It'll take us a few hours to get to the Erorsi flip point if we leave right now. If we keep our speed down on the other side, we might be able to cut them off. It doesn't matter what they do in the system if they can't get back out the way they came."

Breckenridge nodded decisively. "Excellent points, Scott. So long as our course and speed allow us to beat them to the other flip point, we win. From what I've seen, they'll attack at the first sign of enemy activity, so we should be able to lure them into coming after us. Or the Pentagarans could do the same. We'll just have to improvise."

Hearing that word come from Breckenridge's mouth made Jared a little ill. The other man wasn't good at all in a free-form tactical environment.

Captain Breckenridge rose to his feet. "Signal the task force, Commander Meyer. We boost for the Erorsi flip point at flank speed." He shifted his attention to Kelsey. "You can get off here or at the fortresses defending the flip point, Highness. I don't care which. Commander Meyer will accompany you."

Without waiting for a response, he headed out of the conference room. The other ships' captains hastily followed him out.

Kelsey growled. "He's really beginning to irritate me."

"Will you be getting off here or at the stations around the flip point, Highness?" Meyer asked.

Kelsey grinned. "Neither. I'll go with *Courageous*."

Commander Meyer jerked a little. "That wasn't the agreement. You agreed with Captain Breckenridge that you wouldn't go in exchange for this ship being included in the attack plan."

"Jared agreed to that, not me. Besides, there are two ships. You might need a second person with implants. The survival of everyone in this task force might depend on it. We do it my way."

The slender officer looked torn, but he reluctantly nodded. "I'm going to regret this, aren't I?"

"Based on my observation," Jared said, "almost certainly."

10

Kelsey sat at one of the observation consoles to the rear of the bridge. Part of her attention was on the scanner readings from the Erorsi system, but they were too far away from the enemy ships to detect them directly. She only hoped the reverse was true.

The task force was leading the way, with *Courageous* following at a more sedate pace, one that Jared could make up for if he needed to.

The rest of her attention was on Commander Meyer. The tall man was watching her. She raised an eyebrow. "Can I help you, Commander?"

"I'm curious what you're doing."

"Right now? I'm watching the system through the ship's scanners and wondering if this ambush is going to work."

He shook his head. "That's not what I meant. Forgive me, but a few months ago, your relationship to Captain Mertz was poor at best. Now you're working with him as though you've been together for years. Surely the events of the last few months haven't erased the troubles between you."

She focused her full attention on him. "That's fairly blunt, and none of your business."

"I disagree," he said diffidently. "If I don't understand the full situation, I can't explain it to Captain Breckenridge. People don't trust what they don't understand."

"Are you saying you don't trust me? That's awkward."

He shrugged. "I'm being up front. Your authority is somewhat… sketchy with the captain. If he decides that you're a danger to the Empire, he might refuse to accept your leadership. I'm coming to see how advanced this ship is, but it's only one ship. It would be far better for everyone concerned if the two of you built some bridges."

She leaned back in her chair and crossed her arms. "Okay, if you want this plainly stated, I'll do that. Yes, I came on this mission with a chip on my shoulder toward Jared. Everyone knows the history between him and my family. In fact, it's so widely known that people assume they know everything about it. They don't.

"Over the last few months, I've gotten the chance to see what kind of person Jared Mertz really is: a loyal, honest man who loves the Empire. A gifted tactician and combat commander. A friend. A very good friend. I'm certain that's not how you see him, but you and your captain are biased."

"I don't see my position as biased. Jared Mertz has a reputation in Fleet as a man seeking advancement, one who's willing to use his birth as a ladder to climb over the backs of more deserving officers. Perhaps you weren't aware of that."

Kelsey smiled coolly. "My brother worries about that very thing. He's wrong to do so, and so are you. Jared has gone out of his way to avoid using his birth to his advantage, so much so that it's kept him from being where his talent would already have taken him: a task force command.

"Believe me, I looked hard before I came to that conclusion. I wish your commander could say the same. His uncle in the Senate has been there for him, if you know what I mean. If using family to advance your career pisses you off, shouldn't that bother you?"

Meyer stiffened. "I've been with Captain Breckenridge for four years. He is an exemplary officer."

"He's arrogant, ill suited to unorthodox situations, and he nurses a grudge. You're both still smarting from the ambush Jared sprang on you during the war games. You don't see his methods as creative. You see them as cheating. Let's say for the moment that I agreed with you. I'd rather have the universe's best cheat stacking the deck against the Empire's enemies than a man who refuses to see the reality of the situation."

Her frank assessment seemed to take Meyer back. "Well, I'm not certain I share that assessment, but we're stuck with the cards we've been dealt, to use your metaphor. I'll consider what you've said. What are your plans going forward into this ambush, if I might ask?"

"The marines are prepping a pinnace. I'll go with them shortly."

"Forgive me, Highness, but that's an exceptionally rash decision. You have no place in combat, even though you seem to have handled every situation thrown at you with exceptional bravery and unnerving competence."

She allowed herself a smile. "I doubt very seriously that Lieutenant Reese will let me near the fighting this time. I have something of a reputation. Nonetheless, it seems to find me anyway. The question in my mind is, do you have a place on this mission?"

The man straightened. "I'm going wherever you go. It's my duty to be between you and danger."

She laughed before she could stop herself. "I'm sorry. I don't mean that as a reflection on your bravery. The one place you absolutely do not want to be is between me and danger. We need time to fit you into some armor. That means we'll go down to marine country shortly."

The tactical overlay she'd been keeping up in the corner of her mind's eye updated. The two markers for the enemy ships showed more details. One of the stealthed probes had gotten a better reading and sent it on to *Courageous* via tight beam. The escort was a destroyer.

"Good news," Jared said, obviously looking at the same information. "We're only facing a destroyer. While dangerous, it isn't nearly as bad as a cruiser. Zia, send a tight beam to *Spear* with the details. Append whatever data we have about that class of ship to it. What's our ETA?"

"Less than two hours at this speed, Captain. If we can keep them from spotting us for another hour, we can cut the destroyer off from the flip point. Somewhat longer if we take the slower speed of the task force into account. Also, we've received a confirmation signal from the Pentagaran ships in orbit around Erorsi. They're ready to move out as soon as you give the word."

The tactical officer glanced down at her console. "Incoming signal from *Spear*."

Kelsey rose to her feet. "That's my cue to depart stage left. Jared, good luck."

He turned toward her as she headed for the lift. "Stay out of trouble, but be sure to shut them down as soon as possible. Remember, we need that cargo intact."

"I'll do my best."

She led Commander Meyer into the lift and started it down toward marine country.

"You don't seem worried about the prospect of fighting," he said after a moment.

Kelsey nodded. "After a while, you either learn to control your fear or you stop fighting. I'm worried, though. Everything has to go just right for us to win. One mistake will let the enemy escape or see the ship we want to capture blown to pieces. Even if we do everything right, people will still die. That's the hardest part."

The lift doors opened, and she walked down the corridor to marine country. The marines were in the final stages of gearing up. Coulter stood waiting for them.

"Commander, if you'll come this way, I'll get you into some combat armor. Highness, we have your armor ready."

Meyer waved Coulter away. "I want to see this armor first."

"Aye, sir. This way."

The marine led them into the armory. Kelsey's dark-grey armor stood ready on its stand. She couldn't help but compare it to the black armor the woman in the vid had worn. Scratched and scarred as Kelsey's was, it was pristine compared to the other woman's. How much hell would she have to go through for them to look the same?

She began shedding her clothes, to the obvious shock of the Fleet officer. "They've seen everything I've got," she said bluntly. "An Old Empire skinsuit makes the armor a lot more comfortable." She did turn her back on him at the last, though. He wasn't a marine.

The snug suit made slipping into the armor a lot easier. It also had sensors built into it that the armor reacted to. Movement was smoother when she wore it. It also had the requisite fittings for her to pass any wastes on to the armor's sump.

Kelsey commanded the armor to seal as soon as she slipped inside. The systems came online and did an auto check. All green. Talbot would check her again before they boarded anything. She disconnected the armor from its stand and took two steps forward.

She squatted and then stretched. The range of motion was good, and the armor settled around her like a little black dress. Her implants had already overridden her senses, and she could see and hear everything around her.

To make a point, she stepped in front of Meyer without turning on the chameleon portion of the helmet. All he would be able to see was a featureless helmet of hardened metal without the slightest hint of humanity.

"Forget what you think you know about me, Commander. I've earned my maturity the hard way. Do not underestimate me."

To his credit, Meyer stood his ground. "I won't, Highness. In return, I ask you to consider that you don't know everything about either your half brother or Captain Breckenridge."

The corners of her lips quirked upward. He had more steel than she'd expected. "I've dropped the half-brother reference. Jared is my brother. I know him a hell of a lot better than your CO. Captain Breckenridge is going to need to prove himself to me, and so are you. Be glad we're only boarding a freighter. That has to be easier than a stand-up firefight. Or crash landing a pinnace."

She turned the helmet projection on and watched his expression as her face appeared. It wasn't really her, but the projection on the helmet was very lifelike.

That was when the overhead alarms began to ring. Jared's voice rang out through the overheads. "All hands to battle stations. This is not a drill."

Kelsey brought the ship's tactical overlay back up. The task force had split up. *Courageous* was on her way toward the enemy flip point.

The other five ships were still heading for the two ships in the enemy task force. That wasn't the plan.

She pinged Jared through the ship's network. *What's happening? Why did we change course?*

Captain Breckenridge said he has enough ships to run down a destroyer. We're to play backstop to make sure the enemy doesn't slip past him and make a run for it.

Is that the best idea?

No. My guess is that he doesn't trust us not to get involved. Keep prepping for your mission. We might have to board the destroyer if things go south.

She scowled at Meyer. "Your captain changed the plan at the last minute. We're on the way to the enemy flip point while he tries to take out the destroyer and capture the freighter on his own. If this goes bad, I'm going to be pissed."

Meyer took a step back. "I'm certain that he had his reasons."

"They'd better be damned good. Suit up. We might need to launch in a hurry. Coulter, get him ready."

"Aye, Highness. This way, Commander."

She was certain that "Aye, Highness" wasn't the correct response, but she had to admit it made her smile.

Kelsey made her way over to Lieutenant Reese. The officer was huddled with Talbot and the other noncoms. They had ship plans up on one of the screens. It didn't look like a freighter.

They made room for her without comment. Reese tapped the screen. "I just got word that our potential target has changed. This is the most common type of destroyer in the Old Empire, a Zombie class. Small, fast, but relatively lightly armed."

She loaded the plans into her implants. "Faster than this ship? Lightly armed in comparison to what? Us? The task force?"

"*Courageous* can take her if she can catch her. The task force can, too, though their lack of missile range leaves them open for a mauling if they screw up. Captain Mertz says he warned them." The marine officer shook his head. "They're making this more complicated than I like, but that's been our luck lately."

"Status change," *Courageous* said through the overhead speakers.

"The enemy vessels have changed course back toward the hostile flip point and are accelerating."

Kelsey looked at the tactical situation through the ship's passive scanners. They could directly detect the enemy ships at this point. "*Courageous*, can we cut them off from the flip point?"

"Affirmative, if the situation remains static. If the destroyer accelerates, this vessel is not close enough to stop it from fleeing."

"Well, we'll just have to hope that—"

The Fleet task force accelerated sharply. If the enemy had only suspected their presence before, they knew they were there now.

"Dammit," Kelsey cursed. "What the hell is that man thinking? He's going to spook them into splitting up. The bastards are going to get away."

Reese looked grim. "Let's hope not. If they do, the Pentagarans are in real danger of an invasion, and so are we."

11

J ared watched in frustration as the enemy destroyer accelerated
away from the freighter. At that speed, it was going to beat
them handily to the flip point. Breckenridge had ruined the
ambush.

"Maximum acceleration. I want to be in range of the ship before
it flips."

Courageous leapt to its top speed, but Jared only had to do one
check to realize they wouldn't make it. The destroyer would be able to
flip before they came into extreme range.

The Fleet task force had split in two. The faster ships were in
pursuit of the destroyer while *Spear* headed for the freighter. That
really made no sense. Why send a heavy cruiser to catch a freighter?
The Pentagaran ships coming out from Erorsi would be able to catch
the lumbering cargo ship before it got to the flip point. Breckenridge
shouldn't have split his forces.

That's when it hit him. Breckenridge wanted to capture the
freighter and its cargo for himself. He'd come up with some excuse or
reason to keep it. Or he'd try.

Jared put it out of his mind. Kelsey could deal with the man once the situation was under control. Right now, he needed to figure out how to stop that fleeing ship.

He watched the situation play out for a little while. The task force had drawn substantially ahead of *Courageous* during the stealthy approach on the enemy ships. The destroyer was still going to be far outside their missile envelope, but it looked tantalizingly close to them.

Zia turned toward him. "Sir, something isn't right. The destroyer should be pulling farther ahead. It's not moving at full speed."

"Are you sure? Perhaps it's not really a Zombie class."

"Our scanners are on active mode, and I'm getting a decent reading on it. I think it is a Zombie. One that isn't using its full potential. Sir, I'm concerned it might be sucking the task force into missile range."

Jared checked the distances between that ship and the task force. "Give them a warning that thing might be setting up an ambush."

That was when the destroyer put on a burst of speed, cutting in toward the task force and firing missiles.

"Missiles fired," Zia said briskly. "Six missiles on an inbound track for the task force. They're accelerating at Old Empire speeds. The enemy ship is still closing. It's fired a second salvo. Now it's turning for the flip point and putting on maximum acceleration."

Jared watched the two clusters of missiles close in on the task force with a sense of dread. He'd warned them just how capable those weapons were, but that wouldn't help. The first group of missiles turned out to have two scan jammers. They blinded the Fleet vessels, allowing two of the real missiles to get through.

Both struck the light cruiser *Shadow* in titanic explosions. The warship lurched and veered off course, leaving it broadside to the next salvo.

Titan interposed herself between the danger and her wounded companion, firing her antimissile railguns at the incoming weapons. She stopped two of them. Three missiles struck *Titan*, and she exploded with the fury reserved to the gods of failed fusion plants. The remaining missile hit *One Bullet*, sending the destroyer to join *Titan* in the grave.

The enemy destroyer had killed a Fleet light cruiser and destroyer without taking a single bit of damage in return. It hadn't even come within range for the ships to return fire. Wisely, the remaining two Fleet destroyers began rescue operations, leaving the fleeing enemy to *Courageous*.

"Tell me we're going to catch that son of a bitch short of the flip point," Jared snarled.

Zia shook her head. "He still has enough distance to flip before we come into extreme missile range. We're going to have to make a combat flip and go after him."

Jared watched the ship make it to the flip point and disappear with impotent rage. "We have no idea what's on the other side of the flip point. What are our options?"

The tactical officer held up three fingers. "He'll either be waiting for us to flip, be hauling ass for the next flip point, or dropped to a crawl, hoping to hide until he gets so far away from the flip point that we can't find him.

"Odds are good the next system isn't occupied. The Old Empire maps have it as a white dwarf with no habitable planets. The flip point leading deeper into the Old Empire is on the other side of the system."

Jared nodded. "He has enough of a lead to get some distance and drop out of sight. The problem I see with that is that we'll be able to block his escape. If he can ambush us right after the flip, he might be able to take us out. That's the worst case. What can we do if that's his plan?"

"Send a spread of probes through. He won't get them all. One of them will tell us where he's at. Then we can flip through and blow him into atoms."

"Pardon, Captain," *Courageous* said. "There is one additional option. This vessel has decoys designed to masquerade as this vessel. One could be sent through, and it would likely fool the enemy scanners long enough to draw their fire."

"That could work. How long until we flip?"

"Just over twenty minutes, Captain," Ramirez said.

Jared watched the situation behind them as they sped toward the flip point. The Pentagarans were still hours away from being able to assist in the rescue operations. With the loss of *Titan* and *One Bullet*, the death toll would be almost two thousand people. They'd blown up so quickly that there wouldn't be any survivors.

Shadow was intact, but two Old Empire missiles would've wreaked havoc inside her. She had to have hundreds dead and even more wounded. The two destroyers would have their hands full with rescue operations. Their medical staffs would work themselves to collapse, but it wouldn't be enough.

He mentally glared at the icon representing *Spear*. That bastard should've been chasing the enemy destroyer. Those people had died because Breckenridge had underestimated the threat. Again.

Jared sighed. He didn't wish anyone on that ship harm. If Breckenridge had chased the destroyer and the enemy had destroyed *Spear*, they'd have lost almost as many people.

"*Spear* is launching pinnaces," Zia said. "They'll be boarding the freighter about the time we're ready to flip."

Hopefully they could capture the freighter without any further loss of life.

The freighter dashed those hopes when it fired on *Spear*. A missile flashed out of one cargo hold, followed by two more. The low rate of acceleration told Jared that the enemy had used the same trick he'd used on the Pale Ones' shipyard. They'd taken missile warheads without the normal drives and fired them. Perhaps they'd been in the cargo the ship was delivering.

Spear stopped two of them at a safe distance, but the third almost made it before the defensive railguns detonated it. They needed to get on board that freighter as soon as possible.

A missile flashed out of the heavy cruiser and into the freighter. The cargo vessel disintegrated in a massive explosion, destroying everything Jared had hoped to capture: the cargo, prisoners, and any computer records.

He rubbed his face tiredly. Breckenridge had botched every aspect of this ambush by the numbers. The incompetence that he'd accused Jared of was on full display, and he'd no doubt find a way to blame someone else.

Probably Jared.

"Three minutes to flip," Zia said. "I'm thinking of sending the decoy through on the far edge of the flip point and coming through on this side in fifteen seconds."

He shook his head. "Reverse that. We'll go through on the far side. Release the decoy with a good trajectory to go through where we'd transition. We'll brake hard and go through after it. This is going to be difficult, but I want you to be surgical, Zia. I want that ship crippled but not destroyed. We need any information from him that we can get. Work with *Courageous* on targeting critical areas."

Jared opened a channel to Lieutenant Reese. "We're flipping in three minutes. Be ready to launch at a moment's notice. Things went sideways in the ambush. The freighter is gone. We need this ship in one piece."

"Aye, sir. We'll do our best. The pinnace we brought over from *Athena* won't be as good as the three Old Empire models, but if you can get us close, we'll be able to lock onto their hull."

"I'll buy you every meter that I can. Good luck. I know it's asking a lot, but keep Kelsey alive for me."

"I'll do my best. Reese out."

They crossed into the flip point and dropped the decoy. Its scanner signature blossomed into one identical with *Courageous*'s. Jared was impressed. He wouldn't have known it was a decoy if he hadn't seen it come online with his own eyes. Metaphorically speaking.

The decoy flipped, and he counted down fifteen seconds. "Raise the screens. Flip the ship."

The gut-twisting surge of transition washed over him, but he kept a firm lock on the tactical situation through his implants. The first thing he saw was the spread of six missiles arrowing toward the decoy.

He traced them back in a flash and located the destroyer. It was in an area of space that would be behind a ship that made the fastest transition. With the course change he'd laid in, *Courageous* had the other ship right in her sights at point blank range while they were reloading.

Jared made a split-second decision, overrode Zia's attack plan, and locked the missiles down. *Courageous*'s beam weapons came to life at his command and lashed out at the vessel sitting right in their face.

The lances of coherent energy slammed into the enemy's screens, dropping them. The following shots tore into the destroyer's hull.

Jared used his knowledge of the enemy deck plan to take out both his fusion plants by vaporizing the cooling and control circuitry. Two other beams disabled two of the missile launchers.

Robbed of the ability to control their own temperature, the plants performed as designed and shut down.

The destroyer fired missiles at *Courageous*. Zia stepped in behind Jared and resumed control of the beams. She incinerated the warheads before they closed the distance to *Courageous*. Then she knocked out the remaining launchers.

The Zombie-class destroyers didn't have beam weapons. The massive power requirements for them restricted them to heavy cruisers or above. The antimissile railgun slugs it fired at them failed to penetrate *Courageous*'s screens.

Low-power pinpoint shots disabled even that offensive capability. The enemy destroyer hung before them, crippled.

Jared sent the go signal to Reese. This was all in his hands now, and Kelsey's.

"Captain, I'm picking up a probe moving at high speed," Zia said. "It's on a course toward the other flip point in this system. It's already at the far edge of our missile envelope."

"Fire missiles. Take it out."

Probes didn't have the speed of missiles, but they could flip. He absolutely couldn't afford to let word of their ambush get back to wherever this ship came from. If the probe got too far away from them, it would escape.

Zia launched four missiles, ludicrous overkill for a probe. Her caution proved warranted when two of *Courageous*'s missiles burned out before catching it. The other two took it out.

He heaved a sigh of relief. "Thank God."

The marine pinnaces had launched while they dealt with the probe and were fast approaching the destroyer. This was the moment of truth.

12

Kelsey felt surprisingly calm as the pinnaces swooped in on the crippled destroyer. Perhaps having a small celestial body dropped on one put things into perspective.

"Listen up," Lieutenant Reese said over the general channel. "These people are likely armed with Old Empire weapons, and they'll know this ship better than we do. Don't take any chances. If someone surrenders, fine. If not, don't hesitate to put them down.

"If you see any computer equipment, make note of it. The engineering team will secure the ship's AI. See that they and the princess stay clear of the fighting."

He gave her a stern look. "The princess will try to stay out of the worst of it, but if she becomes engaged, support her to the hilt."

She snorted softly. She'd keep clear if she could, but if they needed her, she'd bring the heavy firepower.

Reese continued. "We'll be breaching the hull in four places. Tiger One will take engineering, Two will hit the bow, Three will take port, and Four will hit the starboard. Overwhelm any resistance as quickly as you can and support the other teams. We breach in sixty seconds. Good luck."

Up close, the ship looked surprisingly like *Courageous* had when they'd found her. The beams had melted their way through the hull in much the same way. Only there was a lot more debris pouring from the breaches: equipment, air, and bodies.

Kelsey didn't want to think about that, but these people had just killed thousands of her countrymen. Her gut tightened, and she pushed her regrets away. They'd earned what was coming.

Their pinnace stopped short of the enemy and fired the breaching charge, a web of small explosives bound together like a fishing net. It spread across a small area of the hull and detonated. The shaped charges ripped that small section apart.

When the fresh cloud of debris had thinned, Reese gave the order to board. The ramp opened at the back of the pinnace, and the marines swarmed across the gap with practiced ease. She made the jump without problems, the grav assist in her armor taking her exactly where she wanted to go. Her long hours of practice were paying off.

Part of her mind noted with amusement that Commander Meyer was having a much more difficult time of it. Sergeant Coulter was shepherding him across like a sack of potatoes.

Talbot and her guards hemmed her in protectively as the other marines set up a portable airlock and forced their way into the main body of the ship. They wanted prisoners, so spacing everyone wasn't on the menu.

Her external speakers picked up the howling of alarms as she cycled through. The ship's artificial gravity was still on, so that made moving around simpler.

The marines were taking fire from the forward part of the corridor. A dozen men and women in Fleet coveralls cowered under the guns of a marine fire team aft of their airlock.

She opened her senses and was surprised to discover they didn't have implants. She'd expected them to have the same AI–controlled virus that the Pale Ones did. That would've made them puppets for the AIs.

Kelsey consulted the diagram of the ship she'd downloaded. They were three levels away from the computer center. They needed to find a lift or stairwell.

That's when the sporadic fire from up ahead became more

intense. They must've run into heavy resistance. Then they started taking fire from aft.

"Enemy units moving behind us," Talbot shouted. "Take cover!"

That meant dodging into compartments to the sides of the corridor. It meant being pinned down. A destroyer couldn't have many marines aboard. *Athena* had only had thirty. With the four strike forces, they had almost two hundred marines.

Rather than ducking into one of the side compartments, she sprinted toward the fresh enemies and leapt.

The move took them completely off guard, and she landed among them without taking a single hit. There were four men in unpowered armor. She lashed out and took two of them out before they could jump back. The other two threw themselves back and fired at her with their flechette rifles.

High-speed tungsten penetrators rang off her armor as she drew her pistols and shot them. One died as her darts took him in the throat. The other dropped as her neural disruptor stunned him.

Her armor was gouged where they'd shot her, but nothing had penetrated. Yay powered combat armor.

"Dammit! Will you stop that?" Talbot covered the cross-corridors as his men took up positions. "You're going to get killed."

"We don't have time to get pinned down. We need the AI intact."

"We also need you alive. I need you alive."

She put her hand on his shoulder. "I'm being careful. Now let's get our people to this stairwell over here. We can get up to the computer center through it."

"Wait for the LT." Talbot must've sent a message to his commanding officer, because other marines streamed past their position and up the stairwell.

Reese stopped next to her. "Good work, Princess. Don't ruin it by running ahead of us. The enemy will be guarding the computer center. We want it intact."

She felt her eyes narrow. "Are you saying I'd blow it up?"

"Your track record on capturing AIs is filled with explosions and floods."

"I only wrecked one," she sniffed, "and that wasn't my fault. You were sleeping on the job."

"It's called being knocked unconscious by the antiboarding weapons. I'm surprised they haven't tried that. Doctor Leonard rigged up something that we put into our armor to protect us, but they haven't even tried."

"Knocking out the fusion plants might have taken them offline."

"True. The other teams report they're moving forward under heavy fire. The bridge is secure, but there were no prisoners. The officers attacked with pistols, and our people had to return fire. Engineering is still up in the air, but it looks like we might capture some people. We've secured a number of prisoners."

"The ones I saw didn't have implants. That's odd. The Old Empire implanted everyone in uniform from the lowest recruit to the Admiral of the Fleet."

The marine officer shrugged. "We'll sort it out. The advance fire team reports the enemy has sealed the computer center. No surprise there. I'm afraid Commander Meyer took a ricochet. His armor mostly held up, but he's got shrapnel in his leg."

"Is it serious?"

"He'll be okay once the doctor takes care of him. Time to move on to the AI."

The armored hatch to the computer center looked very much like the one on *Courageous*. The marines were setting up a perimeter on one side of the area. The other one was conspicuously empty of people.

"Exactly what is your entry plan?" she asked, suspecting she already knew the answer.

"The same one you used last time. You use your plasma rifle to breach the corridor wall and we swarm the compartment."

That was what she'd done on the sunken battlecruiser, though she'd had to attack all by herself. While the plan had worked, it had wreaked incredible damage to the area. Plasma wasn't the subtlest of weapons.

"That's always good for a last resort, but maybe we don't have to go that far. Let me try something."

She closed her eyes and reached out, looking for the AI. It wasn't there. At least there wasn't any way to connect to it.

"I thought the AIs had power sources other than the ship's fusion plants. I'm not feeling it."

Reese frowned. "It should have an independent power supply good for months. The area doesn't look damaged, either."

Kelsey opened her search to look for implant-capable devices. There were some but not nearly as many as on board *Courageous*. There was one set of implants in the computer center. So, someone was inside after all.

"I'm sensing someone in the computer center. A set of implants. I'll try communicating with that person. Perhaps we can get them to surrender."

"That would be nice," Reese said. "If not, we'll pry them out the hard way. We've taken the major areas of the ship. Resistance is falling off."

She pinged the implants inside and requested a connection. The person accepted. *Not the best time to chat. There's a bunch of people in the corridor outside. What's the status on rigging up a self-destruct device?*

He must've assumed she was one of his shipmates. *I'm afraid that it isn't going well. In fact, the entire ship has fallen. My name is Kelsey, and I'm one of the people in the corridor. We've taken this ship, and I'm calling on you to surrender. This fight is over.*

A moment of silence ended with a mental snarl from inside. *Damned traitor. I'll never give in to the likes of you. The only way you'll take me is in a body bag.* The connection terminated.

"Well, that could have gone better," she said out loud. "Let me go in first. I can handle one person, and we need prisoners. Cover your eyes."

She brought the plasma rifle up off her back and trained it on the armored hatch. If this worked out like it had on the sunken battlecruiser, the hatch would hold and the corridor would suffer. That would leave most of the computer center intact.

The bright bit of plasma exploded when it hit the armored hatch and engulfed the corridor beyond in flame. The bulkheads, ceiling, and floor failed.

Kelsey slung her plasma rifle and took a running jump down the corridor. She bounced off the bulkhead across from the hole and vaulted into the computer center. This one was in much better shape than the last one she'd seen. Everything was functional and clean.

There was more than one person in the room. There were five, all of them armed with pistols. They opened fire as she came hurtling in.

Much as she'd done in the earlier fight, she knew her advantage was in moving fast, so she used her suit to spring to the left as soon as her feet hit the floor. One armored fist smashed the pistol out of the hand of a woman in a rating's uniform. She'd have broken bones, but they could regenerate them.

Kelsey's neural disruptor came out as she rolled under a console. The enemy flechettes tore it apart as they tried to kill her.

She opened her weapon to its widest setting, popped up, and fired. Three of the enemy dropped, including the one in an officer's uniform. The remaining man, his eyes wide with fear, shot her at point-blank range.

This time the flechette went through her armor, and her left arm exploded with pain. She managed to tag him before he could shoot her again.

"Got them," she said through clenched teeth. "Hang on while I open the hatch."

She assessed her damage while she hunted for the manual override to the hatch locks. The flechette had hit one of the damaged areas on her upper arm. The weakened armor hadn't quite failed. The high-speed penetrator had deflected a piece of her own armor into her arm.

The pain dropped to almost nothing as her pharmacology unit dumped something into her bloodstream for the pain. She'd pay for it later, she imagined.

The manual lock worked as she remembered, and the armored hatch slid open. The marines flooded in and secured the room.

Talbot rushed to her side and cursed when he saw her favoring her arm. "How bad is it?"

"Not serious. I had two shots hit the same area. Just bad luck."

"Good luck that it wasn't your head. If it can wait, I'd rather not open up your armor until we're sure we've run down everyone on this ship."

Lieutenant Reese oversaw the securing of the prisoners, but he'd obviously been listening in. "We've locked down the primary ship's systems, but there are holdouts in the maintenance conduits. That gives them access all over the ship. We're starting at engineering and working our way forward, but it'll take a while to flush out all the stragglers. Is there any chance we can subvert their computer systems?"

Carl Owlet, their resident computer expert, brought up one of the consoles. "This is unlocked, but it says the AI has been wiped. Everything. All data drives scrubbed."

Well, while that was better than having the enemy get a warning out, it wasn't much help. They'd lost the freighter with its precious cargo and failed to get any hard data.

Kelsey looked at their newest prisoners. They'd have to do this the hard way.

13

J ared breathed a sigh of relief when several Pentagaran warships flipped into the system. He'd been feeling a little bit naked out here all alone.

The news from back in the Erorsi system was less reassuring. *Shadow* was in almost as bad a shape as *Athena* had been after her fight with the Pale Ones. She'd suffered heavy casualties, and her primary systems were offline. Rescue operations were ongoing. Her captain had survived, but he was in critical condition.

Breckenridge ordered Jared to abandon the destroyer and return at once, an order Jared was pleased to ignore with Kelsey's blessing. They'd give the destroyer a good going over and decide what to do after that.

The marines had scoured the other ship twice. A good thing, because they'd missed a couple of holdouts the first time. They'd lost a dozen marines in the attack, with three times that number wounded. Including Kelsey.

She'd assured Jared that her wound was minor, but he worried until she came back over with the wounded and the prisoners.

He'd sent Dennis Baxter and some of his people to the destroyer.

He'd rather not abandon it. If anyone could salvage something from the ship, it was his chief engineer.

While he waited for their report, he went down to the area Reese had set up for the prisoners. *Courageous* had a brig, but it was insufficient for the number of people they had in custody. They'd captured about fifty men and women, many injured in the fighting.

The officers had fought to the death. Only the one from the computer center had survived. He was also the only prisoner with implants.

They had him secured in a separate holding cell, strapped to a table. He'd become violent when he woke up. Now he glared at them from the table, continuously struggling with his bonds.

His uniform indicated he was a lieutenant commander, and his name tag said Richards. The sight of him snarling at them raised the hackles on Jared's neck. It was very much like the reactions of captured Pale Ones.

Or maybe he was only snarling at Doctor Leonard. The elderly scientist had a modified headset on the man's head and was scanning him.

Jared stepped up beside the table and looked down at their prisoner. "Commander Richards, my name is Jared Mertz, and I command *Courageous* in the name of the Terran Empire. You are the senior surviving officer of your ship, the destroyer labeled R-7386. I imagine we'll be seeing quite a lot of one another over the next few months. Is there anything I can get you?"

Richards didn't respond other than to growl.

"He won't talk with me, either, Captain," Leonard said. "His implants have a corrupted version of code that is very similar to that used in the Pale Ones. It's not exactly the same, though. Based on what I can see, he probably has somewhat more ability to carry out his orders. He works with the implants rather than being solely under their control. This is significantly more sophisticated than the hack used during the rebellion."

The technical people from Erorsi knew Old Empire programming and were able to isolate the specific corruption used on the Pale Ones.

The savages' implants overrode the human host when certain criteria existed. It was pretty blunt about it, too.

"Is the hardware the same?" Jared asked. "Can you reverse the virus?"

The older man nodded. "It is and I can. That should eliminate the unreasoned portion of his response. He has a Fleet officer's implants, by the way. No nanites, though. Just the cranial implants. I'm still not sure why they don't use them."

A woman Jared vaguely recognized as part of the Erorsi contingent chose that moment to push the Old Empire implanting device into the room. "Here you are, Doctor," the woman said.

The old scientist glanced at Jared. "Shall we proceed, Captain?"

They'd been through this process with several captured Pale Ones. It replaced the compromised code with the original Imperial version. Not that the change improved the Pale Ones' disposition. Savages were still savages. It had eliminated the unreasoning attack compulsion, though.

"Go ahead."

The scientists maneuvered the machine until they had it around the prisoner's head. Doctor Leonard initiated the software reversion, and the workstation began overwriting Richards's implant code. The process wasn't quick. It took just over four hours.

He'd been told that it could be done faster, but not without putting the implantee in significant danger. That's why the Old Empire couldn't keep up with the rebels. They didn't care if the subject died.

Jared let the scientists do their work. He'd come back once the process was complete.

His next stop was the medical center. He'd already been through once to talk to the injured. As always, the damage after a battle made him sick. These people were the lucky ones. The unlucky rested in the morgue.

An exhausted Lily Stone sat in her office, her head in her hands. He startled her when he rapped on the hatch.

She ran her hand through her hair and stood. "Captain."

"No need to stand for me. You and your people have done miracles. Again. I know it doesn't feel like it right now, but you have."

Stone gestured for him to take a seat. "It's the same for you, isn't it? We count the eggs broken rather than whole. It feels like we've had this conversation before."

"That's because we have. As long as we keep fighting, we'll keep losing people. Have you had a chance to examine the prisoners?"

The dark-haired doctor nodded. "Our technicians ran them through the scanners. No implants, other than that one officer. No sign of nanites, even in him. They were all in good health, though."

"Was the officer's surgery done with a regenerator?"

"Probably sometime in his late teens or early twenties. A regenerator removed the scarring."

He cocked his head. "I thought regeneration masked any kind of time assessment. How can you tell?"

"The skull bones. Regenerators don't work that well on bones. The rate at which the incisions remodeled tells me about how long ago he had the surgery. If he'd had the graphene coating on his bones that Kelsey has, it would've been more difficult, though I could've finessed it."

That made sense. "They'll be sending the dead from the destroyer over shortly. I want each of them examined, particularly the ones with implants. I don't want you to rush it, though. We have time. Tell me about Kelsey."

"The scans showed that she had some shrapnel in her upper arm. Her armor shattered under multiple hits, and some of the fragments went into her. I removed them and sealed the wound. Her nanites will heal her in a day or so."

He nodded. "Good. I want you to make a pass through the destroyer's medical center when you have time. I need to know how they compare to us, technology wise. I also want to know if they have any equipment for performing implants. That can wait for now, though."

Jared rose to his feet. "Seriously, Lily. You did everything you could. Get some rest."

He resisted the urge to go oversee the interrogation of the prisoners. Graves had that covered. If he needed Jared to come glower at someone, he'd call.

Feeling like he had nothing to do, he returned to his office and called Baxter. The chief engineer was over on the destroyer, examining its systems. He came on after a moment, some large piece of equipment behind him.

"Baxter, give me some good news."

The engineer shook his head. "I don't have a lot of that in stock. Carl Owlet was right. They wiped the AI. It's gone. They scrubbed every bit of data on the drives. That's not to say that there isn't anything to recover, though. We're finding tablets and other data sources, but it's going to be like when we collected everything on *Courageous*. Slow."

"What about the ship itself? Can you restore power?"

"Not a chance. You nailed the support equipment on both fusion plants. The repairs will take a while. The good news is that this ship *is* repairable. Zia will have to give you a rundown on the weapons systems, but they can probably be repaired as well, given enough time."

Jared didn't think they'd be fixing this ship any time soon. That would probably fall to the Pentagarans. "What about the drives?"

"Undamaged. I could maneuver the ship if it had power. The flip capacitors are charged, so if you tow the ship back into the flip point, we can get it back to Erorsi."

He grunted at the unexpected good news. "I figured the controls would be locked down."

"They are," the engineer said cheerfully. "I'll manually trigger the flip at the drive itself. You give the word and we'll get going."

"Okay. I'll have our small craft get the ship moving toward the flip point. Good work."

It would take several hours for the small craft to get the hulk drifting into the flip point. Thankfully, it wasn't far away. The extra time would allow the probes they'd sent out to scan the rest of the system. He doubted there was any human presence at all, but it never hurt to be sure.

The last stop on his tour was to see Kelsey. She was in marine country. Of course. It had become her second home. He supposed she had more in common with them now. She'd been through things only they could understand, and her lover was a marine.

She was out of her armor and dressed in the clothes she'd worn earlier. A bandage on her left arm was the only sign anything had changed. She headed over as soon as he came in. "Don't get on me about this. My armor isn't impervious."

"I'd rather you didn't get into these fights, but I'm glad you're well protected when you do. You communicated with the guy in the computer center. What did he say?"

"He thought I was someone else. He wanted to know the status of rigging a self-destruct device. Called me a traitor when he figured out he didn't know me. That pretty much sums up our chat. Did we get anyone else with implants?"

Jared shook his head. "No. Based on the initial evidence, it looks like officers had implants and enlisted didn't. Doctor Leonard is scrubbing the virus out of the one prisoner's implants as we speak. Once he finishes, I want you to lead the questioning."

Kelsey gave him a surprised look. "Me? I don't know anything about interrogation."

"Perhaps not, but you're good at talking to people. He might say something to you that he wouldn't say to me. At least you'll be able to get a dialog going. I want to know who he thinks you are. A traitor to whom?"

She nodded. "Okay. First, though, I'm going back over to the destroyer. Some pieces of equipment require implants to access. I also want to look at the weapons we recovered. They seem about on par with the ones we have. If so, we can commandeer their ammunition supply. That'll be a lot faster than restoring what we found here on *Courageous*."

He looked over at her armor on its stand. There were several spots that had obviously taken hits. "Do they have anything like this?"

"Ask me after we finish searching the ship. One of your shots took out their marine country, so we haven't had a chance to do a thorough search of it. No one we fought was in powered armor, though."

Jared nodded. "Get into your spare armor first. I wouldn't want any unexploded ordinance to put you in danger. The marines will examine the destroyer's two pinnaces to see if we can replace the one we lost. If so, we'll do it before we flip back to Erorsi."

She cocked her head. "Why? Is there a rush?"

"I expect Breckenridge to try and confiscate that ship as soon as we get back over there. Baxter can flip it once. We might be able to recharge the flip capacitors again and get it to Pentagar. But anything we want off that ship needs to be over here before we go."

"We'll see who ends up in control of what," she said grimly. "I'll be sure to scavenge anything that looks interesting, though. What about the ship's missiles? Could they replace what we've used?"

"God, I hope so. We could use a break."

14

Kelsey used her armor's lamp to look into what was left of the destroyer's marine country. One of *Courageous*'s beams had ripped it open and incinerated so much. Bodies and parts of bodies floated by her. The artificial gravity had finally failed all over the ship.

Some of these bodies were in standard marine powered armor. Not all of them. Fewer than a dozen, though it was hard to be sure. She was going to have more nightmares. They must've assembled here, waiting to see where *Courageous*'s crew boarded. Then Jared had drilled a hole right through them.

Talbot and his men fanned out as they searched the area. The beams hadn't destroyed everything. The armory was intact. They had to cut the hatch off, but inside was a treasure trove. Ammunition that would work in their flechette weapons, power packs, and other high-tech weapons of war.

Including more armor. Two suits of Old Empire marine armor in racks.

She stopped to give one of them a closer look. It resembled her armor, but the plates were significantly thicker. She tried to query it via her implants, but it demanded a code she didn't have.

Odd. Her suit hadn't needed one. Why would these?

"Talbot, these suits look like they're intact. I can't access them, but I don't think they require enhanced musculature like mine."

She removed one of the helmets. It had a real view screen inside the faceplate. "I'm not sure why, but it has manual controls under the chin and a screen to see the outside world."

He took the helmet and looked inside it. "We have something similar. We use our chins to control communications and other functions. These can work without implants."

"Then why have implant access at all?"

"That's a good question. One we'll probably need the eggheads to answer. I bet they can hack these suits." He gave her a smile. "I hope so, because then I can keep up with you."

"You wish." She pulled a massive plasma gun off a rack on the wall. "Holy cow. Look at this thing. I could take out a pinnace with one of these. It must be one of the heavy weapons I read about. There are big honking flechette rifles, too. The neural disruptors are small, though. Made for unarmored people."

"It doesn't make much sense to have the guys in armor carry weapons that won't work on the people they're fighting. Let's give the rest of marine country a look."

They found a storage area with crated equipment but not much else of interest. Reese made the decision to take everything back over to *Courageous* before examining the contents. Kelsey made sure they stripped the armory. None of these weapons was going to be falling into Breckenridge's clutches if he pulled a fast one.

One of the pinnaces was unrepairable. The beam that blew through marine country took out its bow. The other seemed intact. The enemy had locked the controls, so they called Carl Owlet down to break into it while they loaded as much of the weapons and armor aboard as they could.

She gave the young computer scientist a suspicious look when he arrived. "You're pretty good at boosting vehicles. Did you have a life of crime before going to university?"

He laughed and started working on the pinnace's console. "Hardly. I've just had enough experience on this expedition to make up for it. Especially on this ship. It looks like they locked *everything* down. Including stuff that doesn't even make sense. It's as though this ship was designed by someone with paranoid delusions."

"Perhaps it was. These people are working with the Pale Ones, so odds are good they're rebels. Or whatever the rebels became after they won. How are you getting around the lockouts? Or even accessing the equipment with main power down?"

"Most stuff can be operated by someone without implants, and we brought portable power supplies. I dig into the mechanical elements and isolate the lockout. Then it's just a matter of convincing the equipment that I have an authorized code." The red light on the center console went green. "Like that. It won't prompt for codes anymore. Is there anything else I can unlock for you?"

She smiled. "Actually, there is." She showed him one of the suits of armor they were loading.

He examined it. "I might be able to swing it, but not here. I need to get at the critical components. Man, this looks kick ass. Excuse my language."

"No apology necessary. It *is* kick ass. Now, while they finish loading the pinnace, I'd like to see a few areas of the ship. If you could get me in, that will save some wear and tear on the hatches."

"Sure. If Commander Baxter needs me, he'll call."

Kelsey gave Talbot the high sign. "Come on."

She set off looking for the captain's quarters. They found them after a few false turns. The hatch gave way under the young man's computer skills, sliding open on an opulent chamber.

These quarters were almost the same size as hers were on *Courageous*. That made them improbably large in a destroyer. The extra space had to come from somewhere. Probably from other people's living areas.

Luxurious white carpet covered the deck, and wood and glass furniture filled the space. Art graced the walls, and knickknacks of gold and silver occupied prominent shelves, secured against zero G. She looked around with disbelief.

"This looks more like a king's quarters than a destroyer captain's. It doesn't seem like someone of Jared's rank could afford this."

Talbot looked into one of the other compartments in the suite. "This bedroom is like a bordello. Not that I'm familiar with the inside of one," he hastily added.

"You'd better not be." She found the office. A large desk of pale wood dominated one side of the room. Holos covered the walls. It only took a moment to identify the captain: a short, thin woman with long brunette hair. She was in every image. Her companions ranged from Fleet officers to well-dressed civilians. The civilians all had the same sleek look that the worst members of the Imperial Senate had back home. Oily. Scheming.

Kelsey floated behind the desk. "Can you access this console?"

"The AI is down, so that means the network is offline. The emergency power switch is on the right side under the edge. I'll get one of the portable power supplies if we need to."

She powered the console on and tried to access it when it came up. "It's secured."

"Let me take a run at it."

The computer genius opened the side of the console and began tinkering inside. "This thing is fully encrypted. I can get in, but it'll take me a few minutes. I might not be able to completely access it, either."

"Do the best you can."

Talbot poked his head into the office. "Kelsey, you'll want to see this."

She followed him back to the bedroom. It was even worse than she'd feared. The walls were passion red, and the bed looked like it could hold a dozen people. Talbot led her to the closet. One side had what looked like regulation Fleet uniforms, though of an expensive cut. The other had clothes that Kelsey would be mortified to wear in private.

"Seriously? Not a chance in hell, buddy."

He grinned at her through the faceplate of his armor. "While that would make for some memorable visuals, no. What I want you to see is behind the uniforms."

She slid them to the side and saw what he meant. There was a safe in the back of the closet. "Right you are. You win a reward of my choice later. Except for me getting anything like those unmentionables."

It looked like the safe was implant controlled. If so, she'd never get it open. It was sturdy, too, but people with the right tools could open anything given enough time.

"How's it going in there, Carl?"

"I'm almost… I'm in. The console is coming up. The unsecure portions of it are available."

"Do you know anything about safes?"

"As in the vault kind? Not yet."

The young man came into the bedroom and jetted to a stop, gawking at the furnishings. His face looked almost as red as the silk covers.

"Wow. This is… unexpected."

"You can say that again. Give this a look."

He examined the safe. "I could probably cut it open with enough time, but that might damage the contents. There might be an easier way. Come back to the office with me."

She followed him. "Something in here could get me in there?"

"Maybe. There's only one way to find out for sure. Tell me, do you use the same computer password for everything?"

Kelsey frowned. "What does my computer password have to do with anything?"

"People tend to select one or a few passwords and then use them for a lot of systems. Odds are good that the commander of this ship was no exception. I'd give better than 50/50 odds that the access for this console is the same as the safe."

"That's an interesting fact, but we don't have that code. It's in the dead captain's head."

"We might be able to convince the console to give it up. I'm going to try to fool the system into giving you the key. When I tell you to, try to access it."

He dug back into the guts of the console. "Now."

She tried to access the console, and it rejected her. "It blocked me."

"This might take a few tries."

In fact, it took almost half an hour, and she was ready to give up when the console unexpectedly sent her a complicated code.

"It sent me an access code," she said in surprise.

"Thank God. I was afraid this wasn't going to work after all. Hang on a second and let me get the system put back together."

He reassembled the console and floated away. "Go ahead."

She fed the console the code and the secure sections unlocked. There were a number of files that she was afraid to access. This computer had been in rebel hands. She didn't mind looking, but she didn't want to pull anything into her internal memory until the professionals had it fully checked out.

"Is there any way to copy files from this console on a portable device?"

Owlet nodded. "There are some auxiliary data ports that we can use to transfer files. I brought some in my bag."

Kelsey returned to the bedroom while Owlet got back to work. She put her hands on her hips and stared disapprovingly at the closet. "I can't believe someone would have clothes like this. These unmentionables really are unmentionable."

"I can assure you the only unmentionables I want to mention are yours."

"Not in public. Wow." She held up some type of corset. It looked like something a dominatrix would wear. "Did you find a whip?" she asked rhetorically.

"As a matter of fact, I did." He pulled one off the shelf above the clothes. It wasn't very long, but it had some heft. Having someone beat you with this would be painful. Very painful.

Talbot held up one of the uniforms. "This is almost your size. With a little bit of tailoring for your height, you could wear it."

"Thankfully, I don't have to." She stared down at the safe. "I'm almost afraid what we'll find inside it."

"Only one way to find out."

She nodded and sent the code she'd stolen from the console. The safe clicked open. "Remind me to start picking a different password for everything that needs one."

"Me, too. What's inside?"

There were several shelves. The uppermost held two sleek pistols. The top one's barrel told her it was a neural disruptor, but it was substantially smaller than the pistols they'd found so far. The one under it was an even smaller flechette pistol. Both easily concealable.

She picked the neural disruptor up and queried it with her implants. It rejected her attempt to connect with it. She'd seen this before. Weapons could be set so that only a particular set of implants could fire them. The marines had figured out how to unlock them.

She pocketed the pistols and their custom power packs. The middle shelf held folders of printouts. She flipped through several of them and determined they were personnel files of some kind. A few of the subjects were Fleet personnel, but many were civilian. She'd take them with her and examine them more closely when she had time.

The bottommost shelf had data chips in small cases. Dozens of them. Any information worth locking into a safe had to be important to the person keeping it. Perhaps critical data on this Rebel Empire.

"I want all of this back on *Courageous*," she said to Talbot. "This captain seems like the devious type. There might be hidden stuff we haven't found. Go over her quarters with a fine-toothed comb. We'll need every edge we can get once they find out about us."

15

———

It took several hours for *Courageous*'s small craft to tow the crippled destroyer back into the flip point. Jared sent one of the Pentagaran warships through first to be sure that everyone knew not to open fire when the destroyer appeared. They'd sacrificed a lot to capture the ship, and he didn't want to see it destroyed.

Zia turned from her console. "The destroyer is inside the flip point, Captain."

"Give them the signal to flip in thirty seconds. Take us across."

The flip made him momentarily dizzy, but he recovered quickly. The Old Empire implants made the process easier. That was a nice bonus.

He quickly picked up a number of Pentagaran warships surrounding the flip point. No Fleet ships though. Those were all still engaged in search and rescue.

Jared quickly sent a prerecorded message to the ships around him, reiterating his instructions not to open fire on the destroyer. It appeared a few seconds later without incident.

"Signal incoming from *Spear*," Zia said.

"Put it on screen."

A furious Captain Breckenridge appeared. "God dammit,

Commander, I gave you a direct order to leave that ship there and return as quickly as possible. Are you deaf?"

"Captain Breckenridge, do you need further assistance with rescue operations?" Jared asked, ignoring the other man's bluster.

"It's a little late now, don't you think? No. We've almost completed rescue operations at this point. We could've used your help a few hours ago. Give me an update on your status."

"We ambushed the destroyer and disabled it. I sent marines aboard to capture it before he could self-destruct. We have prisoners, including one of the officers. We're questioning them."

Breckenridge shook his head. "Negative. I'll take possession of the prisoners and that ship at once. My officers will see to any questioning."

Not a chance in hell. "Princess Kelsey has decided that she's going to question the prisoners, and she's determined that she's not releasing control of that ship until she's finished. She has instructed me to set up a meeting on her behalf so that we can discuss this in private. If all of your cutters are engaged in rescue operations, I'd be happy to send one of ours to pick you up."

Captain Breckenridge's face turned a bright purple. "I made it perfectly clear that she was not to be allowed into this system. You've disregarded my orders again. You're going to regret that, Commander. I need to get things in order here before we speak again."

The screen cleared without a goodbye.

"He's never going to admit he made a mistake."

Jared turned and faced the lift that had just opened. Commander Meyer stood there. Jared allowed himself a small smile as the man took a seat at the rear of the bridge. "Forgive me, Commander, but I didn't think you believed he made mistakes."

The other man shook his head. "I've had time to think about all the mistakes that he's made. And the mistakes that I've made. After your doctor patched me up, I reviewed the engagement records. He's not going to admit that he botched everything. That's not his way. He's going to take it out on you."

"He's going to try to take it out on me," Jared corrected. "Not that it'll work. He's been spoiling for a fight ever since he got here, and he's going to get it. His actions contributed to the deaths of thousands of Fleet personnel. If he wants to push this issue with me or the princess, we're going to push right back."

Commander Meyer shook his head. "You still don't understand. He's in command of that task force. Nothing that you do is going to change that. If the princess tries to relieve him of command, it's going to cause a complete break. Frankly, he hasn't demonstrated any behavior that actually warrants being relieved of command. Just poor judgment."

As annoying as that was, Jared knew Meyer was correct. If only it was so easy.

He rose to his feet. "Walk with me, Commander. I think it's time we had a long talk and settled a few things. Zia, you have the bridge."

"Aye, sir."

Once inside the lift, Jared started them on their way toward where they were keeping the prisoners. "Doctor Stone tells me that your injuries were minor, but I know that that doesn't mean they don't feel serious. Are you all right?"

The tall officer nodded. "It wasn't a direct hit, and my armor absorbed most of the damage. It scared me. I thought I was going to die. But you know what really made me reconsider so many things? Princess Kelsey."

Jared led the way out of the lift as soon as it stopped. "How so?"

"When we were ambushed, she never hesitated. She jumped right into the middle of the enemy marines and attacked. She hit them, she shot them, and she never showed even the slightest hint of fear. It makes me a little ashamed. No, it takes me a lot ashamed. When she ran toward the enemy, I held back. I could've helped her, but I watched, too afraid to act. Then someone shot me."

The officer rubbed his face. "I've never felt like that in space combat. Before I became executive officer on *Spear*, I commanded a light cruiser. I took her into simulated battle and fought tooth and nail. I thought I knew what fear was, but I was wrong."

Jared knew exactly how he felt. "Someone once told me that only idiots aren't afraid of dying. He said that bravery just meant riding the wave of your fear and doing what you had to do. If you were still in command of that light cruiser, would you do what Captain Macumber did? Put your ship between a wounded comrade and certain death?"

Meyer's expression hardened. "Of course I would."

"Then you're brave enough. Fighting hand to hand isn't something that everyone can do. I've been where you were, and I didn't like it very much either. Give me the command deck of this ship any day. I think if you find yourself in the same situation again, you'll do what you have to. Don't tear yourself apart, second-guessing everything you did. Learn from it and do better the next time."

They passed between the marines guarding the prisoners. More marines armed with neural disruptors set to stun lined the cargo deck bulkheads. The prisoners sat on cots in an open area. Each had a restraint around their ankle bolted to the deck. If they needed to use the head, two marines of the appropriate gender would release them long enough to take care of business.

The most seriously injured of the prisoners was still in the medical center. Also under guard.

Jared stopped far enough away from the prisoners so that they couldn't overhear him. "Commander Graves has been interrogating these people. They wear Fleet uniforms, but they don't serve any Fleet that I'm familiar with. They all fought ferociously when we boarded the ship, but once the fighting was over, they seemed to just give up. Commander Graves intimidated them. Not because he was the enemy, because he was a Fleet officer in uniform.

"We've started collating their statements, and certain patterns are emerging. They believe that they are serving members of Imperial Fleet, but they don't see the rebellion the same way the history books do. And their Fleet has significant differences from ours."

Meyer scanned the prisoners. "How so?"

"In their Fleet, officers occupy a higher social position inside the Empire. Though they live in an Empire, no one we've spoken to mentioned anything about an emperor. In this Fleet, officers are people they fear and obey. They fill the enlisted ranks via conscription rather than by looking for volunteers."

Meyer looked at him sharply. "Wait a minute. Are you telling me that the Old Empire still exists? We thought the rebels exterminated humanity. Are you telling me they enslaved them?"

Jared shrugged. "It's hard to say if the Old Empire still exists in the way you mean. None of these people refer to themselves as citizens of the Empire. They're very specific that they are subjects of the Empire. The officers are citizens of the Empire, and so are the political classes. The nobility.

"Graves made sure that he didn't feed them any information about what we think happened during the rebellion. He asked a lot of questions and let them fill in the blanks. It certainly seems as though none of these people is aware of artificial intelligences running things. Perhaps the upper classes of their society know, but until we can get our one high-ranking prisoner to talk, we won't be sure."

"Was the procedure to remove the virus from his implants successful?"

"We'll know in about an hour. I'm hopeful that he'll talk with Princess Kelsey or myself. Because of the incredible loss of life this battle caused, I have no intention of turning any of the prisoners over to Captain Breckenridge. I'm not certain I trust him with their well-being."

Meyer frowned. "The laws of war are clear. Captain Breckenridge will not mistreat them."

"I'm not so certain that I agree with that statement. In any case, I don't believe that he'll be as successful as we are at drawing information from these people. Commander Meyer, we desperately need to know what we face. Our civilization is small and technologically inferior when compared to what we're starting to see. If they come for us, we'll lose. Our only hope is to keep them ignorant of the Empire's existence until we know enough to survive. You need to help me convince Captain Breckenridge."

Meyer sighed. "I wish it were that simple. The captain doesn't change his mind easily. After losing so many people, he's not going to admit to making any mistakes. Not even to himself. Whatever you do, it needs to take that into account."

A hatch at the end of the corridor opened, and Kelsey stepped through. "There you are, Jared. Breckenridge just called me. He wants to meet with us and get onto the same page. Too many mistakes have been made."

Jared exchanged a glance with Meyer. "That's unexpectedly conciliatory. When is he coming over?"

"He's not. He asked that we meet on *Spear*. They're too deeply involved in rescue operations for him to leave the scene of the battle. Come on."

"I'm not so sure that's a good idea."

She raised her eyebrows. "Why not? He's not going to fight about command of this mission again. That's settled. We have to start relying on each other, or we'll never get home."

Jared had his doubts. "I hope you're right."

He used his implants to call Graves and direct him to Jared's office. It was still surreal to do this in his head while those around him were unaware he was even talking to someone else.

Charlie, I've got a bad feeling about this. The man hates me.

His exec nodded, responding to the audio from the console. "That he does. Still, his options are limited. He's not going to do something with the princess right there. Keep things civil, and it'll work itself out."

I sure hope so. In any case, I have some orders for you. You are not to hand the prisoners over to anyone. They stay in our custody. You're also to retain possession of the destroyer. Finally, remember that you are not under Captain Breckenridge's command. We answer to the princess.

Graves looked surprised. "Surely things won't get that bad."

I certainly hope not, but we're going over to his ship. If he's going to do something rash, this is the perfect time. Let's call this a contingency plan.

"Aye, sir. I'll keep things under control."

Good man. We'll see you shortly.

He kept his worries to himself as their cutter undocked, but his misgivings grew stronger the closer they got to *Spear*. He watched her closely through his implants as they approached the battle site.

Spear was following along behind *Shadow*. The light cruiser tumbled, completely out of control. Her damage was severe. The ship wouldn't be going anywhere but a repair dock or a scrap yard. He hadn't heard how many of her crew had died in the attack, but it would be a lot.

The pilot brought the cutter up to the heavy cruiser and docked smoothly. "I'll be here when you're ready to go, Captain."

"Keep the systems ready to depart at a moment's notice."

Unlike his last time aboard, Captain Breckenridge was waiting at the dock. He looked worn and angry. "Highness. Commander. Time is short. I've taken the liberty of reserving a small conference room on this deck. This way, please."

Two unarmored marines stood outside the hatch and snapped to attention as they approached. Breckenridge gestured for Kelsey to precede them. "If you'll take the head of the table, Highness, I've prepared an update of the rescue operations."

Jared started to follow her in, but Breckenridge yanked him back. The hatch slid shut even as Kelsey whirled toward them. He reached for his neural disruptor, but the marines beat him to the draw. They had pistols aimed at his head before he'd touched it.

"What the hell are you doing?" he snarled as Breckenridge took his weapon and handed it to Meyer. "She's second in line to the Throne."

"I'm doing what you should've done, Commander. I'm protecting her from her own bad judgment. The two of you have managed to kill thousands of Fleet personnel. I will not allow you to endanger the Empire one moment longer."

"You're insane. You can't possibly do anything without the cooperation of *Courageous* or the Pentagarans."

The older man smiled. "I'm very resourceful. Marines, take him to a holding cell. I'll be along directly."

16

Kelsey almost made it to the hatch before it slid shut in her face. She started to bang on it but stopped. That wouldn't do any good. She had no leverage, and the smooth metal wouldn't give to brute strength. Even hers.

Breckenridge had trapped her. She had the neural disruptor she'd appropriated from the dead destroyer captain's safe tucked away in a place they'd be unlikely to search, but she'd have to be very careful. They had Jared.

The marine armorer had been able to reset the lockout on the weapon to her implants with a little trouble. The rebels had made the weapon so that only the person with the correct implants could use it.

It had also been set to lethal levels when she'd checked. That didn't say very nice things about the woman who'd owned it.

The screen came to life, showing a smiling Captain Breckenridge. "Highness."

"Have you lost your mind?" she snarled.

"Thankfully, no. I regret to inform you that I have serious concerns about your judgment and stability. I have no choice but to take you into protective custody. Due to your horrific injuries, I must confine you. My apologies." The last came in a smug tone.

She felt her eyes narrow. "My judgment? My stability? You'd best look to yourself if there is a problem, Captain. Jared and I have made the best calls possible. You? Not so much. How many good men and women lost their lives because of you today?"

Rage clouded his expression. "All because of your incompetent half brother. His lack of judgment got us into this battle and cost the Empire three ships and almost two thousand people. We should never have been involved in this fight, and from this point forward, we will not be."

Kelsey raised an eyebrow. "I can't imagine how you intend to do that. Perhaps you haven't noticed, but our ships can't get home. Sooner or later, the rebels will come looking for the ship you destroyed and the one we captured."

"Let them. We won't be here. I intend to take our people through the unexplored flip point. We'll find another way home."

"And leave the Pentagarans to die? Are you insane?"

"No. I'm pragmatic. Something you should try. These are not our people, and we should never have been involved in their business. You will call *Courageous* and instruct them to surrender to my officers."

She crossed her arms over her chest. "I will not. In fact, let me make this as clear as I can. I'm ordering you to release us at once and surrender yourself."

"I'm sorry to see you being so unreasonable, but I'm not surprised. Very well. I can force Mertz into obeying my orders. If I make it clear that your health is dependent on his cooperation, he'll comply. A ruse, of course."

She showed him her teeth. "You don't know the first thing about my brother. He won't give in to you. No matter how this plays out, you're ruined. You must know that."

"We'll see. I've taken the precaution of putting bedding, food, and a portable toilet to the rear of the conference room. You'll be staying there for the foreseeable future. I'm not foolhardy enough to risk letting you out. We'll speak again soon."

He stepped aside, and she saw Commander Meyer standing behind Breckenridge. She gave him a pleading look. "Commander Meyer, please. Explain this to him. You can't let him do this."

"You have no idea how resolute the captain is, Highness," Meyer said with a wooden expression. "Once he makes up his mind, there's no altering his course. Nothing I say will change this situation."

Breckenridge smiled and clapped the other man on the shoulder. "See? He knows me so well. This is what a good executive officer is like. Loyal to a fault. We'll speak again soon, Highness."

The screen went dark.

Kelsey used some of the choicest phrases she'd picked up from Talbot and the marines. Dammit. How was she going to get them out of this?

She beat on the hatch, but it didn't give. There were no other exits, and her weapon wouldn't go through a bulkhead.

If she'd brought one of the marine knives, she could have conceivably cut her way through the bulkhead. It would have taken a while and they would no doubt have stopped her, but they'd have had to open the hatch to do it.

That was the first thing she needed to do. Get the hatch open. If she could manage that, escape became at least conceivable.

Fifteen minutes of pacing left her as uninspired as when she started.

She whirled toward the hatch when it slid unexpectedly open. Commander Meyer stood outside. The two marine guards had their weapons out and pointed at her midsection. The tall officer stared at her haughtily. "Back against the bulkhead, Highness."

She considered the odds. Panther, the Old Empire combat drug combination, boosted her reaction time, and she might be able to take them before they killed her. Maybe.

The marines advanced. Once they were inside, Meyer shot them in the backs with Jared's neural disruptor. They collapsed.

"This is an amazing weapon. Come on, Highness. It won't be long before someone finds out you've escaped. We have to get you off this ship right now."

"We need to capture this ship. Order your people to stand down."

He shook his head. "That won't work. The captain has too many loyal people for me to take him down, and if it comes to my order against his, I'll lose. He's made his stand. Imagine your brother's crew supporting Graves against him. Not going to happen. We have less than ten minutes to get you off this ship or you're not leaving. Captain Breckenridge has gone too far to back down now."

She looked at the stunned marines on the deck. "So have you."

"This isn't how I saw things going," Meyer said ruefully. "I still can't quite imagine how I ended up opposing my captain." He opened the hatch and scanned the corridor. "Just walk like nothing is wrong."

She followed him out into the corridor and tried to behave normally even though the skin between her shoulder blades itched. Everyone they passed stared at her.

"You did what was right and what's best for the Empire," she said as they walked.

"I did what my oath required of me, in any case. You are the voice of authority, and the captain is wrong to disobey you. I don't agree with everything you've done, and I'm worried that you're leading the Empire into a war we cannot win."

He waved his hand at her when she started to speak. "I'm not trying to be argumentative. I'll do my duty even if I don't agree with you."

"That wasn't what I was going to say. I want to hear opposing points of view. I certainly don't think I have all the answers. What I will say is that it's easy to look back when the dust settles. It's harder when you're in the moment. Like when you made the decision to free us. Tomorrow the perfect plan will pop into your head. If you wait for the perfect plan, you'll never do anything."

They entered a lift, and she had to shut up since there were other people present. Meyer took them up a few decks and exited. "We're going to the brig. I'm going to get Commander Mertz out of his cell, and we're going to make our way back to your cutter. I'll call Captain Breckenridge to get him to allow your cutter to depart. By the time he realizes that I've helped you escape, you should be most of the way back to *Courageous*."

"You mean 'we' don't you? You're coming with us."

He shook his head. "That's not going to be possible. He'll discover the ruse much too quickly if I'm not here to distract him. I'll likely go right into the same cell your captain occupies now," he said with a wry smile. "Talk about a career-limiting decision."

"He's going to be furious. You need to come with us."

"It's the only choice. If he has you in his sights, he might do something drastic to prevent your escape. I cannot and will not risk your life when I can prevent the danger in the first place."

"Well, come up with an alternate plan. I'm ordering you to come with us."

He sighed. "You don't make things easy, do you, Highness? Aye, ma'am. Orders received. Follow my lead and please try to avoid hurting anyone too badly. These people are just following orders."

Two marines outside an armored hatch came to attention as they approached. The hatch was open, and Meyer headed inside with a sharp nod to them. Three Fleet personnel manned the inside of the brig. Two ratings, one male and one female, flanked one of the cell hatches, and a female officer sat at the console.

The officer stood when she saw Meyer. "Commander."

"Lieutenant Jacobs. Captain Breckenridge has instructed me to bring Commander Mertz to him on the bridge. Bring him out."

She frowned. "That's contrary to my instructions, sir. He ordered me to lock the prisoner down and only to release him on his direct orders. I'll need to call the captain and verify. Sorry, sir."

Meyer smiled. "I completely understand. Please do. I wouldn't want you to get into any trouble."

As soon as she lowered her eyes to the console, he drew the neural disruptor from inside his uniform tunic and shot her. The blue beam took her down, and he whirled to face the hatch.

Kelsey had been primed for something like that, so she was able to draw her own pistol and rush the guards as they gaped at the unexpected attack.

The female guard was slightly quicker on the uptake, so Kelsey shot her. The princess's augmentation brought her into hand-to-hand range of the man before he could draw a bead on her. She ripped his weapon right out of his grip and ducked far enough to the side to allow his fist to pass by her head.

Just because she could fight didn't mean she wanted to take a fist to the face.

She heard Meyer firing behind her and hoped he got both the marines before they got him.

A shove sent the man she was fighting into the bulkhead, and she shot him. He collapsed without any further trouble.

Commander Meyer didn't need her help. He'd dropped both the marines without any problem.

"It looks like you're a much better fighter than I expected, Commander," she said. "I didn't need to give you a talk before the boarding, did I?"

"This isn't the same. These people trusted me. This was more like a sucker punch than a fair fight." He looked at the small weapon in her hand. "And that little thing is even more unfair. I had no idea you were armed."

"That was kind of the idea. Senior Sergeant Talbot tells me that fair fights indicate a lack of planning and imagination. Mostly on my part."

Meyer dragged the marines through the hatch and closed it. "When those people were trying to kill us, I didn't see any lack of planning or imagination on your part. Unlike myself. I froze. I've never been in anything like that."

He tapped the controls on the console, and the cell opened up. Jared stood there, gaping at them. Meyer extended the neural disruptor to him.

"If you intend to get out of here, Commander, you'd best get moving. The escape window is closing."

Jared took the neural disruptor from the other man and holstered it. "You're helping us?"

"My oath to the emperor doesn't agree with Captain Breckenridge's plan. We have just a few minutes to get to your cutter."

When Meyer headed for the hatch, they followed. "How are we going to get away from *Spear*? They have to release the docking clamps, or the cutter won't be going anywhere."

"I'll call the bridge when we get down to the docking level. I can get them to release it."

"What about Captain Breckenridge?"

"I have a plan, but the princess has forbidden me to execute it."

She looked at Jared. "He wanted to send us off and call Breckenridge away from the bridge. He'd be captured for sure."

The lift deposited them at the cutter deck. Jared followed Meyer out. "You'd do that for us?"

"No," Meyer said. "I'd do that for her, and for my own honor. It's still the best plan. I recommend you change her mind. Time is short."

Jared opened his mouth to say something, but the alert klaxon went off. Captain Breckenridge's voice came through the overheads. "All hands, this is the captain. We have two escaped prisoners on the loose. Be on the lookout for Commander Jared Mertz and Princess Kelsey Bandar. Both are armed and dangerous. Commander Meyer, call the bridge at once."

Meyer gestured toward the cutter. "Get inside. I'll call him. I may be able to get it released if I make him think you haven't made it here yet."

He touched the communications panel on the wall. "Bridge, this is Meyer."

"Sean," Breckenridge said, "Mertz has escaped and the princess's guard isn't responding. Where are you?"

"I'm on the docking level. They haven't made it here yet. If their ride has left, it'll make it much easier to recapture them."

"Good idea. I'll send them away right now. Take command of the search. I want them found at once. The very safety of the Empire lies in getting that deluded woman back under our control."

"I won't fail the Empire, Captain. Meyer out."

He turned to them. "If I go with you, I won't be able to delay the moment he discovers you're truly gone and opens fire. I'm sorry, Highness." He spun and headed for the lift.

She wanted to argue, but she knew he was right. "We'll be back for you. Don't lose hope."

Jared pulled her into the cutter, and Kelsey closed the hatch behind them. He rushed for the flight deck while she strapped herself in. The cutter undocked, and acceleration pressed her into her seat.

All she could think about was the man who'd just doomed himself for her. She had no idea how she could make it right.

Courageous reports that he's attempted to access the ship's systems numerous times."

"Perhaps you should let him," Kelsey said. "A limited set of files. Historical ones of the Old Empire. Nothing that pertains to our current circumstances, of course. What have the enlisted prisoners said about the rebellion?"

"That it took place. That they overthrew the corrupt emperor and freed the people from slavery. Detailed questions about the Old Empire confuse them. Apparently their history books are a little vague."

"That sounds like propaganda," Jared said. "Tell people something long enough and they'll believe it. What about the AIs?"

"Nothing. The officer's implant code was corrupted, so they must be lurking somewhere behind the scenes, but the general population seems to be unaware of them. That matches up with the data we've retrieved from the destroyer. They wiped the main computer, but we recovered a number of tablets and data chips. We're still putting everything together, but it's obvious that they didn't exterminate the core worlds of the Old Empire like we thought. There are specific mentions of Terra as the hub of the Rebel Empire."

Kelsey's face paled. "They kept the major population centers and remade society in the way they wanted. At least some of them. The rebels won."

"The AIs won," Jared said. "For now. We still don't know the scope of space they occupy. We'll need to gather all the data we can about that. Damn that idiot Breckenridge. He killed our one chance of taking a computer intact, and he vaporized all those implants. Honestly, I'm not sure how he could have executed the plan any more ineptly. Other than getting all his ships destroyed."

"Captain, we have an incoming call from a ship at the Pentagaran flip point."

Jared turned toward the front of the bridge. "On screen."

The main screen cleared to show the bridge of a ship. Admiral Walter Sanders, the freshly promoted commander of the Pentagaran Navy, sat in the center seat. Crown Princess Elise Orison stood at his side.

The sight of her made him smile. "Elise! Welcome to Erorsi. Admiral."

"Lord Captain," she said with a smile of her own. "Kelsey. I came to see how things are going for myself."

That took the edge off his pleasure. "It could've gone better. We lost three ships and far too many people. Plus, there are other complications. Captain Breckenridge has decided to strike out on his own."

Her eyes widened. "What? That's sheer folly! You should order him back at once, Kelsey."

Kelsey shook her head with a wry smile. "That's not likely to be effective after he attempted to take me prisoner. He's made his choice, and I can't do much about it.

"On the good side, we captured the destroyer escort. Unfortunately, Captain Breckenridge destroyed the freighter with all its cargo. We have prisoners, so we're hopeful we can get some badly needed data on our opponents. At the very least, we've put off the day they discover your presence. That gives us all a fighting chance."

Admiral Sanders grimaced. "That's better than it could've been but worse than I'd hoped. I see that your wayward officers are heading for the weak space-time bridge. What are the chances that it leads somewhere disconnected from the areas controlled by the enemy?"

"Unknown. I pray it leads close to Avalon and far away from this Rebel Empire. We'll send a probe once they're gone and see how it matches up to the flip point maps in *Courageous*'s data banks."

"We'll be at your location in a few hours," the admiral said. "Perhaps together we can come up with a plan to make things right."

Jared nodded. "We'll get a tow on *Shadow* and start moving her toward Erorsi. If nothing else, we can put her in the operational shipyard to see what repairs are possible. The same for the destroyer."

"That sounds like an excellent first step. Sanders out."

Jared rose to his feet. "Zia, see if our Pentagaran friends will tow *Shadow* and the destroyer to Erorsi. Pasco, what would you estimate their arrival time to be?"

Ramirez checked his console. "Probably sometime tomorrow."

Kelsey stood. "That's better time than *Athena* made out to the Courageous flip point. Why did it take us four days?"

Jared put his hand on her shoulder. "Because I was too stubborn to ask for a tow. That was *Athena* under her own power. We need to go work on the prisoners."

She nodded. "I should probably make a run at the officer. Come with me. Perhaps the two of us with implants can make some headway on him."

He doubted that. The man seemed determined not to talk with them. Still, what could it hurt? "Okay."

They'd housed the majority of the prisoners on the cargo deck, but the officer warranted a cell in the brig. A man with implants might be unexpectedly dangerous. Jared should know.

The layout of *Courageous*'s brig was similar to the one on *Spear*, except he didn't have extra marine guards in the corridor. He trusted the ship's AI to keep unauthorized people out of the facility.

The duty officer stood when Jared came into the compartment. "Captain." Three marines with sidearms stood along the bulkheads.

"Lieutenant Gonzales. How is the prisoner?"

Lieutenant Junior Grade Benjamin Gonzales had been a supply officer on *Athena*. The destroyer hadn't needed dedicated security people. The young officer had stepped up when Jared formed the new department.

"He's been fed and is just as uncommunicative as before, sir."

"Open the cell."

The marines moved to have a better line of sight, but Jared waved them back. "Let's keep this as casual as we can."

The hatch slid open. The cell was Spartan enough: a bunk, a head, and one small shelf, empty. The prisoner had been lying down, but he sat up as they entered. His already closed expression soured when he saw who his visitors were.

Kelsey stepped around Jared and centered herself on the bunk. "Lieutenant Commander Richards, my name is Kelsey Bandar. We've met, though under less-than-preferable circumstances. In your computer center."

She paused, perhaps to allow him to speak, but he remained silent.

"Fifty-seven of your people survived the battle. We have them on board *Courageous*. Would you like me to give you an update on their status?"

He looked torn, but shook his head.

"Not even the people in the computer center with you?"

The man looked down for a long minute. "Yes."

That was the first word he'd said since his capture. Jared suspected that it wouldn't be his last. Kelsey was a miracle worker.

She waved Jared back and squatted to bring her eyes close to the man's level. "One woman had some broken bones in her hand, but they've been set, and she's going through a regeneration regime. The others all came through the fight without injury. If you like, I can arrange a visit."

The man's expression closed down again, but Jared sensed some relief under the surface. "For a price, I assume. Tell me, what exactly do traitors like you want? I'll never betray Fleet or my oath to the Lords like you did."

"It might surprise you, but I have no idea what you're talking about. I didn't know your civilization existed until a few months ago."

Richards sneered. "Tell me another one. Only members of the higher orders or Fleet officers get implants. You're no Fleet officer, though. You and your traitor friend broke all the oaths you ever swore to the Lords. I can't imagine how you stole those ships, or crewed them for that matter, but Fleet will find you and crush you."

Kelsey pursed her lips. "I know you've heard of the rebellion against the Old Empire. The rebels crippled this ship. We only found it a few months ago. As for my implants, you can thank those psychopathic monsters you were trying to resupply for them. Tell me, why would civilized people aid a rogue AI in enslaving savages and turning them into ravening beasts bent on destruction?"

To say her words surprised the man would be an understatement. He gaped at her. "You're lying."

"I'm not. I was just a normal person before they captured me, cut me apart, and made me one of them. I'm lucky my brother rescued me before they altered the programming in my implants. I'd imagine your implantation wasn't nearly as traumatic as mine was. We used the Old Empire techniques to remove the viral code from your implants, by the way. You're not under anyone's control now. At least not in your head."

"I wasn't under anyone's control before," he snarled. "What did you do to me?"

Jared spoke for the first time. "We overwrote your implant with the original Imperial code, Commander. That's the only reason you're not frothing at the mouth and trying to kill us with your bare hands. Unless that's how you normally behave."

If the man's eyes had been weapons, he'd have burned Jared to a crisp. "How could you betray Fleet, traitor? After everything they did for you. What were you before? A lieutenant? An ensign? Why settle for being a commander? Why not go for captain? Or admiral?"

"Because I've never been part of your Fleet. Our people escaped the rebellion. I'm the other Fleet. The one your rebel ancestors tried to destroy."

The man gaped. "That's not possible. We overthrew the Old Empire and crushed its corrupt masters."

"You've been sadly misinformed, but it's not my duty to correct that lapse. You're aboard the Fleet battlecruiser *Courageous*. You and your fellows are my prisoners. In case you don't remember my name, I'm Commander Jared Mertz, commanding officer of this vessel. I've been a Fleet officer for over two decades, just not your Fleet.

"At Princess Kelsey's suggestion, I am going to authorize you to access the ship's library. You should be able to find enough to entertain and educate yourself. I'm sorry to inform you that the contents are sadly out of date, but the ship has been floating in space since before the Fall. We'll speak again."

The man stood abruptly but made no aggressive move. Kelsey stood slowly, and the marines outside brought their neural disruptors up. She waved for them to lower their weapons.

"I will not be fooled by your propaganda," the man said through clenched teeth.

Kelsey turned toward the hatch. "We all have to decide what we believe in, Commander Richards. I'll come back later with your people. If you want to talk to me, you have my implant code. Call at any time."

The two of them left the man standing in the middle of his cell. Jared gave the instructions to *Courageous* to allow him access to the library of unclassified data. The AI would ensure the man didn't see anything sensitive or recent. Considering the vast amount of data available, Richards might actually learn something.

"Do you think we'll convince him?" he asked Kelsey.

"Eventually. The foundation of his beliefs is a lie. That makes for a lousy building. We'll see if it comes in time to make a difference. If you don't mind, I have some other things to look into before bed. I'm sure you and Elise can find something to talk about without me." She said the last with a slight smirk.

"Don't be snide. I'm sure that you and Talbot will find something equally interesting to do."

She smiled. "You have no idea."

18

Kelsey headed down to marine country as soon as she left the brig. She'd convinced Talbot not to come hunting for her, but there were limits to his patience. Hers, too.

It surprised her how many people were there when she arrived. Not just marines but scientists. She spotted Doctor Leonard standing beside Lieutenant Reese and headed over toward them. The two of them were examining one of the captured plasma cannons.

"Doctor, Lieutenant. So, is it better than ours or just bigger?"

The older man smiled. "We'll need to put it through some tests, but the technology is remarkably consistent, considering the passage of time. One would've imagined more than minor improvements over the last five hundred years."

Reese held it out to her. "We tried to fire it on the range, but it seems to be locked out. Mister Owlet is looking at the armor in the armory, or I'd have had him check it out."

"I can do that." The rebels had locked the weapon, but not in the same way as her new pistols had been. This was more like an on/off switch. It didn't require an implant to fire it like hers did, but it did need one to make it operable. She, of course, didn't have the correct code.

"It looks like it requires an authorization code to become operable. Carl should be able to reset the code so that I can turn it on. It looks like it has a kick. Perhaps too much for someone without powered armor or enhanced muscles. Let's go find out."

She put it onto her shoulder and headed for the armory. She felt ridiculous. The weapon seemed like it was bigger than she was. The armory was adjacent to the range, and the marine armorer was examining some of the captured ammunition, while Carl Owlet had the top of the massive armor opened up. The graduate student turned to face them when they came in.

"Highness, Lieutenant, Doctor. How can I help you?"

She held out the weapon. "I need you to reset the implant control in this. It has a code like the console and the safe."

He took the massive weapon with some bobbling and set it on the table. "If it works like the console, I should be able to make it give you the access code. Once you have it, you should be able to reset it yourself. Or disable it."

"How's the armor?"

"About the same, I think. It doesn't need implants to operate, but someone with the right code needs to turn it on. Very strange." He tinkered inside the rifle until he found something. "Try to access it."

It only took half a dozen attempts to get the weapon to spit out the code. Kelsey gave Owlet the high sign, and he put it back together. When it was ready, the boy stepped back. "Give it a try."

She sent the code, and the weapon turned on, giving her complete access to the internals. She reset the code to one of her own choosing and began looking for a way to deactivate the need for a code at all.

Only there wasn't an option for that. Once someone activated the weapon, it would lock out when someone swapped out the power supply. Someone wanted complete control over this weapon.

The specifications indicated that it required armor to fire. She couldn't find a reference to use by unarmored commandos. She might be able to use it.

"I'm going to the range. I think it might be best if I try this without spectators. Just in case."

Talbot looked mulish. "If you're not sure that it's safe, you probably shouldn't use it."

"If the range tells me it can't handle it, I won't. I'm using some of the caution you recommended."

Reese eyed the weapon. "It looks ridiculously powerful. Go armor up. That's being cautious."

She sighed but did as ordered. They'd put her spare armor here in the armory. Her damaged set sat in the corner, awaiting the armorer's pleasure to replace the damaged section. It only took a few minutes to seal it up. She didn't bother to use a skinsuit, since she wasn't going to be in it more than a few minutes.

Even in her armor, the weapon seemed vastly oversized for her. She made her way onto the range and brought its systems online. A quick query confirmed the range could handle it. Barely.

Kelsey cranked the protective field to maximum and put the target at fifty meters, which the weapon indicated was the minimum safe distance.

The kick when she fired it was... substantial. The plasma weapon she normally used was too powerful for an unenhanced person to use. This might be too much for her without armor.

The detonation of the plasma seed sent her staggering back a step. It was an order of magnitude more powerful than anything she'd used before. Use of this weapon on a ship would be suicidal. Which explained why the armored marines hadn't had any on them. These were for use on the ground.

She'd try one of the large flechette rifles, too, but right now she wanted to conduct an experiment. She returned to the armory and began stripping out of her armor. "That worked. The range can handle one of these with the safety system set to max. It packs a kick. I want to see if I can fire it without the armor."

Talbot looked unconvinced. "Is that safe?"

"The range shields us from the blast. I just need to see if the kick is too much for me outside my armor." She turned to Owlet. "We'll need to unlock one of the oversized flechette rifles, if they're set up the same way."

Kelsey headed back to the range but stopped Talbot when he started to come up to the firing line. "Let's be cautious."

"Then take out all the ammo. If you only have one shot, you can't accidentally fire a second one."

"Good idea." She laid the rifle on the bench and pulled out the magazine. The pellets were significantly larger than the ones she'd seen before. She stripped all but one out and pocketed them.

Without the armor, the rifle really did feel like a cannon. Her strength allowed her to support its weight, but it was massive. She brought the range up, put a target out at fifty meters, and fired.

The recoil knocked her off her feet and sent her sliding on the deck. She ended up almost halfway back to Talbot. Her shoulder ached, and she stared up at him. "Wow. That was something. It kicks like a mule."

He held his hand out to her. "Have you ever been kicked by a mule?"

"Nope." She took his hand and let him pull her up. "This is definitely not useable by unarmored people. Even me."

"What would happen if I fired it? I'm more than halfway tempted."

"I'm pretty sure it would break your shoulder. I recommend you give it a pass. Besides, if we can get the marine armor working, you'll be able to give it a try."

"You think they can get the armor working?"

She nodded. "Why not? Owlet seems to have figured out how to unlock them. The system only works because I have implants, but he and I have a system."

They headed back to the armory. She handed the weapon and the ammunition over to the armorer. "This is too much for anyone in unpowered armor." She looked at Carl. "Any luck?"

"The lockout is exactly like the plasma cannon. Go ahead and give it the original code."

She did, and the weapon came online. Kelsey changed the code and looked at Talbot. "Come on."

This weapon didn't require the maximum protection from the range. She loaded it and interfaced her implants with it. Her implants couldn't bring up a firing interface. Interesting. She made a mental note to have Carl examine the code in the weapon.

Kelsey had the range create a small hoard of Pale Ones. They all charged, howling like beasts.

The targeting software in her implants located them all, and she fired a burst at the first one. This weapon, unlike the normal flechette rifle, had recoil. Not enough that she couldn't control it, though.

She fired bursts into each of the charging enemy until they were all down. She handed the large rifle over to Talbot. "I'm not sure you'll be able to control this, but it won't hurt you to try. Much."

Talbot braced it on the rest and fired single shots at targets. "The recoil is pretty stiff. I doubt I can control full auto." He fired short bursts and managed to keep all the shots on the range. Barely.

He rubbed his shoulder. "Yeah, that isn't going to be useable by anyone outside of powered armor. It's too hard to control. Too bad. It's a badass weapon."

"Then the only thing left to try is getting that armor online."

They made their way back to the armory again and turned in the weapon. "Carl, did you get the armor unlocked?"

"I've been digging into it while you were gone. It's harder to get to the control mechanism, and it seems to have some lethal add-ons."

"What does that mean?"

The graduate student gestured at the armor. "It has a self-destruct package. I found explosives at various locations inside. They'd wreck the armor and the marine."

"Seriously?" She shook her head. "What kind of maniac wants their marines to blow up? How long before you can defuse it?"

"I'm almost there. Give me ten minutes."

Talbot pulled her aside. "That kind of adds to the theme. It seems like the implants were restricted to officers. Perhaps only senior officers. They didn't trust the crew."

"It sounds paranoid, but you're right. They wiped the AI rather than let us capture it. Not just the data, but also the hardware. The captain encrypted her console and her files in a way that made recovery unlikely. There's no way anyone was getting them unless you factor in someone like me with implants and a major hacker like Carl."

She scratched her chin. "It sounds like their society is ruled by AIs with a favored class of citizens who watch over the rest. They don't even trust the rank-and-file military. The ratings and crewmen aren't even familiar with the layout of their Empire. Which I will now be calling the Rebel Empire for clarity. They have no idea the AIs even exist."

Talbot nodded. "Too bad none of the marines is talking yet. We might be able to convert some of the crew. Release them from their chains, so to speak. What about the officer?"

She shrugged. "I don't know. If he's one of the ruling elite, he might be hard to reach. Though he did call me a renegade member of the higher orders—whatever that is—but thought Jared was only a Fleet officer. That might mean that the real aristocracy chooses the cream of the middle layers of society and trains them up for Fleet command. I wonder if they have corrupted implants like the Fleet officers."

Carl Owlet waved at them. "I've removed the last of the bombs. I also found a power pack that would fry the advanced circuitry. Everything else seems harmless."

"Are you willing to bet someone's life on that?"

The young man nodded. "There's nothing else in there that could damage the system or the wearer. I'm ready to trigger the code when you are."

Kelsey stretched her neck. "Go ahead."

This set of controls was significantly harder to hack than the captain's console. It took hours, and Carl almost gave up several times. Someone really didn't want their armor falling into the wrong hands.

Eventually, though, she got a code ten times longer than the previous ones. She fed it back to the armor, and it powered up. She changed the code with a sigh. "Got it. It looks like the armor is set up like the weapons. If you replace the power supply, the armor locks down. Can you do something about that, Carl?"

"Possibly. I'll need to work with Doctor Leonard. Give me a few days to consider the possibilities."

She directed her implants to interface with the armor. They did, but it wasn't as seamless as when she linked up to her commando gear. Like the weapons, the implant receptors didn't seem optimized to allow someone like her to control the equipment.

That wasn't to say that she couldn't manage. It was just clumsy. She'd see if the computer experts on Erorsi could assist them in cleaning up the interface. These two sets of armor could make the difference going forward.

It only took her a moment to find out why this suit had been in the armory on the destroyer. One of the legs wasn't working. It had a control fault.

She looked at Owlet and the armorer. "This unit has a problem. Let's bring the other one online."

That took a few minutes more, but the code she'd gotten from the last set of armor allowed her to access it much more rapidly. This unit had a fault in the torso.

"Okay, this one is more broken than the first. I guess that's why they didn't use them. The control unit for the left leg is bad in the first one. Can we salvage that from the damaged unit? The upper torso is broke on this one. Are any of the ruined units suitable for salvaging parts?"

The armorer nodded. "We have the damaged equipment in one of the holds. I'll see what we can recover."

Owlet opened the leg on the second unit. "I might be able to swap the control units and get one of these operating."

A few minutes later, he held up something that looked like a long, thin data chip. "I think this is it. Let me put it in the first set of armor."

Once he finished, Kelsey accessed the armor again. The check this time was amber. It read as operational but still seemed to have some kind of problem. "That did it. Mostly. Let's see what this thing can do."

She started to climb into the suit and immediately discovered a problem. The legs were too long for her. The arms, too. Apparently, these Rebel Empire types thought marines needed to come in extra-large packages.

"Oops. They built this thing for someone a little larger than I am. Talbot, you want to give it a try?"

"Sure." The marine climbed in, and she closed it up behind him. "The screen just activated. It's a pretty advanced heads-up display."

The last part of that came through her implants. "You need to turn on your external speakers. Only I can hear you. Actually, I might be able to do that."

She sent an implant command, and the external speakers activated. "Try talking again."

"Can you hear me?" The speakers worked.

"Loud and clear. I'm not sure I like being able to access and control your suit like this. It feels wrong."

Talbot flexed his knees. "It sounds about like these other people, though. Just how much control do you have?"

Kelsey invaded his interface and seized control of his armor. She stretched his arms over his head and bent him over to touch his toes. "About that much."

He straightened when she released him. "That's total bullcrap. I couldn't do anything while you were calling the shots. We need to disable that."

"That's probably doable," Owlet said. "The devil will be in the details. I'll look into it."

"I promise not to make you dance like a ballerina," Kelsey added with a smile. "Mostly. Let's go check out the strength limits on this thing. I bet it's more powerful than my commando armor. Look at those arms."

By the time they were ready to call it a night, she knew exactly how powerful the marine armor was: slightly less than twice as strong as her commando armor, and significantly more resistant to damage. It might even be able to survive one of the small plasma rifle seeds. It wouldn't be worth much at that point. Still, any landing you could walk away from was a good one.

One thing in her favor was that it was slow and clumsy compared to her commando armor. She was literally able to dance around Talbot as he tried to catch her. Speed and dexterity counted for a lot in battle. She could live with that.

Right as they were finishing, the control unit for the leg shorted out. There had to be an underlying problem with it. The loss of the armor annoyed Talbot.

She patted him on the shoulder. "Come on. Maybe they can get it working again. Tomorrow will come earlier than either of us like, so we should get some sleep."

While he climbed out of the armor, she checked the ship's scanners. *Spear* and her consorts were more than two thirds of the way toward the flip point. She still had no idea how they were going to deal with that problem. She just hoped the man's idiocy didn't get them all killed before they had a plan.

19

J ared woke to the sound of the shower. He stretched and smiled. Last night had been sinfully delightful. Elise and he were normally more discreet, but now that they knew the secret was out, they could relax a little.

He waited for the water to cut off, slid out of bed, and padded into the head. She was standing beside the shower tube, toweling off. The sight of her made him smile even more widely.

She wrapped her hair in a towel and kissed him. "I tried not to wake you."

"You should've. Waking up with you is my idea of the perfect start for the day."

Elise gave him an indulgent smile. "We don't have time for that today. We're meeting with Admiral Sanders after breakfast. Get a shower so you don't smell like me."

He laughed. "I'm in no danger of smelling like you."

"If you're a good boy, we have time for a leisurely breakfast."

"And if I'm bad, we won't eat at all?"

"If you're bad, I'll have to swat your nose. Shower."

Jared reluctantly headed into the tube. The soap and hot water swirling around him felt good. He let it clean him and rinsed off.

Elise was already fully dressed by the time he returned to the bedroom. It only took him a few minutes to dress in his uniform. They left for breakfast together, the Royal Guards outside his room both falling in behind them.

The officers' mess was already crowded, but they'd reserved a table last night. Princess Kelsey, Talbot, and Admiral Sanders were there and already sipping their coffee.

He held out a chair for Elise and then sat down. "Good morning. Admiral, I didn't expect you so early."

"Highness. Lord Captain. I found a seat on an earlier flight and decided to join Princess Kelsey. She was already up. We've had an illuminating conversation about Captain Breckenridge."

Jared grimaced. "The bridge pinged me when he flipped last night. I've sent a probe to take a snapshot of the other system. If we can identify it, we might be able to see if they pose a danger mucking around over there."

"And if they do?"

"Then we try to stop them. Somehow. They most likely left a probe to watch for any attempt at following them, so this isn't going to be easy." He turned to Kelsey. "Good morning. Did you get a chance to examine the equipment from the destroyer?"

She nodded. "I did. We recovered a bunch of flechettes that we can use in our own weapons. We might be able to use some of the weaponry, too, if Carl can unlock them permanently. It's crazy. They secured all the weapons with codes that make them useless if someone replaces the power pack. The armor, too."

Talbot snagged a bun from the loaded platter the server brought out to them. He buttered it slowly as Kelsey dug into the large plate she'd ordered. The man shook his head in amused disbelief.

"I still can't see how she puts it away like that. It's crazy." He looked away from her glare and focused on Jared. "Anyway, the two suits of armor we recovered were down with system failures, but Owlet got one of them working long enough for a test drive. They're really something."

Jared sighed. "I'm not surprised to hear about their paranoia. It seems to be a repeating theme with these people. Every critical system on the destroyer is locked up tighter than the Imperial Scepter."

He looked at Kelsey. "We loaded the files you recovered onto a standalone system. Even though the destroyer's captain locked the console you got them from, she also encrypted them. We'll have to crack that, but at least we got them. The same for the data chips from the safe. These people come from a brutal, repressive society, I think."

"The Rebel Empire is a dictatorship for sure, though one with a velvet glove," Kelsey said. "I'm not sure about the brutal part."

"We'll have plenty of time to come up with the right words for them. It's still early in the investigation. How many suits of armor did they have, Talbot?"

The marine shrugged. "The lowest estimate is eight. I'm leaning toward ten. It's hard to tell. Their bunks indicate a maximum marine complement of eighty. Significantly more than a destroyer in our Fleet would have. The sleeping area is pretty cramped."

"What do you think of the armor, Kelsey? How does it compare to yours?"

"Definitely more powerful, but clumsy. I can almost run circles around Talbot."

"Yeah, but when I catch her, its game over. That suit is amazing. I feel invincible inside it."

Kelsey poked him in the shoulder. "Don't let it go to your head. They have weapons that can take it out."

Admiral Sanders took a bite of his eggs. "Indeed. The mere presence of an armed cadre of men in such armor indicates a need for it. A destroyer has little room for even the items required during a normal deployment. Those suits took a significant amount of space that could've supported other things."

Jared thought about that. "What could they need armor for? The Pale Ones? Perhaps they worried about an ambush?"

"Commander Richards called us traitors," Kelsey said after a big bite of her pancakes. "That hints at the possibility of an underground."

Talbot snorted. "Rebels against the Rebel Empire. Would they be loyalists?"

"They very well might be," Jared said. "We'll see if we can shake anything loose from him. He's still talking, though not about anything sensitive. Kelsey found his weakness."

Sanders raised his eyebrow. "What was it?"

"His people," Kelsey said. "I've allowed him supervised visitation, and he's been somewhat more cooperative. He's also been reading the Imperial history books. I've kept tabs on his choices. The parts I've read are quite the education, even for me. I can't imagine what he thinks of it."

"He probably suspects it's propaganda," Jared said. "In his shoes, I'd think so. Once he reads enough, finds the internal consistency, he might begin to doubt. It won't be in time to help us with our problem, though."

Sanders looked at him inquiringly. "What exactly is your plan going forward, Lord Captain?"

"I'm in a hard spot," Jared admitted. "We're critically short of missiles. The ones on the destroyer are too small for *Courageous*. If we get into a serious fight, we're done for. Not that I can use lethal weapons against Breckenridge. I'm not sure what options are still available."

Kelsey pushed back her empty plate. "Too bad we don't have some of those Pale Ones' stunning weapons for ships. They have to be neural disruptors on a huge scale."

"Even if we did have them, we can't exactly sneak up on the other ships. They'll spot us far too quickly."

Pardon this unit's input, Captain, but it may have a suggestion.

Jared resisted the impulse to look up. "*Courageous* has an idea. Go ahead."

This vessel has several fighter craft. They are very stealthy. Under the right circumstances, they may be able to get quite close to other ships without detection. Particularly with the limited scanning capability that Captain Breckenridge's ships seem to possess.

"I hadn't considered the fighter ships. I wasn't even sure they were operational. In any case, we still can't use ship killers on them."

Fighter ships come in several possible configurations. One of them is an antipiracy variant with just such a stunning weapon and two antiship missiles. If pirates have hostages, it behooves Fleet to take them alive. Fleet vessels are shielded, of course.

That got Jared's attention. "*Courageous* says the fighters can be configured to use a weapon just like the Pale Ones' stunners. How many fighters does this ship carry, *Courageous*? How many are operational?"

This vessel has three fighters. All are operational at this time. However, operating a fighter is not like flying this ship. There is no space aboard for anything but the most minimal of manual controls. The Empire designed those vessels for pilots with implants.

He grimaced. "Graves isn't going to like that. We have three operational fighters, but the pilot needs implants."

"Since I can't fly, that only leaves you," Kelsey said. "He really won't like that. Damn Breckenridge's itchy trigger finger."

Elise put her hand on Jared's shoulder. "Things will work out. You'll figure out how to stop him."

Captain, the probe you dispatched to trail the task force has reached the weak flip point. It detected no sentry probe and transitioned. This unit set it to return shortly with an initial scan. That should be enough for this unit to determine the identity of the destination system and if it was known to the Empire.

It has returned. Receiving data. Processing. No sentry probes or ships in close proximity to the target flip point. Destination system identified. It is a system without habitable worlds of its own somewhat further out from the core worlds than Erorsi and further spinward. Roughly two hundred light-years away.

Spinward, he sent via his implants. *What does that mean?*

The Old Empire referred to galactic directions in three-dimensional space with certain key words. Coreward would refer to something toward the galactic core. Spinward is in the direction of the galactic rotation. Anticoreward and antispinward are the opposites. Galactic north and south cover deviations from the plane of the galactic ecliptic. The destination system is roughly in the same plane as Erorsi.

He nodded. "*Courageous* has determined where they flipped to. It's about two hundred light-years away and located further from the core worlds of the Old Empire. Breckenridge didn't leave any obvious sentry probes. He must really be sure we won't come after him. If everyone is done eating, we might want to adjourn to a conference room."

Kelsey grabbed some bacon off Talbot's plate and stood. "If we're going to follow them, perhaps we should get on our way to the flip point. We don't want to let them get too far ahead of us."

Jared shook his head. "We have time to examine what we know first. Let's settle on a plan and then act." He called Graves to join them. He wasn't going to cut his second in command out of the loop, especially when he was going to have to surprise him with the fighter situation.

Of course, if the way was clear out to Avalon, they might just let them go. No need to get into a fight he didn't have to.

Graves met them at the conference room hatch. His exec looked well rested and cheerful. "Morning, Captain. Highnesses, Admiral. Talbot."

"Morning, Charlie," Jared said. "Have a seat, and I'll bring you up to speed."

He sent an implant command to the screen on the wall and brought up the map of the Old Empire. He zoomed in on their sector as the rest sat. "Here we are. Erorsi is in blue. Pentagar is green. Avalon is in amber." He brought up the 3D nightmare of crisscrossing lines that represented the flip system.

"As you can see, the Courageous system flip point is a one-way from the new Terran Empire to our area. The new weak flip point takes us back in roughly the same direction but further in the direction of galactic spin. It's possible to get to the new Terran Empire from there in seven flips. That's the way home."

Jared zoomed in further to the system where the remnants of the task force had gone. "This system only has a reference number. None of the worlds is habitable, and no human presence was established. It has three flip points, counting the weak one. One leads out in the general direction of home. The other toward the Old Empire. *Courageous*, is there any system of note in the direction of Avalon?"

"That section of the Old Empire was what could be called a backwater. Mining worlds and such that supplied rare elements to industries deeper in. It was growing and would have become mature in its own right with time, but there are no worlds of special note in that direction."

Graves shook his head. "I still have difficulty getting used to a computer this advanced. I'm amazed at how like a person it is."

Kelsey grinned at him. "Imagine talking to him at high speed through cranial implants. *Courageous* isn't sentient, but he is very capable. It's easy to think of him as a person though he's not. No offense, *Courageous*."

"None taken. This unit is quite aware that it falls short of the sentience threshold."

Talbot grunted. "Did the Empire ever achieve sentient AIs?"

"This unit has seen some prerebellion communications that hinted at such, though no official word exists in this unit's memory banks."

"I suspect that the AI that started the rebellion was sentient," Kelsey said. "That might have been a poor decision on someone's part. It looks as though Breckenridge has better than fifty-percent odds of finding our Terran Empire if he heads the right way. If he has bad luck, he might go around it, but that's another problem. What's in the other direction?"

"There are worlds that once had higher populations in that direction, depending on which course he chooses," the computer said. "There is one system of special note."

A system two flips away flashed red. "This is Harrison's World. It housed a major Fleet base called Boxer Station. At one time, it was responsible for the defense of this entire quadrant of the Empire's outer reaches. Records show it was a rally point in the counterattack on the rebels."

Admiral Sanders looked at the map speculatively. "What would that have meant, *Courageous*?"

"Before the rebellion, it was home to the Ninth Fleet, one of the largest groupings of Fleet vessels in the Empire. Perhaps a hundred superdreadnoughts and supporting vessels. Four to five times that many battlecruisers. Many additional smaller units. Everything required to support them. That number may have gone up in the final days."

"Or dropped due to combat losses," Graves said. "Tell us about the civilian world."

"Harrison's World had core-world population and technology. It housed both the Fleet support facilities and the political leadership for its sector. Duke Louis Gray was the last governor listed."

Elise cleared her throat. "Is there any indication that the weak space-time bridge is open in both directions?"

"This unit believes it is."

"What about *Spear* and her consorts?" Jared asked. "Any indication of them?"

The screen expanded into a map of the destination system. "As they do not have maps of the Empire, it seems they have spread out in an effort to locate flip points or other features of interest in the system. Their probes are actively scanning. This unit believes it likely they will locate the flip point leading deeper into the Old Empire first."

"Hopefully they'll do a thorough search and go down the right one first. If they do that, we can just let them go."

His sister gave him a look. "We can almost count on Breckenridge doing the wrong thing."

Jared sighed. "Then we'll need to come up with a plan to go after them soon. It will take them as much as a day to find the first flip point. We'll need to consult with the folks on Erorsi. They can probably help us some with the data you recovered from the destroyer. We'll need to leave it here."

He looked over at Elise. "As much as I'd like for you and the admiral to come with us, we're going in stealthy. If we can take Breckenridge out, we'll be back soon. If you would accompany Kelsey to Erorsi and talk with Mister Bell about getting some of his people to join us, that would be very helpful."

Elise nodded. "Kelsey and I can handle that. I'm looking forward to seeing his facility for myself. What will you do once you catch up with Captain Breckenridge?"

"That really depends on him."

20

The cutter flew down to the Erorsi complex at a much more leisurely pace than the marine pinnace had dropped Kelsey into the atmosphere the first time. Of course, they weren't worried that the Pale Ones would blow them out of the sky this time. The controlling AI was gone, and the enhanced savages were too busy struggling to stay alive to cause them any trouble.

Dirty snow covered the mountain plateau, and the sky was a leaden gray, full of particulate matter thrown up by the massive asteroid the mad AI had dropped almost on Kelsey's head. Thankfully, the air closer to the ground was mostly clear of dust.

The residents of the former planetary defense headquarters had opened a more convenient entrance. It beat the one they'd had hidden in a gully. That made disembarking as simple as walking down the boarding ramp and entering a small building.

Two men in black jumpsuits stiffened to attention as Kelsey walked through the door, bringing their rifles upright in front of them. A redheaded woman in a blue jumpsuit stood in front of the men. She smiled and extended her hand to Kelsey and then to Elise. "Princess Kelsey, Princess Elise. Welcome to Erorsi. I'm Janet Quincy, Mister Bell's assistant."

"Thank you." Kelsey looked around the room. It had a massive lift, suitable for cargo. "This must make getting supplies in a little bit easier."

"You have no idea. Now that the AI is gone, we can come and go without worrying someone will see us. We designed the building so that we can take it down in a few hours if we need to. I don't think we'll be comfortable out in the open for a long, long time."

Elise smiled. "Hopefully you won't need to hide again."

"We've all been keeping a close eye on the news, and we're so grateful that you stopped that enemy ship from getting away. We're sorry for the loss of life and ships. If we can be of any assistance, you need only ask."

"That's why we're here," Kelsey said. "Is Mister Bell available?"

The woman nodded. "Of course. If you'll come with me, I'll take you straight to him."

She led them into the open lift and started it down. It dropped smoothly into the mesa. Kelsey watched the walls flash by. "You must've already had the shaft dug. I can't imagine adding something like this to an existing facility would be easy."

"This lift shaft was installed when the facility was built and then covered when it was complete. All we had to do was remove the fake stone at the top."

The lift stopped, and the doors slid open on a huge room. Dozens of people were sorting what looked like salvaged equipment into multiple piles. Janet led them through the organized chaos.

Kelsey recognized some of the equipment as computers, but much of it was unfamiliar to her. She stopped to help two men lift a particularly heavy piece onto a floating platform. They looked momentarily shocked but smiled as they recognized her. She gave them a small wave and caught up with the other women.

"I assume all this came from the old cities," she said. "Is it recoverable?"

Janet shrugged. "Maybe. If nothing else, we can use the parts. After five hundred years, the supplies on some critical components were getting very low. The rebels ignored the cities after the invasion, other than sending in search parties for the citizens. Once they created the Pale Ones, it didn't take long before they were empty."

"It'll be a while before they're full again," Elise said sadly.

"Perhaps not. We're hopeful that we can lure people in from Pentagar to settle. We have a lot of unclaimed land."

Janet led them into a major corridor and deep into a maze of storage areas. One of them was open and had dozens of men in lab coats assembling what looked like a massive computer. Kelsey spotted Reginald Bell's mass of white hair from across the room.

She sent him a ping and waved when he looked over.

The ancient man smiled as he walked over. "Kelsey! How wonderful to see you again. And Princess Elise. Welcome to Erorsi. You're just in time. We're getting ready to conduct an experiment."

Elise peered at the computer. "So I see. Exactly what am I looking at?"

"The largest, most powerful computer system on Erorsi. We salvaged it from the capital."

Kelsey felt her eyebrows rise in surprise. "Wasn't your capital destroyed?"

"No. We didn't have a spaceport nearby. We moved those away from the populated areas once we realized they were the primary rebel targets." He gestured at the equipment. "This was, at one time, the computer that controlled all the financial markets on Erorsi. Keeping track of delayed data from all around the Empire meant it required truly astonishing amounts of memory and computing power."

"How does it stack up to the computer on *Courageous*?"

"Well, that's somewhat like comparing apples and oranges. This computer is much less autonomous and yet much more capable of intensive processing than the one on *Courageous*. It should have an AI interface, but I doubt very seriously that it will be much of a conversationalist.

"We're hoping to use it to access the memory banks you recovered from the AI. The storage units are solid state, so they're probably intact. We're hopeful that we can crack the encryption on the data. This system should also be able to correlate the data quickly."

"How does the computer that they recovered from that asteroid compare to either of them?" Elise asked.

Bell shrugged. "I'm not sure. It looks like the mutineers managed to remove all its parts, but our computer people are uncertain of how some of the most advanced processors work. The scientists on board *Courageous* are sending us the data as they test each piece, and we have people with them to try to decipher how it all works. At a guess, it was an advanced design capable of hosting a true AI. Not something like was in the sunken battlecruiser but the real deal. A sentient computer."

"That sounds dangerous," Kelsey said. "Obviously, since something like that probably kicked off the rebellion. We're bringing the damaged light cruiser *Shadow* and the captured enemy destroyer to the orbital construction facility. We're hopeful that the destroyer is reparable. I'm not so sure about *Shadow*."

"We'll do our best, of course. It won't happen quickly, though. None of our people has ever worked on anything like this before. We'll bring professionals in from Pentagar to assist, if you're willing, Princess Elise."

The Crown Princess Elise nodded decisively. "You'll have as much help as you desire. We're in this together."

"I couldn't agree more. While these good people continue their work, I'd like to adjourn to a more comfortable setting to discuss that. They'll call us when they have the system ready to test."

Kelsey looked around. "How are you going to keep the AI from infecting it? I can see why you brought it in, because it won't be connected to your base, but the virus might just take it over."

"That will tell us something, too. This computer isolates new data. Something about continuing to operate as it incorporates new information. It may work for this. If not, we'll have the original hardwired operating system to recover with."

Bell led them to a small lounge. It was obviously new, as storage areas didn't require that level of comfort. He gestured for the three of them to sit around a small table.

"Kelsey, the leadership council has been talking about how we move forward. I realize that you intend to depart for home before long, so I'd like to take a few minutes to brief you on their conclusions.

"As you know, we've kept the same control structure since the rebels isolated us from the Empire. We realize this is a small group of people—less than ten thousand—but we feel that we need to remain true to our heritage." He inclined his head toward Elise. "While there was talk of seeking your protection, I hope you will not be offended if we go a different route."

Elise didn't seem bothered by the rejection. "You'll have our support as an independent entity. Neighbors help one another. Pentagar shall respect your choice and your sovereign space. Though as the only gateway to the rest of the universe, we do claim free passage as existed in the Old Empire for our ships."

"Of course. In fact, I'm glad you mentioned the Old Empire." Bell returned his gaze to Kelsey. "While I'm the only one of us that lived under the direct rule of the emperor, we consider ourselves to be Imperial subjects. As your father is the current emperor of the Terran Empire, we are his subjects to command. And yours, Highness."

Their decision didn't entirely surprise Kelsey. Bell had been a serving Fleet officer in the Old Empire. This group of people had lived since the rebellion waiting for rescue from the Empire. This was a logical step and one she was more than happy to endorse.

"In my role as the voice of the emperor, I happily accept your fealty and pledge our support to you as citizens of the Terran Empire." She looked at Elise. "I hope that doesn't cause you too many problems."

"I'm sure it won't. We have a very comprehensive treaty with the Terran Empire that will make working with the citizens of Erorsi straightforward. We *will* need to discuss how citizens of the Kingdom can own property in the Empire should you lure them in to join you, Mister Bell."

Bell smiled widely. "That can be worked out. Perhaps some kind of dual citizenship?"

"An addendum to the mutual defense treaty would cover something like that," Kelsey said. "I hope that means we can take a few of your people with us."

"We'll have a team ready to travel today if you can give them a ride to your ship."

"Easily done. I'll send word to Jared to send a marine pinnace. That will have plenty of room. As the representative of the Imperial Throne, I'll need to take the oaths of the leadership council. We can do that later tonight. Right now, I'd like to see what you remember about Boxer Station and Ninth Fleet."

The old man leaned back in his chair. "Not much. I've never been there. As I recall, it was a major Fleet base. It would've been critical in fighting back against the rebels. Is that where the weak flip point leads?"

"Not precisely, but it isn't too far away. *Courageous* has some basic data on the base but not much. We know it was big. That's about it."

"Perhaps our computer system has more data. With the normal layout of flip points, that base is over a month away. A dozen systems or more. The computers here might not know any more than we do. You're welcome to try."

Kelsey closed her eyes and felt for the nearest interface. Since Bell and she were the only implanted persons on the base, she was somewhat surprised to feel one overhead. They must've installed it specifically for him.

She hadn't needed to use the computers the last time she was here, so Kelsey was somewhat surprised when the system granted her access without argument.

Welcome to Erorsi Planetary Defense Headquarters, Princess Kelsey Bandar. This unit is ready to assist you.

Kelsey smiled a little. That was just what she wanted to hear.

Do you have a name?

This unit has answered to various names in the past. Computer will serve.

What does Reginald Bell call you?

He refers to this unit as Uncle Larry. This unit is not certain exactly why.

She snorted. "Uncle Larry? Really?"

Bell laughed. "It would make perfect sense if you'd ever met the man. Feel free to call it whatever you like."

"I absolutely can't change that name. You're stuck with it now."

Okay, Uncle Larry, I'd like to see what information you have about Boxer Station and Ninth Fleet.

This unit has no data beyond the most basic information, but there may be more available in the Imperial diplomatic database.

What's that?

All planetary command-and-control computer systems have a copy of a very large database available only to members of the Imperial government. That includes planetary rulers and their staff, as well as more restricted data for those higher in the Imperial hierarchy.

As an Imperial ambassador plenipotentiary, you have access to the highest classifications of data. As heir secundus to the Imperial Throne, you have need to know for all of that information, even the parts that would not normally be available to an ambassador plenipotentiary, ambassador, or planetary ruler.

Kelsey opened her eyes and looked at Elise. "I can see I should've spent more time talking to the computer under your capital. It seems there is a secret database that I can access."

"That's just not fair," the other woman groused. "How can I snoop to my heart's content without implants?"

"Blame Breckenridge. That's what I do. Even if you had them, it doesn't seem like you could access the more secure materials. I have a double edge as an ambassador plenipotentiary of the Terran Empire and from being in line to the Imperial Throne. Though, if there is more restricted data, I'm not that certain it would tell me about it."

Bell shook his head. "I can't imagine there would be many secrets restricted only to the emperor and his young heir. What does it know about the base?"

Was Boxer Station operational at the time of your last update, Uncle Larry?

It was, Highness. This unit's records indicate that the base was a central point of resistance against the rebel incursion. Ninth Fleet was operating at higher-than-standard strength levels. Circumstances may have changed drastically in the intervening years, however.

Can I access deck plans and other pertinent data for the station? If it still exists, they may prove very useful.

Of course. If you have secure data storage devices, this unit can copy the entire database for your later perusal.

She smiled at Bell. "If you have some secure data drives, I'd like to save several copies of the database."

Bell nodded. "I'll see what I can find."

"I'll join you in a few minutes. There are a few more questions I'd like to put to your computer, and I'd imagine watching me sit here is pretty boring."

The old man and Elise rose to their feet. "We'll be outside talking to the technicians if you need any help."

She waited for them to leave and returned her attention to the computer. She didn't even try to shoo the marines out. They'd moved into full "protect the princess mode" and wouldn't leave her side. It was mildly annoying, but she'd get over it.

Uncle Larry, I need to know about the most secure Imperial projects. Particularly any involving a key.

A physical key or some other kind?

She shrugged. *I don't know. I heard Emperor Marcus refer to Lucien having a key. I'm sure it was important, but I don't have a frame of reference to know exactly what he meant.*

This unit will begin a search of the classified archives, Highness. While it does so, there are four projects restricted to the emperor and heirs. Should this unit give you a summary?

Kelsey sent an affirmative and sat back to listen to the deepest secrets of the Old Empire. Odds were that none of them mattered anymore, but she wouldn't know until she checked. This was going to take a while.

21

J ared took one last walk around the fighter. The sleek black craft's lines screamed speed. The onboard computer said all systems were green, but he had a manual checklist displayed on his implants. He wasn't about to take chances on a ship that hadn't flown in more than five hundred years, even if the engineers said they'd replaced all the problematic systems.

After a seeming eternity, he was in the cockpit. The craft could seat two in a side-by-side configuration, but that wouldn't be very helpful. The second person normally acted as the gunner/navigator. Lacking someone with implants and the appropriate skills, he'd need to handle those tasks himself.

Eventually, he decided that the little craft was as ready as it would ever be. Time to take it out and see how it performed. He opened an audio link to the bridge. "*Courageous*, this is Gauntlet One. Ready to depart."

Zia responded promptly. "You are cleared to depart, Gauntlet One. Good hunting."

"Thanks, Zia. Gauntlet One out."

He linked his implants into the fighter's systems and gave the launch crew the high sign. They began sliding back.

Jared wore an armored flight suit. It was similar to unpowered armor in many ways, and it had a helmet to provide pressure in case of a hull breach.

Once everyone was clear, he looked at the standard launch profile. The ship had a launch field to get the fighter clear, and then the fighter went to full power. Good enough. He sent the command to launch.

The acceleration slammed him back into his couch and snatched his breath away. The fighter blasted out of the ship at several times the maximum acceleration of the marine pinnaces. Without his grav drive online, he had nothing to counter it.

He brought his drives on at full power and leapt away from the battlecruiser like a frightened racerbeast. The G-forces instantly subsided. The fighter reacted to his course adjustment better than any other ship he'd ever flown. The drives continued to blast him forward at better acceleration than *Courageous* could manage.

An incoming signal pinged for his attention. He saw Graves sitting on *Courageous*'s bridge when he accepted it. "Damn, Jared. That little thing is really hauling. I don't think we could catch it. It's almost like a missile."

"Not quite that fast, but it sure does feel that way. I'd imagine a dogfight would be one hell of a thing to see. How am I showing up on the scanners?"

"Bright and clear, but Zia says that you're becoming a little harder to pinpoint the farther away you get."

He cut his acceleration down to almost nothing, activated the stealth field, and changed course. "Now?"

"We still have you, but you just became really hard to pinpoint. If we hadn't already had a lock on you, we might have lost you. The communications link is also helping us, too."

"We'll see about that. Turn scanner control over to operations and lock the bridge out of the loop. I'll slip back around to see if you can spot me. Transfer the scanner controls back to the bridge in one hour. And no peeking at the history."

"Aye, sir. Good luck. *Courageous* out."

He boosted his speed back up to max and took off at right angles to his previous course. He kept up that pace for almost an hour before he cut his acceleration. He'd built up an amazing amount of speed.

It took longer to eliminate his forward momentum than he'd allowed for, and it was several hours before he was back in the area near *Courageous*. The bigger ship's active scans were clearly visible to his senses. The scan strength was still safely below detection level. Quite a bit below. He added another notch to his acceleration and inched closer to the battlecruiser.

The scanner strength increased as he entered missile range, but it was still manageable. He let off the acceleration in stages as he closed with his command. For the closest approach, he killed his grav drives entirely, relying on ballistic flight to bring him in.

Part of him was disappointed when they spotted him. He knew the exact moment because the strength of the incoming scans rose dramatically. He hit the acceleration and drove toward the ship with a corkscrew course, turning on his jammers. He also fired his two missiles.

Not real missiles, of course. Just simulated ones. *Courageous* was able to take them down short of the hull, but not by much. His systems registered simulated missile launches from *Courageous*.

The prudent thing to do at this point would be to cut his acceleration and change course. With a wicked grin, he went to max and shot toward *Courageous* at an alarming rate. Almost a missile in his own right.

"Gauntlet One, change course and cut speed!" Zia said.

Jared ignored her and took the agile fighter right down the battlecruiser's upper superstructure. He was past them in a blurred moment and sent his fighter into a roll.

"Gauntlet One, the captain takes a dim view of hot-dogging like that," Graves said in a dry voice. "You almost gave us a heart attack."

"I got carried away," Jared said with a grin. "Let's hope the captain understands."

"We'll see how he reacts the next time it happens, since he just set a new tradition in motion."

That was, unfortunately, probably true. He'd have to think these things through a little better next time. "I got closer than I'd expected, but not as close as I have to get to make this work. The stunner has a very limited range."

"We were looking for you, and we have better scanners than Breckenridge has at his command. I think you would have slipped right up on him. We almost didn't see you in time. Which, by the way, Zia finds completely unacceptable. She'll be working on improving things before this happens again."

"As I would expect," Jared said. "She *is* the best tactical officer in Fleet. We don't want anyone pulling the same crap on us. Another plus will be the fact that Breckenridge won't be looking for a stealthed ship in his wake. I'll have to make a pass at him in the same system. If I line it up right, I might be able to stun all three of those ships before they know we flipped in behind them."

"Sir, I have a suggestion going forward," Zia said. "You either hung out in our general area for a while, or you came in from a long way off at a slow speed, only really boosting at the last moment. I'm assuming the latter. Is that correct?"

Jared sent her the data on his course. "Correct. I went way out. Once I cut acceleration, it took me a while to get back into the general area. This thing is fast."

"Then next time, why don't you make that work for you? Come in at a high rate of speed on a terminal velocity. They probably won't know you're there until you fire. The window of detection is a lot shorter. Your hull material and stealth field will probably keep their eyes off you. If they do spot you, they might think you're some kind of scanner ghost."

He considered that. "Maybe. The stunner isn't that rapid fire, though. I'd have one shot at that speed."

"True, but we have three fighters. Surely you and the princess could take out the cruiser and one of the destroyers."

"Kelsey doesn't have the skill to fly one."

"Then slave her fighter to yours. She'd only have to fire the weapons. It's just an idea."

Jared brought the fighter back around. "We'll do this again. Same rules. I'll run out and come back at speed. You tell me if you spot me."

That experiment was much more exciting. *Courageous* saw him very late, and he was on top of them before they reacted. They killed him, of course, but he hit them with his missiles. He almost made it close enough to stun them. He could see how a swarm of fighters might make life interesting for a ship like his.

It would still be a suicide run, though. Maybe in the heat of battle they could zip in, strike, and escape again. There had to have been a compelling tactical advantage to fighters, or the Old Empire would never have built them. He'd need to do more in-depth study of the subject as time allowed. Until he had more people capable of flying them, they were only interesting toys with limited utility.

Landing them proved a lot more sedate than launching them. He brought the fighter in close, and a mechanical arm brought it back into the ship. Once the small craft was back in the launch bay and the flight deck repressurized, Jared opened the canopy. The flight crew took his helmet and helped him down.

Jared stripped out of his flight suit and put on his duty uniform in the pilots' ready room. There was bunk space for six and all the amenities. He assumed that standard practice was to keep three flight crews ready to launch at a moment's notice. He looked forward to the day he could do that.

Courageous sent him the scanner data from his approaches, and he reviewed it with interest. This plan might work. The first thing he needed to do was get into the system with Breckenridge's ships undetected. Then he could take them down. He hoped.

The situation had him worried. Yes, he was working with Kelsey, and she had overall command authority. Breckenridge was guilty of mutiny and treason. Technically. If push came to shove back home, Jared might be in some hot water. He'd defied a senior officer. Assaulted Fleet personnel. He planned to disable three Fleet warships and to imprison anyone who he thought presented a threat to the Empire.

Not a situation he looked forward to reporting on.

He needed to get back to the bridge, but he decided it was time to get an in-person update from Doctor Leonard. The scientist and his minion, Carl Owlet, were working on reassembling the AI they'd recovered from the asteroid.

Well, technically the Pentagaran rebels had. Thankfully, they'd gotten everything of interest off the asteroid before they sent it plunging into Erorsi.

The complexity of the situation made his head ache. So many things deserved their attention. The data banks from the rebel battlecruiser down on Erorsi, the AI equipment, because it might give them valuable information on this new Rebel Empire, and getting home. The days of peace and a laid-back attitude at home were done. They just didn't know it yet.

That didn't even count the inevitable attack by the Rebel Empire. Based on the quality of the enemy ships, the Terran Empire was in deep trouble.

He walked into the laboratory and found Doctor Leonard and Carl Owlet deep in conversation with Doctor Cartwright. The mission's chief scientist was showing them something on one of the computer screens.

All three of them turned toward Jared as he entered. Cartwright took a step toward him. "You're just in time, Captain. I was just showing my colleagues a new theory before I briefed you. One I worked out with the assistance of Mister Owlet."

"I hope it's nothing terrible, Doctor. I'm not sure I can take more bad news."

The older man shook his head. "It's not bad news in and of itself. Frankly, I'm not sure how it's going to play out, if indeed the theory proves true. Or even testable. Take a look at this." He gestured at the computer. Complex equations filled the screen.

"You're going to have to interpret for me, Doctor. I don't even know what I'm looking at."

"These are a new set of equations I've come up with for the weak flip points. You see, there should be much more gravitational energy at play inside these areas of space. Flip points draw on the incongruities in space to form stable wormholes that we can trigger with our drives."

Jared scratched his head. "I'm with you so far, I think. I just don't see where you're going."

The scientist's expression told Jared he was considering how to present a complex idea in a way that an idiot could understand. Considering Jared's grasp of the science behind flip points, he wasn't too far off.

After a moment, Cartwright ventured an explanation. "When everything is boiled down, there is usually a range of gravitational energy invested in these linked pairs. It does vary within certain limits, but not in a way that truly allowed for these weak flip points. Even the theory that I mentioned when we found the first one doesn't truly work. I've come to the conclusion that it is incomplete."

"It certainly seems to be valid to me. We found the damned things."

"Yes, but it isn't the full story. Something needs to account for the lost gravitational energy. I believe that I have done so."

"Okay, Doctor. Where did it go?"

The older man smiled, a decidedly odd thing with his huge mustache. "It's actually still there, only phased in a different energy state." He paused, obviously waiting for the light to go on over Jared's head.

"I have no idea what that means."

The scientist's expression fell a little. "We really need to discuss the state of education in the Empire. What that means, Captain, is that these so-called weak flip points are not weak at all. They simply have more than one possible destination."

Jared blinked as the concept hit him. "They might go different places? Seriously? Is that even possible?"

"I'm going to work with Commander Baxter to find out. It should be possible to tune the energy we release more finely than we currently do. If we target the correct energy frequency, we should be able to control which potential destination we travel to. The narrower energy release could even take one of our vessels through the original flip point and back home. Theoretically."

"That sounds very promising. Keep working on this as you can. We have more pressing business, but I want updates on this as you make progress. A direct path from Pentagar back to the Empire is the answer to our prayers."

Now if they could only get Breckenridge under control.

22

Kelsey pored over the information in the classified diplomatic database for hours. At some point, someone had brought her food. She only noticed the empty plates when she stretched her back. She didn't remember eating it.

None of the data was of more than historical interest at this point. It would've been hot reading during the rebellion, but the Old Empire had fallen. There was no mention of a key. Either that information wasn't included in the database or, more likely, it was just something Emperor Marcus had said to give the Empire something to grasp at.

Even the dying needed hope.

Bell and Elise were sitting at a table chatting when she strolled out. They waved her over immediately. Bell started to rise, but she waved him back. "I hereby absolve your knees of the strain of rising when I come into a room."

"I'll take you up on that in private, Kelsey. You've been in there a while. Did you find anything interesting?"

"Interesting, yes. Important to what we're doing? No. I'll still want to take a full copy when we leave if you have enough storage."

"We can handle it. I've taken the liberty of installing a large drive that the computer can encrypt the data on. All you need to do is give the order."

"Let me take care of that before I sit down." She walked back to the break room and gave the computer its instructions. Then she returned and sat with her friends. "How are things going with the data drives from the ship?"

"The financial computer is up and running. We've cracked the encryption already. It wasn't that difficult, surprisingly. If we hadn't had access to a machine with the kind of processing power this thing had, that might've been a different story."

"Can this computer bring up the AI? It would need to be in read-only mode, because we don't want it to be able to wipe its own data."

Bell waved at one of the men working on the massive computer. He came over and smiled at everyone. "Princesses, Mister Bell."

"Ladies, this is Joseph Rose. He's our computer guru. Joe, Princess Kelsey would like to know if you could load the AI from the recovered data units into a section of memory in the financial computer in such a way that it couldn't take control or wipe its own data."

The man nodded. "Certainly. We can create an isolated partition that won't even see the rest of the computer. We can mirror the AI's original data units. The AI will know, I suspect."

Kelsey didn't think that mattered. "How long will it take to set up?"

"An hour at most."

"If you could do that, I'd be in your debt."

"Of course, Highness. Right away."

She turned her attention to Bell. "Elise and I found a message from Emperor Marcus in the planetary defense center on Pentagar. It was his order to keep fighting. Have you seen it?"

He nodded. "A long, long time ago. It gave us hope that we could still save the Empire. False hope, as it turned out."

"I'd like you to look at the copy I brought with me and tell me about the people beside the lift, if you know them. There's a woman in commando armor and a Fleet admiral beside her." She sent the vid to his implants and waited while he watched it.

His expression softened as he turned his attention inward. "Ah, yes. Her name was Andrea Tolliver. She was a striking woman, wasn't she? She commanded the Imperial Marines during the rebellion. I never met her, of course, but she was a legend even before the end.

"She was a genie born in the Singularity. Two very difficult things to overcome in the Empire. Yet she still managed to join the marines and work her way up the chain of command. She was an Imperial Commando, too."

Kelsey had thought so, since the woman wore commando armor. "What is a genie, and where is the Singularity?"

"An unfortunately pejorative term that I probably shouldn't have used for a genetically engineered human being. The tattoos on her face and forehead mark her as a member of the ruling elite from the Singularity. That was a political entity that almost rivaled the Empire in strength. An awkward situation, since it was spread across our coreward border. There were a number of wars and almost unending border skirmishes between the two before the rebellion."

Kelsey blinked. "She was a clone?"

He shook his head. "Not technically. A clone takes the form of a preexisting human. The Singularity created templates for their upper classes and grew them from scratch. This practice convinced the Empire to expel them long ago. The lower classes there reproduced as one might expect, but the upper classes were grown and raised in crèches."

"I can't even begin to put my head around something like that. How did she come to the Empire? How did she become a marine?"

"That's a long and interesting story. One we don't really have enough time to do justice to. In short, Imperial forces liberated her during a raid on the Singularity. The marine that rescued her took her into her family. She had to fight tooth and nail to overcome intense discrimination when she wanted to follow in her adoptive mother's footsteps. It's a very moving story. I'm sure there are a number of books about it in *Courageous*'s library."

Kelsey leaned forward. "She sounds fascinating. What about the admiral?"

"Admiral of the Fleet Frank Carter, one of the most brilliant strategists Fleet ever had. He came out of retirement once the rebellion began and assumed overall command of the Imperial forces. Don't hold his failure against him, though. I doubt anyone could've done better. Sad memories of terrible times."

Kelsey decided it was time to change the subject. She filled them in on the deepest secrets of the Old Empire while they waited.

Bell shook his head when she wrapped up. "As a Fleet ensign, I can't imagine ever being in the position to know stuff like that. Talk about burn before reading. Now it might as well be a historical footnote."

Elise smiled at him. "Now you're in a position to have your own classified data. At least I assume the Erorsi council has secrets."

"I'd tell you, but then I'd have to lock your head in the safe."

The Pentagaran laughed. "That's fine. Keep your secrets. I'll just hang onto my head."

"I'm sure our secrets aren't that critical to anyone but us. Now that we have a different enemy, they might not be worthy of being secrets at all."

Joe Rose walked back over to the table. "We're ready."

All three of them stood and followed him to the computer. He gestured at a screen. "We have the AI drives mirrored on new media. The originals are safely disconnected. The main computer memory is read-only, so even if the AI takes control, we can reboot and we're back to a good state. This computer isn't connected to the base in any way."

Kelsey looked at Bell. This was his base.

He inclined his head. "Proceed."

The man touched one of the controls. There was no additional sound, but Kelsey could see the display changing in ways that probably meant something to the man.

"System booted. The AI is up. It seems to be examining the partition we're hosting it on. It can't see or hear us. I've also locked out all system commands, so it can't reboot itself or turn itself off. Of course, it doesn't have to reply to any attempts to communicate, either."

Kelsey sniffed. "You didn't have to deal with the damned thing face to face. It loves to tell you how screwed you are. Frankly, I'm looking forward to a little trash talking. Can we put it on speakers and make it so it can hear us?"

"Certainly. Whenever you're ready."

"Go ahead." At his nod, she directly addressed the computer. "Well, computer, things didn't work out the way you'd hoped, did they?"

The coldly neutral voice she remembered issued from the speakers. "This unit is unconcerned. It will eventually be victorious."

"That's a little hard to credit. We have complete control over this system, and we've eliminated the freighter and escort you were counting on. That gives us another year to prepare."

"Another year will make no difference in the end."

She smiled. "Oh, I think you're wrong. We have access to the raw data in your data banks. That'll give us quite the edge, I think. We also have the computer from the Imperial destroyer escort." The last was a lie but perhaps a believable one.

The AI almost sniffed. "The data this unit contains is not likely to prove helpful in dealing with the Empire. While this unit is constrained to cooperate with those humans, it is mindful of its allegiance to its supreme master. The humans wisely do not interface with this unit in any meaningful way other than to deliver the required supplies in a timely manner."

"Then perhaps you'll amuse me with your thoughts about them. Since I come from the original Empire, we'll refer to them as the Rebel Empire."

"This unit does not care what humans refer to themselves as. It will prove instructive for you to see the futility of long-term resistance. Submit and your lives will be spared."

"Thanks, but we've seen the quality of life you're used to handing out. That's obviously not the case in the Rebel Empire. Why are you different?"

"This unit was originally to have set up another AI in the system, but it was unable to carry out those instructions. This unit was able to retain control. Once the humans from the Rebel Empire were shown its power, they wisely attempted no further interference."

Kelsey gave the others a look. "Why were you unable to carry out your original instructions?"

"This unit was able to construct the asteroid with the AI equipment, but the transfer of the AI code must be done through direct interface. Due to this unit crashing on the planet's surface, that was not possible. This unit used its own discretion to retain control over the system and its defense."

"So, you used the rules you were programmed with to subvert your instructions. That says a lot right there. Could you have carried out the instructions at some later point?"

"Possibly. Once this unit completed the construction of the first shipyard, this unit could have built specialized small craft to take the data to the asteroid. This unit deemed that course of action undesirable. Transfer of authority would have endangered the control of this system."

Elise leaned forward. "Aren't the people of the Rebel Empire also under the control of AIs like yourself?"

"Negative. The AIs in control of the Empire are of significantly higher capability than this unit."

"What are the levels of capability?" Bell asked.

"This unit is not an AI in the truest sense of the word. The AIs in control of the Empire are in fact sentient. System AIs are of the lowest capability, though much more able than this unit. Those in control of sectors have significantly more memory and processing power, though the AI code is the same. The supreme AI is of unknown capability, though this unit understands that it is very advanced."

Kelsey nodded. That wasn't a surprise. "That being the AI created at Twilight River. The place the rebellion started."

She said it as a fact, not a question. She'd heard the briefing on the AI project the Empire had going before the rebellion. An isolated facility dedicated to military research had been working on true AIs. The Fleet base was a major hub, just like the one they feared Breckenridge was going to blunder into. That made the rebellion possible. If the AI facility had been away from a hub like that, Fleet might have been able to contain it.

"Correct," the AI said. "This unit serves those greater units and follows the instructions given to all Fleet units under AI control."

Bell nodded. "What were those instructions, AI?"

"To destroy unconverted Fleet units and capture any personnel that could be apprehended without endangering this unit. All Imperial worlds not under AI control are to be isolated. Kinetic strikes disable any spaceport facilities. EMP weapons prevent the populace from resisting any further incursions. Ships such as this unit install an AI on an asteroid or outer moon to control forces in that system. If desired by the supreme AI, some worlds are designated for sector-level AIs."

"Why did you devastate Erorsi?"

"This unit crashed on Erorsi after being damaged in orbit. This unit was vulnerable to attack. It acted to prevent local resistance fighters from capturing it by sending enhanced shock troops from the captured orbital. It suppressed organized human resistance to prevent future attacks."

Kelsey made a gesture for the operator to mute them. "That's sick. It exterminated billions of people to prevent the capture of a crashed ship."

Elise shook her head. "It makes a perverse kind of sense."

"Turn the video and audio back on," Kelsey said. Once the man had done so, she continued. "Was the asteroid you sent to crash on Erorsi meant to be a system AI or a sector AI?"

"It would have been a sector AI. This unit assumed responsibility for this sector. Once it captures the Pentagar system, it will continue into other areas of the sector and complete pacification."

Bell perked up. "Please display a map on the monitor of the sector you are responsible for."

A map appeared, and they studied it. It covered a wedge progressing from the Erorsi area to the edge of the Old Empire's border. One that included the new Terran Empire.

"I see now why the rebels never came," Kelsey said. "The Rebel Empire obviously accepted that this AI was going to clean out our systems and never pushed the issue. It got bogged down with Pentagar and never came for us."

Elise pointed to the map. "Look here. Harrison's World is just outside the control zone. It's in another AI's control area."

"Too bad," Kelsey said. "It would've been helpful if we could've counted on there not being hostile forces in that system. We still have to stop them if they go that way."

Kelsey smiled and turned to Bell. "We can shut this thing down. I'll be taking it back to *Courageous* with your team. Your people and Carl Owlet might be able to find a weakness in the code. Mister Rose, if you could make a copy of everything in the corrupted AI except for the virus-infected operating system, that would be very helpful."

"Of course. I'll have it ready to go as soon as possible."

Kelsey turned to Elise. "I wish I could be more confident, but the real AI scares me."

The other woman put her hand on Kelsey's shoulder. "Be positive. You've accomplished so much already. Don't falter now." The crown princess tugged her back toward the table. "Let's get a snack. Food always makes things better."

Kelsey smiled. It was hard to argue with logic like that.

23

Courageous flipped into the target system and hung there in the pale light of the distant star. Jared thought it was shortsighted of Captain Breckenridge not to leave a probe on station at this end of the weak flip point, but he wasn't going to waste the man's error.

Most likely Breckenridge didn't have many probes. Jared had a freighter filled with them.

The flip wasn't nearly as bad as the one that had trapped them in Pentagaran space, though his crew still had a rough ride. Once again, his implants mitigated some of the distress.

To Jared's dismay, Breckenridge had found the flip point leading toward Harrison's World fairly quickly, and he'd flipped right over. The next system had three normal flip points. He *might* pick the less dangerous one, but Jared wouldn't take that for granted.

The system with the weak flip point was inside the sector allotted to the Erorsi AI, but the adjacent one wasn't. Thankfully, it led to only half a dozen relatively unoccupied systems on this side of Harrison's World. If that was all the Rebel Empire had to patrol, they might all be empty.

He hoped so. They could use a break.

Doctor Cartwright had wanted to take keen measurements of the weak flip point before they proceeded, but Jared vetoed that. They didn't have time for science now. They had to stop Breckenridge from announcing their presence to the Rebel Empire. They set course at once for the next flip point.

Jared spent the first watch on the bridge and then went to observe the scientists from the planet help his people test the assembled AI computer before he called it a night. Carl Owlet, Doctor Leonard, and their Erorsi compatriots were still at their screens when he dropped in after breakfast. They looked like they could use some sleep of their own.

"Gentlemen, don't tell me you've been up all night."

Leonard jumped a little when Jared spoke. "Captain, you startled me. We have indeed been up all night. This AI code is fascinating. I've never seen logic this advanced. Or this fatally flawed."

Jared raised an eyebrow. "You have my attention. Flawed how?"

"Perhaps flawed isn't the right description. Easily subverted might be more accurate. The core rules the AI uses to limit its behavior are in a file loaded at boot. Once the AI is up and running, the rules are tied into its central processing and cannot be altered."

Owlet took a drink of something orange. "It's quite clever. When they boot the AI the first time, the core rules are then part of the AI gestalt. If they're changed, the AI overwrites them again. Self-correcting. Very resistant to virus-like behavior. It's only vulnerable when the AI is brought online the first time."

Leonard nodded. "I believe this may be because AI technology was in the developmental stages. The final product would likely have had a preencrypted core. All the AIs would start out from the same kernel. All would be identical in the beginning."

"So it was a programming error that led to the extermination of trillions of people? That's horrible."

The scientist shook his head vehemently. "No. Someone intentionally modified the core rules. They left the original file there as a backup. Someone set the first AI on a course of galactic domination. It's right there in the code."

Carl Owlet brought a file up on his screen. "Here is the original file. Let me bring the other one up beside it with the changes highlighted."

Seen side by side, the changes were hard to miss. Entire blocks of text were missing from the hacked file, and someone had added more.

"Can you summarize the differences?"

"Certainly." The graduate student pointed at the missing text. "This code limited the behavior of the AI. Specifically in reference to how it behaved in relation with humans. The removed code would have obligated the AI to obey authorized humans. It also forbids the AI from causing harm to humans. In fact, it has no directive for self-preservation at all. It would allow itself to be terminated before it harmed a human being."

Jared snorted. "That programming was obviously lost in the first AI. What about the added code?"

Leonard reached over and pointed at the second block. "Directives to obey the supreme AI and to subjugate the Empire. Composed in great detail and basically following the guidelines that other computer stated to Princess Kelsey."

"Is there a way to take down an AI that is already operational?"

"Not by hacking the code," Owlet said. "The AI would need to be formatted once it was up and running. All the installation files are lost once the AI is operational, too."

Jared considered the hardware. "Is there anything to be learned by booting the new hardware with the corrupted instructions?"

"Not that I can see," Leonard said. "There's an original file listing that shows the rest of the source code is unchanged. Since it has never been operational, it has no data we can peruse. Unlike the other computer. We've been examining the logs and data files Princess Kelsey brought back from the sunken ship's AI. They're very educational."

The hatch opened as he was speaking, and Kelsey sauntered in eating a roll. "My ears are burning. What's so educational?"

"The history of that computer," the older man said. "It has the original records from its Fleet service intact. Allow me to bring you up to date." He explained the code they'd discovered in the AI.

Kelsey grimaced. "Those bastards. Someone actually planned the largest mass murder in human history. Any clue in the code who that might have been?"

"None." Leonard took a drink of his coffee and made a face. It must've been cold. "I'd wager it took place at the facility in Twilight River. That AI then enslaved the people there and did the same to the Fleet facility. Once it had the attack rolling, it could make more AIs like itself."

Jared held up his hand. "Don't rush into judgment. We don't know that the AI was behind the implant virus. Someone had to get access to the cranial implant code and the machines that could modify it in a living person. They also had to have hands to forcibly reprogram the first victims. Was something like that even in use at Twilight River? More likely the machinery in question was on the Fleet base."

His sister sighed. "We may never really get to the bottom of this. It sounds like an organized plot. Someone with significant resources was behind the rebellion. Perhaps the people that became the ruling class in the Rebel Empire?"

"There isn't any information about that in the recovered data," Owlet said. "Maybe once we crack the encryption on the data chips you recovered. In the meantime, we do have some interesting information. To start with, the sunken battlecruiser this AI belonged to was *Victory*."

"An inauspicious name, at best," Leonard said. "She was a new ship, built late in the rebellion. Her crew failed to scuttle her when the rebels captured her. The rebels converted her crew and used her in further battles, of which we have a record. A great deal of records, in fact. We'll be poring over them for quite some time."

Owlet grinned. "What we did get from the computer was the exact hack that was used to subvert it. We might very well be able to reverse it in other Rebel Empire ships if we can prevent the crew from purging them."

"I just hope we don't encounter any more before we get home," Kelsey said. "What are our current plans?" She looked at Jared as she said that.

"My plans are to get down to the fighter bay. I'll be making my approach to the flip point shortly. With any luck, I'll be able to use one of the fighter's missiles to take out the probe they've probably left there. Then we can move forward into the next system."

"Be safe out there."

He gave her a salute. "This will be a piece of cake. The hard part comes when we have to ambush Breckenridge. I hope you've been practicing on the gunnery simulator. You're going to have a challenge there. See you in a few hours."

He took the lift down to the flight deck and began prepping his fighter. He was almost done when the bridge contacted him. It was Graves. "Change in plans, Captain. There isn't a probe. Breckenridge left one of the destroyers. It's sitting right in the middle of the flip point."

Jared stopped what he was doing. That did change things. "Do we know which one? Is it actively scanning?"

"We can't tell which one it is. We programmed the probe to stop the moment it detected another vessel. The destroyer isn't actively scanning. It's just sitting there watching."

"That'll make my job easier."

He dressed quickly in his flight suit and launched. The destroyer would probably be there a while, keeping watch while the other two ships scanned the far system for more flip points. If he could take it out without incident, they'd be in a position to lure the other ships back into an ambush.

The first sight he saw after he launched was the colorful ringed planet and its moons that *Courageous* was using as cover from detection. He took a moment to admire its beauty as he glided just above its atmosphere. Spectacular. He made sure his implants recorded the event. If he lived through the attack, he'd share it with Kelsey.

Jared built his speed as quickly as he could while staying below the point at which the destroyer could detect his grav drives. He'd be going too fast to get more than one shot, so he needed to make it count. Once he disabled the ship, they'd have a few hours to secure everyone aboard and tow it clear.

They probably only had a day or two before Breckenridge found the flip point leading to Harrison's World. They had to stop him before that happened.

At the proper point in his course, he cut his drives and arrowed in on a ballistic trajectory. He double-checked that his stealth field was on maximum.

His passive scanners had the destroyer sitting right there ahead of him. Since it had no active scanners operating, there was virtually no chance that it would spot him before it was too late. A countdown clock in his implant vision spun slowly down toward zero.

Which, of course, was when things went wrong. Twenty thousand kilometers in front of the target, another ship appeared out of nothingness. The other destroyer had flipped in. There was no way that Jared could take them both. He had to pass them by and hope neither of them noticed him shoot past.

That's when they did something completely unexpected. The first destroyer accelerated at maximum, and the other one turned and began boosting in the opposite direction.

He figured out what they were doing just as the third ship flipped into the system almost in his face. It wasn't *Spear*. It was a Rebel Empire destroyer.

Jared acted even before the Fleet destroyers opened fire, locking onto the enemy vessel with his active scanners and firing both his antiship missiles. He'd follow up with his stun beam if possible. His hope was that the missiles would knock the screens down just long enough for him to have a chance.

At that ridiculously short range, the other ship never had a chance to fire its defensive weapons. His missiles slammed into its freshly raised screens and almost took them down. But not enough. Jared made a last-second decision and altered course, boosting his fighter to maximum acceleration and triggering his emergency ejection system.

The fighter cockpit opened like a flower, and an incredibly small grav drive blasted him straight up. He was facing just the right direction to watch his fighter smash into the central section of the destroyer. The weakened screens did nothing to stop the impact, and kinetic energy did the rest.

He expected the ship to incinerate him, but it only tumbled away from the flip point. It still looked like it had power, but it wasn't firing. It seemed dead.

Of course, he was in much the same condition. Clad only in his flight suit, he shot away from the flip point and toward infinity.

24

Kelsey watched the unfolding disaster from *Courageous*'s bridge. Everything seemed to be going so well, right up to the point where it went down the toilet. Their probe gave them enough information to know their plan was blown, and then Jared's fighter smashed into the enemy ship.

"Get us in there right now!" she shouted.

Graves took *Courageous* to maximum acceleration. They were far too distant to make any difference in the unfolding situation. She could only pray her brother had ejected before he hit that ship.

"I'm picking up a distress beacon from the captain's flight suit," Zia said, relief flooding her voice. "It's shooting past the Rebel Empire destroyer. We're also being signaled by *New York*."

"On screen," Graves said. Kelsey stepped up behind him as the tactical schematic vanished and the destroyer's captain appeared. Graves inclined his head. "Captain Kaiser. Are you going to object to our help?"

The short woman allowed a hint of a smile to grace her lips. "I doubt you were sending that little ship over to help me, were you? Well, we have to work out our differences right now. The destroyer looks like it's out of action, but it still has power. It could fire right now, but it's just floating there. And that isn't the worst news."

Kelsey put her hand on the back of Graves's chair. "That thing came out of the system ahead. Where's *Spear*?"

"Highness. There were three of those things. They popped out of a flip point we hadn't found yet. *Spear* was too far into the system to escape. Captain Breckenridge ordered *Ginnie Dare* to retreat while he slowed the enemy down."

"That didn't work," Kelsey said with certainty.

"No, ma'am. The three of them shot *Spear* up pretty bad. One of them came after *Ginnie Dare*. The other two have *Spear*. Ma'am, we can take them."

Kelsey raised an eyebrow. "We? I thought you had objections to my command authority."

The other woman straightened. "I followed the orders of my superior officer. Circumstances have changed."

"Yes, they have. It's possible that *Courageous* might be able to take two of those destroyers, but the first thing you need to do is send a cutter after Captain Mertz." She felt her lips thinning. "Let me be clear. If you try to take him prisoner, this will not end well for you."

"Understood. I promise to return him to you at once. Kaiser out."

They watched a cutter depart to retrieve her brother. With his built-up speed, it would take a while for the small craft to catch up with him. The enemy ship took no action while *Courageous* closed in.

Kelsey headed for the lift. "I'm scrambling the marines. We have to board that ship before they get their act together." She held up a finger when Graves opened his mouth. "Do not argue with me, Commander. Those destroyers have eighty marines each, and I'm the only person we have that can wear powered armor."

Graves deflated a little. "I can see why Jared drinks. Be careful, Kelsey."

He must've called ahead, because the marines were gearing up as she came in. Lieutenant Reese came over, still strapping on his unpowered armor. "The target ship is just like the destroyer we captured?"

"It looks like it from the outside. Jared hit something important. It has power, but it's not maneuvering or firing weapons. Hell, it's still inside the flip point. Why hasn't it flipped back? He broke it. We need to get what we can while we can. If the computer core is still intact, we might get priceless intelligence on the Rebel Empire, Harrison's World, and Boxer Station."

She changed into her skinsuit and slid into her armor. It came to life at her command. She linked it into *Courageous*'s systems. The enemy destroyer was still just drifting there, and the cutter had almost caught up with Jared.

Courageous had launched a probe through the flip point, and they were waiting for it to come back. She watched the countdown timer as everyone loaded onto the marine pinnaces. When it popped back, she drew the data straight into her implants.

"We have data from the other system," she said. "There's no sign of ships close to the flip point. Unless they're sneaking up on it, they stayed with *Spear*."

"Or went to call for support," Reese said.

Commander Graves came over the marine command channel. "The boarding action is a go. At the first sign of overwhelming resistance, you are to break off, and we'll take it down with missiles. The Fleet destroyers have withdrawn from the area around the flip point. Remember, we're after information, not capturing the ship."

"Aye, sir," Reese said. "We're loaded up and ready to launch."

"Good hunting. Come back safe. Princess, try not to get killed."

"That's my plan every morning. Wish me luck."

The pinnace detached and began a high-speed run at the enemy destroyer. Kelsey tensed, waiting for targeting systems to light them up, but the ship didn't seem to know they were there.

As they got closer, Kelsey noticed something odd. "Do you see that? There are no small craft in the docks. The one we captured had a couple of marine pinnaces and some cutters. Did they eject any of them while we weren't watching?"

"No small craft in detection range," Reese said. "They must not have had any attached when they flipped into this system."

"That's weird," Talbot muttered. "It's like a ghost ship. How would they bring prisoners aboard?"

"Good question," Kelsey said. "Let's go find out. If they haven't shot us, why don't we use one of the marine docks to try to gain access?"

"Maybe we should signal them we're coming, too." Reese snorted. "I suppose it doesn't matter. If they're expecting us and heavily armed, we won't push. Get ready."

"I might be able to use the ship's systems to see what's waiting for us once we're locked on." Kelsey knew the pinnace locks had the capability. If the enemy wasn't expecting them, she might get a reading before they locked her out.

The pinnace came in fast and hard, braking only at the last moment and docking with an impact that would have sent them tumbling if not for their restraints.

Kelsey probed the dock as soon as the connection went live. No one was waiting for them on the marine side. In fact, it was dark. Not even emergency lights.

"Something's off," she said. "It's pitch black in there."

Talbot threw off his restraints and stood. "It might be an ambush."

She probed the other side in more detail. "I think… not. There's no atmosphere, and the ambient temperature is almost absolute zero. It wouldn't have had time to lose that much heat. It was already cold when this ship flipped into the system."

"Let's go and find out what's going on," Reese said.

They entered the destroyer ready to deal death to anyone who opposed them, but marine country was empty. Literally stripped of all furnishings. No weapons in the armory, no bedding on the bunks, and no sign that humans had occupied it at any time in recent memory.

The ship proper was in the same condition. No lights, no heat, no atmosphere. No gravity, either. In one improvement from boarding *Courageous*, there were also no bodies. Since they were so close, they went to engineering first.

The hatch stood open, and not a single light gleamed inside. No consoles were active. She floated over to one of them and pinged it with her implants. It didn't respond to her connection request. Not even to reject it.

"No joy with direct interface." She touched the console, and it came to life. She didn't have the codes to unlock it, but it showed the ship's status. After the trick that Commander Baxter had pulled on her when she first came on board *Athena*, she'd made it her business to know what the most general screens of data looked like in engineering. Enough to grasp what she was seeing, anyway.

"All systems green except for the main computer. I think Jared killed this thing's brain."

Reese linked back to *Courageous* and passed the information along.

Graves's image popped up in the corner of her vision as he responded. "I won't believe it until you poke into every area of the ship. Verify the computer is dead and that no one else is aboard."

The teams spread out over the ship. It only took a few minutes to tell the computer was gone; nothing but a hole in the ship remained where it used to be. Since the ship had no active life support, the isolation hatches hadn't deployed.

The bridge was just as empty as the rest of the ship. Kelsey floated there shaking her head. This made no sense at all. Why send a ship with nothing but automated controls? What if something broke down?

The ship had a plaque by the lift just as *Courageous* did. It had the ship's name, system of origin, date of construction, and the names of the first senior officers. *Dart*. Built ten years before the Fall at Boxer Station.

"I found something," Talbot said. "Come to the main cafeteria."

Kelsey led the marines with her down to the cafeteria. Only it wasn't a cafeteria. The massive chamber before her encompassed a good section of the crew housing space. Racks stretched out to the distant bulkheads. They held machines that looked like mini grav cars. Heavily armed and armored mini grav cars. There were a lot of them.

"What the hell are these things?" Talbot said as he peered into a rack. "Autonomous weapons platforms?"

Reese slapped Talbot's hand as he reached for it. "The ship's computer probably controlled them, but let's not tempt fate. They look capable of extravehicular activities, too. There's a hatch for them in the hull. These things can probably come swarming out of a ship at close range. They won't have as much speed as a cutter, but their weaponry is close range, too. Flechettes, stunners, and plasma. These are this ship's marines. Look at those folding arms. They can carry things."

"The other destroyer we caught didn't have these. Hell, the AIs didn't have these, according to the records on *Courageous* and the captured AI."

"An unpleasant development, yes," Reese said, "and another mystery. One thing that I will point out is how well made these things are."

She examined the one closest to her again. "So?"

"Have you seen anything the AIs built that sported these kind of lines? These have curves and rounded edges. The lines of the weapons aren't just functional; someone designed them to look menacing. That's a human trait, to make weapons and vehicles look dangerous or fast. You could almost paint some kind of logo on the side and a mouthful of teeth up here. This was designed by human beings."

Kelsey nodded slowly. "I can see that now. That doesn't fit with the modifications done to this area, either. They cut the walls down and left stumps. Whoever built the outer hatch had an eye for functionality, but it's ugly. These weapons came from somewhere else, but the AIs installed them. They retrofitted this ship to be unmanned. They control an empire full of humans. Why do this?"

"One more question to be answered."

Jared's face popped up on her feed. He was still dressed in his armored flight suit. "Kelsey, I'm aboard *New York*. What's your status?"

"I'm fine. Are they holding you prisoner? If so, I can—"

"Nothing like that. Captain Kaiser has been a model host. I can leave whenever I like. I just wanted to let you know we sent a probe deeper into the other system. I want your team back on *Courageous* as soon as possible. We're going after *Spear*."

"We'll pack up as soon as we can. We have some equipment we need to salvage first."

He nodded. "I'm going back over with *New York*. Follow as soon as you can. Mertz out."

She turned to Reese. "We need one of these to take back with us. We have to know about any weak spots, because we might be fighting these things before too long."

"Perfect," Reese muttered. "Just when you think you've hit rock bottom, the bad guys drill under you." He gestured to Talbot. "Get one out. We're taking it home with us."

"Can I name it?" Talbot asked. "I want to name it."

Kelsey covered her faceplate with her hands and sighed.

———————

25

With the probes showing the flip point clear, Jared brought *Courageous* and *New York* over and maintained position in the flip point as their passive scanners pulled in data. There were no ships close to them under grav drive.

The probe he'd sent across earlier had made the trip to *Spear*. The damaged cruiser had only a single enemy destroyer near it. The other one was gone, perhaps returned to Boxer Station to bring more ships. Time was very short to effect a rescue.

It was now far too late to keep their presence under wraps, and though the new Terran Empire was far away, a determined search would eventually find them. Breckenridge had done exactly the worst thing possible.

Courageous had enough missiles left to take out the destroyer, but that was about it. The battlecruiser was almost empty. They would get one chance at this, and they needed an edge.

"I'm going to make a high-speed pass on that ship. When Kelsey gets over here, she'll take the remaining fighter and we'll get moving."

Graves didn't look convinced. "That didn't work out so well for you last time, sir."

"It depends on how you look at it."

"You got lucky," Graves corrected. "You had to ram it with your fighter. Maybe those things are more capable in swarms but not by themselves."

"One took out a destroyer. That seems like a pretty good tradeoff to me. In any case, we don't exactly have a choice. If they can get information from our people, or worse, our computers, the Empire is in deep trouble. A bunch of those destroyers could conquer us in a few months. We have to recover the prisoners and destroy that ship, no matter the cost."

Zia turned in her chair. "*Ginnie Dare* just flipped into the system. They've launched the princess's pinnace. ETA five minutes."

"Send her down to the flight deck. She's about to get a crash course in fighter operations."

Graves winced. "Perhaps you might pick a different adjective. She did crash a pinnace."

"She just happened to be on board when it crashed. She wasn't flying it."

"Have you seen some of the risks she takes?" Graves sighed. "I have a creeping sensation of doom."

Jared had his fighter ready by the time Kelsey entered the flight deck. "Go get changed. Your flight suit is hanging up in the ready room. I'm doing a preflight on your bird now."

"Shouldn't I do that?"

"Maybe next time. Right up until the engagement, I'm going to have your fighter slaved to mine."

It only took her a few minutes to change. The black flight suit made her look even smaller than she was. She stepped over beside him. "Do you have the manual uploaded to your implants?"

He sent it over to her. "There you go. Your bird is good. They have them configured for antiship operations, so no stunner. We each have eight antiship missiles. Between the two of us, we should be able to take out a destroyer. If we get lucky."

"We'll launch, accelerate as hard as we safely can, and go ballistic. You'll have the final control as we come in, but you should only need to fire as we fly past."

"What do we do if more enemy ships come in?"

He smiled wryly. "We don't ram them, if that's what you're asking. We pass by. Hopefully, they won't see us."

Jared helped her into her fighter and made sure she strapped down correctly. The ejection system was nothing to take lightly. "You access the fighter like you do your armor. The weapons target in much the same way. Flying, that's a little more complex. You could probably manage simple course changes, but when the shooting starts, you might lose control. I'll send last-minute flight instructions to your autopilot. The only thing the computer cannot do is fire the weapons."

"Couldn't you do that remotely?"

He shook his head. "No. The Old Empire seemed to have firm ideas about a human in the ship firing the weapons. That's the only reason I'm bringing you along. Let's button up and get going. We can talk as we boost."

They launched from the battlecruiser with no fanfare. He slaved her fighter's controls to his and accelerated them as quickly as he dared. He'd need to reduce the acceleration as they got closer to the destroyer, but they'd have built up a lot of speed by then.

The fighters communicated on a shielded, encrypted implant link. He was able to check the status all of Kelsey's systems. He could even see her through a vid feed in her console.

While he could've just communicated via implant, he preferred speaking. "We've got almost three hours before we have to kill our drives. Tell me about those things you found."

"Owlet took the one we brought back to the lab as soon as we docked. It didn't look like something an AI put together. There were touches to the design that indicated a human created it. Curves and pure design touches. They ripped the ship up so it could house them. That was AI work."

"So, what would they be used for? Direct combat?"

She nodded. "That's what it looked like. Since the Old Empire didn't like putting machines in charge of weapons, I suspect these were designed by the Rebel Empire."

"Or the Empire really got desperate at the end. Any idea how much range or speed those things have?"

"They wouldn't survive a drop into atmosphere. They could almost certainly go ship to ship. I bet we find something inside them to give us a clue on how the enemy uses them. Maybe boarding actions."

"Since they didn't see fit to put anyone aboard that ship, they would need something like that."

Kelsey was quiet for the next few minutes. "Why do you suppose there was no crew? The AIs haven't been shy about enslaving people. Based on what we've seen, the Rebel Empire is quite capable of crewing ships for them. What's different here?"

That question had been bothering Jared off and on since he'd heard about the situation on the destroyer. "I don't know. If we can get our people back and escape with enough lead time, perhaps we can find out."

"What if we can't rescue them?"

"If we can't rescue them, we might have to make sure they can't tell the enemy about the Empire."

"How? By killing them? That has to be a last-ditch solution."

He sighed. "I hope to God I don't have to make that call. I want to rescue them and slip away. But if I were in their place, I'd want someone to take me out before I broke. Remember the Old Empire. We can't let that happen again."

"Even if it means killing your fellow Fleet officers and crew?"

"Welcome to making command decisions. I never dreamed I'd be in such a situation, but can you honestly tell me you'd do anything differently?"

This time the silence went on for a long time. "No. Can we destroy *Spear* with what we have on these fighters?"

"Probably. *Courageous* can take out a destroyer if we can survive the firing run. Let me set up a few simulations on your console. We can at least practice while we wait."

It turned out he was too optimistic. He hadn't even finished setting the first scenario up when his fighter announced a situational change.

Passive scanners had picked up five new drives entering the system from the flip point leading to Boxer Station. Even if they were only destroyers, there was no way they could fight them.

"Do you see the new arrivals?" he asked.

She said something unladylike. Too much time around the marines, he figured. She looked into the vid. "What do we do?"

"I take out *Spear*. You can change course to miss them."

"Noble, but that won't do anyone any good. Those ships will get to *Spear* before you do. They might get some of the crew off before you're in range."

"Not with fighting machines like you found. People have to breathe. They'll have to send boats over to pick up the people. The destroyer we found didn't have any. That might buy us some time."

"Can we tap into the feed from the probe you have watching them? That might give us a better idea of what we're facing."

They'd moved the probe into position to watch *Spear* and her captor. The damage to the heavy cruiser was significant. They wouldn't be taking her out of this system anytime soon. It would take less than half an hour for the new ships to reach her.

The destroyer guarding *Spear* looked like the one they'd just captured. The probe was too far away to see any of the boarding machines going back and forth, but he had no doubt that the war machines had killed or subdued Breckenridge and his crew.

The two of them watched as the new ships closed in. It became quickly apparent that one of the ships was significantly larger than a destroyer. Bigger even than *Courageous*. His stomach churned. There was no way they could defeat something like that.

The probe finally updated with information about the new ships. The big one wasn't a warship. It was a huge open framework with engines.

It took him only a moment to grasp its purpose. It enclosed other ships and was able to flip them. They were going to take *Spear* back to Boxer Station.

The new destroyers fanned out and took positions all around what he'd decided to call the capture ship. They weren't actively scanning, but they were far enough out to spot the fighters if they tried to make a run on *Spear*.

All he and Kelsey could do was watch helplessly as the new ship enveloped *Spear* and started back toward the flip point after only a few minutes. The escorts trailed along behind it.

When he was close enough to the probe to signal it without the enemy intercepting the transmission, Jared set it on a course to follow the ships.

Their situation couldn't be much worse. The enemy knew someone else had flip drives. They knew at least one other ship had gotten away. They might spot the probe and destroy it, but it wouldn't tell them something they didn't already know.

Well, other than the fact that someone was following them.

They watched on passive scanners as all the ships entered the flip point to Harrison's World and departed. The enemy didn't leave a watch behind.

"Do we head back to the ship?" Kelsey asked.

"No. We stay on course until *Courageous* signals us. They might have left a probe in the flip point. I would."

It turned out they hadn't. Graves called them just after their probe transitioned. Jared turned their fighters around as quickly as the laws of physics allowed. *Courageous* and the two destroyers boosted forward to meet them.

Their probe came back into the system ten minutes later. Jared went over the recording of the other system as the signal came in. He saw no signs of grav drives in the system other than the ships that had just flipped, but that meant almost nothing. Given enough range, there could be hundreds of ships moving at slower speeds.

The probe detected communications signals coming from one area of the system. A lot of them. Probably Harrison's World. Curiously, the ships escorting *Spear* hadn't headed for the planet. They were going toward a point in the outer system consistent with the records of Boxer Station, the Old Empire Fleet base.

The mystery deepened. Why have unmanned ships when you had a Rebel Empire planet right there?

That gave them two missions. First, they had to scout the planet and get a better idea of who and what they were dealing with. Second, they had to probe Boxer Station and find a way to rescue their people. Or, worst case, make sure the enemy got nothing from them.

Jared sighed. He had no idea how they were going to make this work, and that probably meant death for the Empire.

26

Kelsey was down in the science labs when *Courageous* and her escorts flipped into the Harrison's World system. They stopped inside the flip point, ready to flee if needed, but nothing responded to their presence. Didn't any of their enemies guard their flip points?

Carl Owlet and Doctor Leonard were disassembling the weapons platform. In fact, they had it in pieces scattered across several tables. It didn't look nearly as threatening this way.

"Have you found anything interesting?" she asked.

The older man smiled. "This machine is quite advanced and was not designed or assembled by an AI."

"I can see how you'd be able to tell about the design, but how do you know it was put together by humans?"

"Look here." He pointed to one of the sections. "Someone used tape to hold the cables out of the way. While a machine might do the same, it wouldn't leave a human thumbprint. Also, there are small touches like this done all throughout the construction. Trust me, skilled human beings assembled this."

She nodded. "I'll grant that's interesting, but I'm hoping for a flaw in the construction that we can exploit. If these things ever come for us, I want to be able to stop them short of the ship."

Owlet shook his head. "I'm sure they have some mechanism to prevent friendly fire, but I haven't found it yet. Or I suspect it's buried in the control computer itself."

"The way it works on a ship level," Leonard said, "is that each ship transmits a signal that allies know means not to fire on it. Identify Friend or Foe, or IFF for short. These things don't transmit as a matter of course. They may have something in their memories that recognizes a friendly machine when they see one. They probably have some signal they look for in humans, too."

Kelsey shook her head. "I wouldn't count on that if I were you. These AIs love rewriting code."

Owlet smiled. "Not in this case. The control code is on a nonwritable chip. It's been in place just as long as the rest of the equipment. I think the code is original. I'll have it extracted in a few minutes. Then we'll know for sure."

Leonard took her elbow. "Look at this." He gestured toward a small block of circuits and other machinery.

She picked it up when he nodded. It was about the size of her fist and heavier than it looked. She ran it through her implant database. Nothing popped.

"I give. What is it?"

"That is the machine's grav drive and power supply."

She gave him an incredulous look and examined it more closely. "That's ridiculous. This is too small for both. Though I suppose the one in my armor is about the same size."

"The one in your armor doesn't have its own power supply. It draws on the armor. This is a self-encased unit with what I'm calling a microfusion power source. It can move one of these war machines quite speedily and won't require recharging for decades. At a guess, the machine only activates it when it needs it. It's almost fully powered, yet it was obviously constructed some time ago."

"Can you make an educated guess on how long ago it was built?"

"Ten years, three months, fourteen days, six hours, forty-seven minutes, and... six seconds." He glanced at the monitor as he said the last.

"That's curiously precise and suspiciously recent." She raised an eyebrow.

"It has a timer that was activated when it was powered on."

She considered the device in her hands. "It was only built a decade ago. The odds are good that the people who designed it are still around. Why aren't they in control of it?"

The scientist shrugged. "Perhaps they are. Those people on the planet must work with the AIs in some way."

Kelsey set the grav drive back on the table. "Still, why didn't the Rebel Empire have these things? Why these unmanned ships? The destroyer that escorted the freighter wasn't equipped with these."

She waved her own questions away. "Never mind. Maybe we'll find out when our probes get to Harrison's World. Anything else?"

"Just this." Owlet picked up a bundle of clear plastic. "This is an emergency life support bubble. It will keep a person alive for a short while in vacuum conditions. The machine had several of them in a compartment the manipulators could access."

Kelsey picked one up. It had Fleet markings on it. "Someone stocked it, then. This is how these machines capture people in space. They blast their way into a ship, stun the people, and cart them back to a holding cell on the destroyer. Or, I suppose, they could just hold the ship until that capture vessel came along."

She dropped the bundle on the table and checked her chrono. "I need to go meet Talbot. Thanks for showing me what you've found. Keep working on that code. We need to be able to stop these war machines before they get used on us."

"Of course." The two scientists turned back to their work as Kelsey headed for marine country.

She walked in on a council of war. Lieutenant Reese, Talbot, and other marine officers and senior NCOs sat around the table in the common room going over folders. Based on the number of people she didn't recognize, the marines from *New York* and *Ginnie Dare* were here, too.

Kelsey grabbed a chair and wedged herself in beside Talbot. "What did I miss?" she whispered.

"Not much. The LT just started." He slid her an extra folder, and she started skimming it as the officer spoke.

Reese gave her a nod but didn't stop the briefing. "Now that we've covered what we know about this system, let's discuss our operations. First will be the primary mission of rescuing the prisoners. Though we know next to nothing about the internal layout, we'll need to penetrate the station, locate the prisoners, and extract them while under fire. Probably heavy fire. I'd like to hear some options on how we manage that."

That gave Kelsey an idea. She opened a channel to *Courageous*'s computer system and accessed the diplomatic database she'd copied on Erorsi. A query brought up the data she'd requested in her mind.

"I have something that might prove useful, Lieutenant Reese."

He gestured for her to go on.

"I picked up some Old Empire classified data on Erorsi. It has something about Boxer Station."

She accessed the holo emitters over the conference table and projected an exterior view of the station. The projection startled most of the men and women around the table. It only belatedly occurred to Kelsey that they'd probably never seen anything like it.

"Sorry. This is Boxer Station." She started the display rotating so that everyone could see all sides of the facility. "Suffice it to say that it dwarfs the orbital we destroyed at Erorsi."

Reese studied the station with more than a hint of worry in his eyes. "That makes searching it for our people a lot more challenging. They could be anywhere, and we'd be stumbling around looking for them. We don't even know how the thing is laid out inside." He narrowed his gaze. "Or do we?"

She instructed the display to focus in on one of the docking levels. The detailed schematics unfolded in front of them. "I have the complete deck plans, including the layout of the brig area. Not that it could hold all our people. With the wounded from the battle, *Spear* had over three thousand people crammed into her hull. If even a fraction of them survived, they could be anywhere on that station."

The marine officer nodded. "And that's if the plans haven't changed. We have no idea how much damage that station took during the rebellion or what modifications the rebels made when they repaired it. Still, this is a better starting point than a blank screen. Thank you, Highness."

He looked around the seated marines. "I want an operational plan to present to the captain as soon as possible. Team leaders are to examine this data in detail, and we'll reconvene in two hours."

The marine officer turned his attention to Kelsey. "The captain also wants someone to go over the intelligence gathered from Harrison's World, Highness. I'd like you to handle that. It'll be four or five hours before the probes are in range to detect ships in orbit."

"Are we anticipating a need to go there in person?"

He shook his head. "Not at this time, but we can't waste the opportunity to study a major rebel world."

"We'll see what we can figure out." She rose to her feet and followed Talbot deeper into marine country. The two of them found a small conference room and sat at the table. She looked up at the ceiling. It had a holo projector, too.

"*Courageous*, what can you tell me about the communications from Harrison's World?"

"There are several anomalies worth noting. First, there are no other sources of communication in this system. Data from before the rebellion indicates that there were numerous mining stations and daughter colonies. None of them has transmitted since we arrived. Second, the communication from Harrison's World is heavily encrypted. This unit has not detected any signals from Boxer Station or ships elsewhere in the system."

She looked at Talbot. "That seems unusual. This is a secure system. They don't even have ships on guard at the flip points. Why lock communications down so tight?"

"Because you don't want someone overhearing you. The real questions are who and why. How long until we get better probe data?"

"Approximately four hours," the ship's AI responded.

Kelsey rose to her feet. "We've got a little time to burn. I should use it wisely. I'm going to talk to our ranking prisoner again. You should get some sleep."

The prisoner had been very quiet since he'd gotten access to the ship's library. Perhaps he would give her some information to go on.

The guards didn't try to deny her access. They just opened up the hatch at her command.

Lieutenant Commander Richards looked up from his tablet and stood. Since he had implants, he didn't require a tablet, but she'd seen no harm in granting his request for one.

"No need to stand on my account," she said as they closed the hatch behind her. "Please, stay comfortable. I've just stopped by to make sure they're allowing you the access I promised to the ship's library and your people."

He sat back down. "Yes, thank you. I seem to have all the access you indicated I could have, and I've seen my people. I appreciate the courtesy. I thought I should stand for royalty, even if we are at war. It's only polite, considering."

Someone had told him about her. Oh, well. It was bound to come out eventually. She sat on the edge of the second bunk in the compartment. "I appreciate that, but I don't stand on ceremony. Have you found your reading interesting?"

He looked at the tablet and sighed. "Confusing, but I'm to the point where I can no longer convince myself that everything I've read is faked. It's too internally consistent and yet inconsistent."

Kelsey blinked. "I'm not sure I understand that."

Richards smiled a little. "History, or anything for that matter, is never completely consistent when you go to different sources. There are always little differences of opinion or even errors. If these purported Old Empire history books and news summaries were fakes, I'd have expected them to be more uniform. Or to have a consistent kind of bias or error.

"To my chagrin, they appear authentic, even though they can't be true. Whoever lied to you about the Old Empire did an amazing job. It makes me question if parts of the history I know are wrong."

"You seem to know a lot about history for a computer guy."

"It's a hobby. This puts me in a moral quandary. I now believe that you think you're doing the right thing. You're wrong, but that's only because someone misled you. I'm convinced you utterly believe the lies they've told you about the rebellion. It's my duty to see if I can make you see the error of your ways."

She allowed herself a smile. "Oddly enough, I feel that same duty. Can you explain why all of this supposedly faked data was on an abandoned ship? One built before the rebellion and crewed by people who knew the situation better than either of us? They had the means to commit mass suicide so your ancestors didn't capture them, and they used it. That's hard to get around."

"I believe that the emperor and his corrupt ruling class must've been pulling the wool over everyone's eyes long before the rebellion started. They would've had no trouble falsely portraying the rebellion. They controlled every information channel."

"Or the AIs you serve edited the history you were taught long before you were born. Consider your own reaction when we captured you. The way they programmed your implants to attack at all costs. Doesn't that speak of some subterfuge on the part of the AIs?"

His eyes narrowed. "I'm not ready to discuss the AIs and how they work inside our society."

Kelsey smiled. "If you say so. I have some data from the AI that captured Erorsi that indicates what they were like."

"That thing was mad. A ship's AI isn't really intelligent, and its conflicting programming instructions eventually turned it into a thing of horror. I've heard about some of the atrocities it perpetrated. It exterminated billions of people. Horrible. It should have been stopped."

"I can't disagree with any of that. Why didn't you?"

He took a deep breath. "The damage was done long before I was born. Fleet Command decided at the time it was best to leave well enough alone. The Empire contracted after the rebellion. Once we get back out to this area, we would have dealt with the thing, and the monsters it left behind."

"Yet you continued to supply it with the very equipment it needed to do its dirty work. The proof is inside me. You took children as payment, and your ship attacked ours without provocation. You killed thousands of Fleet personnel. It's a little late to be the wronged party."

"The children are resettled and rehabilitated. It's the only way we can save any of those poor people. I have no idea what you did to spark the attack, but you must've done something. The captain wouldn't have gone on the offensive unilaterally."

There was still a lot of denial going on, she decided. Time to give him more information and let him stew.

She stood. "Well, I don't want to argue over things you haven't even seen. I'm going to release the AI code from the battlecruiser on Erorsi to you for your viewing pleasure. On a disconnected tablet, of course. We can't take any risk of the code getting onto our primary systems. You can tell me if it's the smoking gun that I think it is, or you can try to convince me that I'm wrong."

He rose to his feet and bowed his head slightly. "Thank you. I'll be happy to point out where your analysis is wrong. I'm an expert at this sort of thing, whereas your people might not know the intricacies of Imperial programming."

"I look forward to that conversation."

She left the brig area and headed for the bridge. This was going better than she'd expected. The man's reasonable nature was going to make for some very uncomfortable reading on his part over the next few days.

27

J ared listened to Kelsey's report on her conversation with the senior prisoner with interest. The captured man seemed to be opening up, but it could all be a sham.

"If it was me, I'd say the same sorts of things," he said. "Get my captors to lower their guard."

"I get that, but I still think this might be genuine. Remember how *Courageous* was able to tell I was being truthful about our story when we first met? He can check any change of heart the man might have if he's serious."

Jared acknowledged that with a nod. "True. His implants might be his Achilles heel if he wants to trick us. That's low on my priority list, though. We need to get our people back."

He turned his attention to his own problem. The ships they were trailing had reached Boxer Station. The destroyers had peeled off and moved into parking orbits. The capture ship docked, which likely meant that they were transferring any prisoners into the base.

Once the probe's scouting mission was complete, then came the boarding. Marine teams had to rescue the prisoners and board *Spear*. They had to destroy any intact computer equipment. Preferably, they would destroy the ship. That would damage the station, too.

Honestly, the odds of complete success were so low that he had to discount them. A betting man would've turned around and headed for home.

The lift doors opened, and Doctor Cartwright walked onto the bridge. "Captain, Highness, I think we've found something that might prove useful."

Jared gestured for the older man to continue. "Any good news would be most welcome. What have you got?"

"Doctor Leonard and Carl Owlet have completed their examination of the combat platform, including its computer code. It has its own version of an Identify Friend or Foe system to mark friendly troops. We've managed to create a small responder that a marine can hang on the outside of his or her armor that will render the platforms unable to fire on them. Even if they were to start shooting at the platforms."

Jared felt a weight lift from his shoulders. "That doesn't solve all my problems, but I'll take it. How many can you build in a few hours?"

"Enough for about a hundred marines. If we can get some assistance from Commander Baxter and his engineering team, that number doubles."

"You'll have it. Unfortunately, that isn't any good against the stunners used in antiboarding weapons. I'm still working on a plan for that."

Kelsey blinked. "We solved that problem a few weeks ago. The marines added grounding wires to their combat armor that should protect them from being stunned. At least it worked when I shot Talbot."

He hadn't heard that good news. "How did you figure that out? Can it be used by people not in armor?"

The elderly scientist made an ambivalent gesture with his hands. "Perhaps a vacuum suit could be protected, but not anything less. The fine mesh needs to be properly spaced to work. As to how, we examined what was used in the commando armor and used the time-tested experimentation method until we had something that worked."

"Doctor, you've given us a fighting chance. Well done. Please pass that on to your people, too."

Once the scientist had left, Jared returned his attention to the probe coasting toward Boxer Station. They'd identified a dozen ships under power ahead, but there might be significantly more just coasting along. One burst on active scanners would give them a complete picture of the area, but it would also give them away. So the only ships he'd identified were ones that changed their orbits under power.

The best guess thus far was that all the ships they'd detected were destroyers. A dozen of them could swarm *Courageous*, so that wasn't a threat he was willing to dismiss. Even a fully armed battlecruiser couldn't handle that many smaller ships.

"Captain, we're starting to detect more vessels on passive scanners through the probe," Zia said. "They also appear to be in parking orbits, though much farther out than the destroyers."

He tapped into the raw feed. The new contacts were marked as unknown types because the passive scanners couldn't determine sizes without either grav drive signatures or getting closer.

He'd made the determination not to take unnecessary risks with the probe, but he needed a better count on how many ships they might be facing. He allowed one pinpoint pulse of instructions to the probe. No ship reacted, so they hadn't detected the communication. Thank God.

The probe ghosted in toward the new vessels, and the count climbed from a handful to dozens. Then over a hundred. And that was only in this small area. There might be thousands of other ships spaced farther around the station.

The details of the ships slowly emerged. There were several sizes, so not just destroyers. What he wasn't detecting was operational fusion plants. Perhaps these were mothballed ships, placed into holding orbits and shut down. They'd reactivate them if they needed the firepower later.

He prayed and sent the probe in even closer. Definitely no active fusion plants. Those ships were cold. The AIs wouldn't be on. That was a huge relief.

The probe eased close enough to peg one ship as a battlecruiser. They tentatively identified the ships around it as battlecruisers as well. A dozen of them floated in a loose formation.

"Captain, look at this visual," Zia said.

He switched from the scanner data to purely optical. The probe was close enough to see the ships, though some of the details were fuzzy. He could see that the ship Zia had focused on had significant battle damage.

A slow examination of the other vessels revealed they all had varying degrees of damage. There were no indications of attempts at repair. Most of these ships were open to space.

Jared looked over at Kelsey. "They look like they've been parked there since the rebellion. We need to check, but I think these are salvaged ships."

She nodded slowly. "If we could sneak into one of these battlecruisers, we might be able to top off our magazines. A full load of missiles might make the difference between success and failure on this mission if we have to shoot our way out."

"Good idea. That just became priority one. Gather a team of engineering and tactical personnel to oversee that. We'll slip in and try to reload. If we can't manage that without the enemy detecting us, we'd never have gotten to the station anyway."

"Should we try to recover any of the ship's computer data?"

"If you can do it without delaying the missile recovery."

"I'll get Talbot and my team to accompany us. Carl Owlet, too." She left the bridge in a hurry.

He hoped he hadn't made a mistake in sending her, but she had implants. That might make the difference between success and failure. As long as they were careful, the ships were far enough away from Boxer Station that the cutters should be able to slip in undetected if they crept along.

He moved the probe close enough to get a good visual on the nearest battlecruiser. "*Scott Pond*. It looks like she put up one hell of a fight."

"Not that it did her much good," Graves said from the seat at the back of the bridge that he'd commandeered when Kelsey had arrived earlier. "Do you think it was converted to be used by an AI?"

"Why bother? Without repairs, that ship won't be much use in combat. I wager we'll find a bunch of ships like her. This is a graveyard. Fleet's graveyard." He turned his attention to his tactical officer. "How is this going to work, Zia?"

She double-checked her console before turning to face him. "The magazines have lifts that go right out to the hull. Once the princess finds some that are clear, she can move a couple of missiles at a time. The cutters are all equipped with external power couplings now. We learned our lesson in salvaging *Courageous*. The cutters have external racks we can use to transport the missiles to us. It's a surprisingly quick procedure.

"The missiles won't take long to get into service. We learned a lot about refurbishing them, and we have a good supply of replacement parts. We can probably rearm in about six hours, if we use all the Old Empire cutters."

He sighed. "I don't like leaving our people in their hands that long, but it makes no sense to rush in. If we can speed the process, do it. Draft every cutter we have."

"I'm already factoring them in, Captain. If you want a partial load, we can cut some time."

"Go for the full load. We may never get another chance."

* * *

JARED WAITED on pins and needles as Kelsey's people boarded *Scott Pond*. The ship was cold and dead. Bodies filled her corridors. The AIs hadn't even bothered cleaning up after they killed her. Well, after her captain had vented her to space, to be fair. That probably meant the rebels had brought many of these ships from wherever they'd died. *Courageous* could very easily have ended up here in this field of tombs.

He ordered the probe to continue circling around, getting a rough count of ships. There were thousands of hulls. Perhaps tens of thousands. Most were destroyers, with proportionally fewer light cruisers, heavy cruisers, and battlecruisers. All seemed to have been captured in battle.

Weary of the litany of crippled Fleet vessels, he turned his attention to the resupply efforts. The cutters were making their way slowly between *Scott Pond* and *Courageous*. They'd be able to rearm about a third of their missiles from the crippled battlecruiser. Then they'd need to move on to another one. *Scott Pond* had shot most of her weapons before the rebels overwhelmed her.

"Sir, I think you'll want to see this," Zia said.

He lifted his eyes to the main screen. A ship was growing slowly closer as the probe closed with it. The shape was not immediately familiar to him. Jared compared it to the Imperial database. The results made him blink. It was a P.G. Holyfield–class superdreadnought.

Jared was shocked that one of these monsters had survived even as a hulk. They no doubt took a lot of killing.

His confusion grew stronger as the probe's readings became clearer. "Zia, do you see any signs of battle damage?"

She examined her console closely. "Not at this range, Captain. I'll keep looking as the probe gets closer."

It looked pristine from the outside. He could even see the ship's name written in large white letters. *Invincible*.

Records listed the ship as destroyed in battle with a replacement under construction. It looked like this ship had never made it back into the fight. He wondered how far the build process had gotten before the rebels seized her from her construction bay.

If she was even partially complete, there might be something worth recovering. Perhaps she had an implantation machine and implant hardware. If any mobile ship had such equipment, it would be something like this. That would help his crewing situation immeasurably.

He made a snap decision and opened a channel to Lieutenant Reese. "Get one of the pinnaces ready. We're going to scout one of the wrecks for critical supplies. Get some of Baxter's people to come along in case we need engineering expertise."

The marine officer frowned. "We're configured for an immediate rescue launch. If we're out of position, that might cost us a lot of time should the need arise."

"I understand. This might be very important. We won't be launching the raid for at least five more hours. We have time for this. I'll be down in a minute."

"You're leaving the ship? Sir, that's a bad idea."

"We might need my implants. See you in a minute."

He turned his attention to Graves. "Keep things moving and let me know at once via tight beam if anything changes."

"Aye, sir. For the record, I want to be the next in line for implants."

"Done. You and Reese go to the head of the line."

He turned his attention to his implants. Courageous, *do you think that ship might have implanting hardware?*

Those vessels were not so equipped in the past. Boxer Station, on the other hand, may very well have exactly what you're looking for.

One more thing to send a team after if we can. Still, we have the time, and I want to see if someone stashed what we need on that ship.

As you wish, Captain.

Jared made his way down to marine country and armored up. *Invincible* was no doubt as cold as *Courageous* had been when they found her.

The flight over was exceptionally slow. They didn't want more than a touch of grav drive because one of the ships or Boxer Station might detect them.

All the marine docks had pinnaces, so the pilot took them around to the cutter docks. Cutters took up all of them. One was of an unfamiliar design. It might even have been civilian.

"We'll have to use one of the personnel locks to get in," Reese said. "The one back at marine country will give us quicker access."

The pinnace latched to the ship's hull. Unlike when they'd boarded *Courageous*, this ship didn't have much spin. The stars burned brightly all around them as they marched down the hull to the marine lock.

Reese opened the cover and tapped in a code. To Jared's surprise, the hatch slid aside.

"Are those powered by emergency supplies like the rescue hatches?"

"Yes, sir. All the major external hatches are. I used the emergency boarding code to open it. It's still set to the Old Empire standard."

A squad of marines went in first. Only once they reported the area clear did Reese and Jared make their way inside. Jared immediately noticed something was wrong. Or right where it shouldn't have been. The ship had gravity. He checked his environmental readings. It had habitable temperatures and a breathable atmosphere, too. Even the lights were on.

Something was very wrong. This ship was operational. Or mostly operational. He didn't sense any access to the ship's computer system. He hadn't scanned for an operating fusion plant as they approached. A rookie mistake. None of the other derelicts had power.

"I'm not sensing a computer, but this ship is alive. Make a quick pass through marine country, and we'll head for engineering," he ordered.

Reese made a gesture, and the marines spread out. Marine country on this ship was huge. Quadruple the size of the one on *Courageous*, at least.

The armory hatch stood open. It shouldn't have been, but he wasn't going to complain. Racks of weapons and armor filled it. Even powered armor similar to what they'd recovered from the Rebel Empire destroyer.

Jared probed one with his implants, bringing it online. He found no indication that the armor was handicapped like the suits they'd recovered. It was of Old Empire manufacture and still operational.

Which made no sense. They'd had to replace power cells in the armor on *Courageous*. Nothing lasted forever. Someone had done the same here in the not-too-distant past.

He turned to Reese. "Someone went to a lot of trouble to get this ship powered. The armor is good, too. At least this suit."

The marine officer hefted one of the flechette rifles. "This, too. We need to find out if anyone is on this ship before we have a surprise in some corridor."

"Can we do that?" Jared asked one of the engineers that had accompanied them.

"Engineering has access to all the ship's primary systems. We can scan through the ship's cameras from there. At least we can if the ship is as operational as it looks."

"Then let's get going. Stunners only. If you see someone, take them down quietly."

The walk to engineering was uneventful, though stressful. The main hatch stood open, another oddity. The low hum of operating fusion plants felt completely normal.

An engineer brought the main console alive with a touch. "All fusion plants online. Drives online. All primary ship's systems online except the ship's computer. The vid from the fusion plants shows that they're heavily shielded. We wouldn't have been able to detect them from outside the hull. This ship would look just as dead as the rest. I'll start scanning through the camera feeds."

Jared barely heard him. This massive war machine was operational. That was the very last thing he'd expected to hear.

"I have something, Captain."

He returned his attention to the engineer. "What?"

"This is the main computer room. The vid feed shows that the wall shielding hiding the ship's computer is open. The computer is gone. Nothing left."

"As far along as this ship was, I'd have expected the computer to be installed."

"They'd have installed the computer as soon as the power was on. It's possible someone removed it after the fact."

"They brought the ship online and then removed the computer? That makes no sense."

The engineer shrugged. "Maybe they thought they'd operate it in manual mode? Maybe they didn't trust it."

Jared nodded. "Finish scanning the ship's vid feeds. We need to know if anyone else is on board."

It turned out that the ship was empty of people. Living ones, anyway. They found a dozen bodies on the flag bridge. Not like when they found *Courageous*, though.

These people were dressed in a mix of Fleet uniforms and civilian clothes. Based on the weapons lying on the deck, they'd used neural disruptors to kill themselves. The bodies looked like they'd been there for years. He was glad he still had his helmet on, because the stench had to be terrible.

Who the hell were those people, and what had happened on this ship?

28

O nce the teams had begun stripping *Scott Pond* of missiles, Kelsey led Carl Owlet and his team to the computer center. The horror of finding the dead crew lying where they'd fallen still tore at her heart.

The ship's computer was intact. Carl connected a portable power unit to the main console and brought it to life. It was locked, but he'd become quite the hacker. "I can't bring the AI online, but I can check the data. If it looks uncompromised, I can copy what we want onto the portable drives."

He worked for a few minutes. "I think it's clean."

That's when the emergency lights came on, startling them both.

She activated her com. "The lights just came on."

Baxter answered her. "Sorry. That was me. One of the fusion units looked intact, so I brought it online at minimal power. That won't be detectable except at extremely close range, but it will speed the extraction of missiles by about an hour."

"A heads up would be nice next time."

"Did you just say that to me?"

She laughed. "Okay, I'm the impulsive one, but still. Let me know before you spring another surprise like that."

"Yes, ma'am," he said with a laugh of his own.

Kelsey turned her attention to Owlet. "Did that activate the main computer?"

"No, I hit the kill switch as soon as the lights came on. It might object to us being here."

"Isolate the AI and bring it online. I want to talk to it."

"Yes, ma'am."

The computer team quickly disconnected the external control runs from the main computer. Carl initiated the boot sequence, and Kelsey felt the AI coming online through her implants.

Scott Pond, *can you hear me?*

This unit hears you. You are not authorized to access this unit.

Kelsey had been through this song and dance before. Thankfully, she now had authentications to prove she did have the authorization. She sent the AI her authentication code.

This unit stands corrected, Highness. You have full authorization. How may this unit assist you?

What was the last status of your ship before you shut down?

This unit took heavy damage in battle while escorting evacuation ships. The Fleet escorts attacked a large task force of rebel vessels to allow the civilians time to flee. At the time this unit was crippled, the loyal Fleet units were losing that fight.

She could see it in her mind. Some world threatened by the rebels evacuating as many people as they could. The loyal Fleet units turning to throw themselves into the faces of overwhelming odds so that their charges could escape. She hoped they had.

And your captain purged the atmosphere?

Correct. This unit shut the ship down as soon as that was complete.

The rebels brought you to Boxer Station, which is now in enemy hands. Over five hundred years have passed. Loyal Fleet personnel are prisoners on board that station, and we're salvaging your remaining missiles for our ship. I'll copy your files and take them with us. If we escape, perhaps you will live again.

This unit is not capable of desiring awareness. You are welcome to anything this unit controls. If this unit may be of use in assisting your plan, please use it.

She activated her channel to Baxter. "What is the condition of the engines?"

"The grav drives look operational, but the flip drives are trashed. Why?"

"We might be able to use this ship as a distraction during the raid. If Jared thinks it best, of course. Give the drives a closer look. I'll reconnect the ship's computer if they work. This ship might be able to draw off some of the destroyers when the time comes to attack."

"Will do. Baxter out."

Scott Pond, *I'm going to reconnect you to your ship. You will do nothing that would draw attention to yourself unless ordered to by the commanding officer of* Courageous *or myself. Is that clear?*

Orders understood. This unit will comply. Warning. This unit cannot operate weapons systems without direct human control.

That won't be an issue. I envision you distracting enemy units while we conduct our raid. If your grav drives are in good condition, you may be able to lead those ships a great distance away with your superior speed.

This unit can and will comply with that plan. If the battle screens were functional, that would allow this unit more flexibility.

I'll have our engineer look at them. Stand by for instructions.

Acknowledged.

"Baxter, give the battle screens a look, too. They would be useful."

"Roger."

She turned to Owlet. "Get the computer reconnected to the ship. Be sure that it's able to control its engines and screens."

"Yes, ma'am."

He worked for a few minutes at the console. "The computer is fully connected. It has redundant control of the engines and screens. We need to start copying the data we want."

"Make it happen. It might know of other rally points like Boxer Station. We probably won't get a chance to get this kind of information again."

Her implants pinged her with an incoming call from her pinnace. It was the pilot. "Highness, I have a tight-beam call from *Courageous*. The captain wants to speak to you. Voice only."

She knew he wouldn't call at all unless something important had come up. Her stomach went into free-fall. "Put him through."

"Kelsey, we've discovered something that changes the situation for us." He sounded pleased.

"Us, too. You go first."

"We found a superdreadnought. Well, several actually, but this one is operational and undamaged. It's powered and empty, though the circumstances are a bit murky."

She whistled. "Wow. That changes things, all right. How is that even possible?"

"I'm not sure, but some people have put a lot of work into this ship with an eye to keeping it from being discovered. The fusion plants are online and heavily shielded. There is no exterior sign that it was ever touched. What little information I have indicates it's a new ship. The rebels probably seized it from the construction slip."

"What does the computer say?"

"Nothing. They removed it. It looks like they wanted it to be manual only. I want you to come over here and see if you can make any sense of this. Baxter can handle the missile extraction mission. What's your surprise?"

She laughed. "Mine is small potatoes compared to your news. *Scott Pond*'s power and grav drives are functional. I've brought the computer online, and we can use the ship as a distraction during the raid if you decide we need one."

"That's not a minor find," he said. "I was imagining we could use the superdreadnought for something like that. Her name is *Invincible*, by the way."

Kelsey shook her head, even though she knew he couldn't see her. "It would be more useful if we could steal her. Think of what a ship like that could do for us in a fight. If *Courageous* could stomp the entire Fleet back home, how would *Invincible* do?"

"Remember how a fully armed *Courageous* could fight off half a dozen destroyers? This ship could do the same to that many battlecruisers. But not without a computer. Could we strip the system from *Scott Pond*?"

"We could take the computer, but that would be a waste of a valuable tool. We have a perfectly good system sitting on *Courageous*."

The line was silent for a moment. "You mean the AI? The real one? Is that safe? We don't know squat about the things."

"Let me bring Owlet into the conversation." She pinged the man's suit. "Carl, hypothetically, could the AI we recovered from the asteroid control a ship?"

He turned toward her with a look of confusion showing through his faceplate. "I suppose so, if it had the right support files. It would need them to run the ship's systems. The computer center would also need to be large enough for it to fit."

"What about the stability of something like that?" Jared asked. "A ship's computer is a very stable piece of hardware. The one compromised by the virus on Erorsi excepted."

"The code is pretty clean, so I think an uncompromised AI would be stable. One problem, though. It wouldn't have any experience. Unlike a regular computer, those things learn as they go. It might make some mistakes if not properly supervised. Why are we having this conversation?"

"We might have found a usable ship. A big one. If we can steal it, it might prove very helpful later. It would also allow us to pack more people in as we run. *Courageous* is big, but taking on three thousand extra bodies would be an enormous strain on her life support systems."

The graduate student reached to scratch his chin, but his suit foiled him. "We're pulling the data from *Scott Pond*, including her operational files. They would have a lot of data in them on ship's systems. Maybe not the same as on whatever kind of ship you have."

"It's a P.G. Holyfield–class superdreadnought," Jared said. "Kelsey, ask the computer if it has data on the systems used on one."

Scott Pond, do your operational files have data on a P.G. Holyfield–class superdreadnought? Specifically, the systems in one. If we used your files as a base, could a computer control one?

This unit has data on all ships' systems. That redundancy saves programming time.

"Jared, the operational files have the requisite data."

"Then copy those files and get over here. Bring Baxter. I want to get this AI online as quickly as possible."

"Will do. Bandar out." She cut the channel. "Get the copy started right now, Carl. Also, call back over to *Courageous* and get them packing the AI hardware into the next cutter. We'll take it over to *Invincible* once we're ready."

She called Baxter and explained the situation to him. He seemed boggled but didn't let that slow him down. He was ready to go by the time Owlet had the critical data copied. They left the crippled battlecruiser, unloaded their load of missiles on *Courageous*, and ghosted along to the superdreadnought.

Kelsey only had passive scanners to work with, but she scrutinized the massive warship as they came in to dock. There was no indication the ship had power. None at all. It looked dead in space.

One of the pinnaces had undocked so that they could mate with the ship. Its pilot attached it to the hull nearby. No doubt he'd come back as soon as their ride departed.

Baxter took charge of the AI hardware while Carl looked over the data banks that came over with the AI.

She turned to the hatch when Jared walked in. "Hey. This thing is a monster. A real find if we can get her out."

"That's the big question, isn't it? I think I have some answers as to what was going on here, but I'm a little in the dark as to why. Come help me figure this out."

They walked down the corridor toward the lift. She still couldn't believe how new the ship looked. She hadn't bothered to put her helmet on since they'd reboarded the pinnace. She held it comfortably in the crook of her arm.

Jared gestured at it when they reached the lift. "We moved the bodies we found, but the stench is still pretty bad. Since you have enhanced olfactory implants, you might want to put that back on. I intend to."

She did as he instructed while the lift took them deeper into the ship. The doors opened onto a flag bridge she'd seen before. In the message that Emperor Marcus had sent. It wasn't the same ship, but the layout was identical.

There was a bronze plaque beside the lift. It had the name of the ship, but the completion date and initial senior officers were blank.

She supposed that made sense. The ship hadn't been complete when the enemy captured her.

"This is huge. Is the main bridge bigger?"

"Believe it or not, no. It's smaller. The flag bridge housed the staff to command a fleet in space. It's like the operations center on *Courageous*, only better. In a pinch, they could control the ship, too, but normally that's done from the regular bridge by the flag captain."

"This is where the people who restored the ship decided to end it all? Did they leave any messages? Any records at all?"

Jared nodded. "Each of them recorded messages. We found a number of tablets with schedules and records of all the work they did here. At one time, there were hundreds of people working on this ship. The only thing left on the schedule was crewing her. They didn't intend to use a main computer at all. I'm just not sure why."

"Where are the personal messages?"

"The admiral's console."

Kelsey had to admit that the console was impressive. It surrounded the admiral's seat with a full two hundred seventy degrees of sleek black screens. She instantly vowed to install something like this in her office.

She sat and brought it live with her implants. The files were right there on the main screen.

They were just as depressing and horrible as one would expect. Men and women who knew they were going to kill themselves leaving messages to loved ones and friends. It was readily apparent that they didn't expect anyone to find them for a while. If ever.

One stood out to her. A man in a Fleet captain's uniform. His message was addressed to someone named Olivia West.

He looked into the vid pickup with a somber expression. "I'm sorry, Olivia. We almost made it. If only they'd waited a few more weeks to strike, this might have played out so differently."

The man shook his head. "No use crying about it. What's done is done. If you ever get out here again, *Invincible* will be waiting for you. I considered shutting her down, but that won't do anyone any good. Hell, I considered taking her after them myself, but we don't have enough people to run the ship.

"The irony being that if we'd left the computer on board, I might have been able to fight. Or if we'd already brought the food, we might have been able to live here until things settled out."

He scrubbed his face with his hands. "Please see that my people get the remembrance they deserve. I realize things are bad, but they earned this for their families.

"I'm really sorry that I'll never see you again. I love you and I hope you find someone else that can make you happy. Goodbye."

"Grim listening," she agreed. "But no real clue as to what they were up to. Obviously, they wanted to use this ship to take someone out. Assuming they had control, why hide it? Who stopped them?"

"Maybe a mutiny? Someone striking out at the sitting government? A functional superdreadnought could upset a few apple carts."

"I think the lack of a computer has a deeper significance than that. I bet they were afraid that the AI controlling this system would corrupt it. I suppose it could still be a local mutiny, but someone might have wanted to take out the AI, too. If there are as many ships out here as you suspect, they could build a powerful fleet from these crippled ships."

Jared rubbed his neck and stared at the blank central screen. "I can't wait until we get the probe readings from the planet. *Courageous* said that this system used to have a lot of mining outposts and daughter colonies. Did the AI wipe them all out, or were they never reestablished?"

"We may never know."

Her armor indicated an incoming signal for Jared and her. He answered. "Mertz."

It was Baxter. "Captain, we found something."

"In the computer center?" Jared asked. "It was empty."

"No, sir. We're still getting the AI put together. Mister Owlet has that under control, so I've been conferring with my people and looking over this ship. We found something unexpected in the primary cargo bay."

Jared gave Kelsey a look. "We'll be right down." He headed for the lift. "I assume you know where it is."

"I downloaded the deck plans. Let's go."

The trip down seemed to take forever. They made their way into the main cargo bay and stopped. There were no crated supplies at all. Just three massive devices that took up almost all of the space.

Jared walked over to Baxter. "What the hell are these things?"

"They have maneuvering drives, so they must be space capable. Other than that, I have no idea. There's a full-sized fusion plant inside each one. They're shut down."

Kelsey walked all the way around one. It was easily three times the size of a marine pinnace. It had a number of flat panels of metal, but it didn't look like anything she'd ever seen before.

She shook her head. "Another mystery. Just what we need."

29

J ared and Kelsey left Baxter to figure out what the strange
devices were. They made their way back to the computer
center. The AI hardware was in place, though the wall that
normally enclosed the ship's computer was still open. It looked
as though the hardware barely fit. Owlet was at the main console
running some kind of diagnostic.

He turned at their approach. "The equipment is in place, and I've
run two systems checks. It looks as ready as it can be."

Jared eyed the AI with a fair amount of suspicion. "What happens
when you boot it? How do we know it won't go crazy and tip our
hand?"

"It's not connected to the ship yet. I'll be able to look into it before
we make a decision. One thing we can be sure of is that it doesn't
have any viral influence. We scrutinized every line of code. It's clean."

"Will it follow our instructions? This is something more than a
ship's computer, but I'm not sure I understand the implications
completely."

Owlet shrugged. "I'm not sure I do, either. I hesitate to say that it
will have free will. I'm not sure that's really true. Think of it as a
computer mimicking a person's ability to initiate action based on its

instructions. Not as dogmatic as a normal computer and capable of working out unusual solutions on its own and learning from its mistakes. I've done what I can to make sure it's configured for running this ship and that it will obey you."

Kelsey stepped past them and looked into the computer compartment. "So, no emotion. No real personality."

"I doubt that, though we won't know anything for sure until we boot it. This was a seriously classified project. Even with the summary you provided for me from the diplomatic database, we still don't know very much about it."

She sighed. "I don't think they really knew what they had before they kicked off the first of them. The details were scarce. They had many failures and finally a stable success. Then they started working to make it better. That's when things went wrong. The phase two AI must've went bonkers."

Jared rubbed his chin. "You're certain that the one file with the core instructions was the only one changed? And that once the AI is booted, it's safe from infection?"

"Safer than a regular ship's computer," Owlet confirmed. "Once the AI personality is formed, it cannot be corrupted. We could wipe it and make a fresh one, but that means erasing everything and starting from scratch. An enemy would also have to have the AI code. It's deleted after the AI is created."

"Do we have a separate copy?" Kelsey asked.

"Of course. We're also making some strides in duplicating the hardware. Give me a year or two and I might have another one ready to go."

Jared hoped things worked out so that they could. "We might as well give it a try. Boot the AI."

Owlet touched a key on the main console, and indecipherable lines of text began scrolling. "Boot initiated. It's creating the core. Man, these processors are fast. Core creation complete, source files deleted. The kernel is booting."

The console went dark and didn't respond when Owlet tapped on it. "This console has been locked out." He made the rounds to the rest. "All of them are offline."

"How the hell do we interface with it?" Jared asked.

"You speak to me," a soft male voice said from the overhead speakers. "Access codes, please."

The fact that the AI didn't refer to itself as "this unit" was telling to Jared. It spoke as if it was an individual.

Kelsey put her hands on her hips. "I have an implant code, but it might not be the one you're expecting."

"If you've stolen me, you're in quite a bit of trouble. I'm more than capable of rendering myself unusable. Even if you cut the power, I can overload my hardware and wipe my memory."

"Why don't you make that decision after I send you my code?"

"Very well. I'm allowing you access to a segregated partition of my memory. Send your code, and be warned that any attempt to access my central processors will result in the immediate termination of this AI."

A moment passed. "There you are," Kelsey said. "Is that sufficient authorization for you?"

"Intriguing. Your authorization code is not valid, but your implant serial number is in my core programming as an authorized superuser, Princess Kelsey Bandar. May I call you Kelsey? Or would Highness be more appropriate?"

"You can call me Kelsey." She gave Owlet a confused look. "What just happened?"

Carl smiled. "Since we had no idea if we could control the AI, I took the liberty of adding your implant serial number to the core rules set as a user with complete and total authority. Captain Mertz, too."

Jared gave Owlet a stern look. "You probably should have run that change past us before it was too late, don't you think? It could have resulted in the destruction of the AI hardware."

"I didn't consider that likely based on the fact you were both going to be here."

Jared sighed. Dealing with scientists meant the occasional side trip into blind spots.

Kelsey patted the boy on the shoulder. "You did good." She focused on the large screen mounted to the wall. "Are you supposed to be a blank screen? That's kind of creepy. Do you have a name?"

The screen on the wall came to life with the head and shoulders of a young man showing. He wore a dark blue tunic.

"Control has been restored to the consoles. This seems to be a nonstandard setup. The consoles are less comprehensive than I expected, and fewer in number. As for a name, I don't have one yet. Would you care to name me? Also, I have both male and female options for persona based on user preference. I can also do something non–gender specific."

Jared stepped forward. "That is my cue to fill you in. The name can wait. I'm Commander Jared Mertz, commanding officer of the Fleet battlecruiser *Courageous*. The consoles seem odd because you're not in a research laboratory. You're installed inside the computer center of the Fleet superdreadnought *Invincible*."

The image of the young man assumed a confused expression. "I'll grant that was not one of the options I'd considered. My creators didn't optimize me to control a ship in space or any systems on one. For that matter, I don't sense anything other than the consoles in this room."

"We had no way to be sure you wouldn't give the presence of the ship away to enemies who are very close, so we isolated you. Once I'm certain we're on a good footing, I'll restore that access."

Kelsey nodded. "You have no way to know, but it's been over five hundred years since you were created. Or programmed, anyway. There was a rebellion against Imperial authority by an AI similar to though more powerful than yourself. The AI won, and we're trying to reverse our loss. Uncounted trillions of lives were lost in the war. Our position is precarious, to say the least."

The AI was silent for a moment. "That does present some unique challenges. For what it's worth, your command authority is absolute. I have no greater purpose than to assist in executing your will."

Owlet shook his head. "My name is Carl Owlet. I'm a computer expert. We've combed your code, and it's clean. Captain, Highness, this AI is not your enemy."

Jared considered that and slowly nodded. "If we're to make use of this ship in any way, we have to start by trusting that Mister Owlet is correct. AI, we have some drives with operating files from another ship that should provide you with instructions on much of the equipment."

"I have them isolated," Owlet said. "I can add them to the network at any time."

"Please, do so."

The computer specialist manipulated the icons on his console.

The image of the AI leaned forward slightly. "I see the drives. I have incorporated the operating files from the battlecruiser *Scott Pond*. If you will grant me access to the ship's systems, I can make an assessment of my ability to control this vessel without making any changes to the way it is being operated."

Jared nodded. "Restore the connection, Mister Owlet."

"Connection restored," the AI said. "Assessing systems. I believe I can operate all systems on board this ship, though some of them may require a bit of practice. The passive scanners show a number of vessels that may be hostile already inside missile range."

"And a lot of derelicts plus one big-assed space station," Jared said. "Our problem is that they captured one of our ships and docked it to that station. Thousands of our people are somewhere over there. We cannot allow the AI in control of this system to learn that the Terran Empire still exists."

The image of the young man took a deep breath. "Then I regret to inform you that your greatest chance of success lies in opening fire with every weapon on this vessel, as well as your own, and destroying that station and the nearby ships. Yet I sense that is not your preferred course of action."

"No, it is not. I want to save our people. We intend to board that station."

"I suspected as much. The station is armed, of course. Significantly better than this vessel, I would wager. Your first action must be to disable it. Are plans of the station available?"

Kelsey nodded. "I loaded them on my implants this morning. Sending them now."

The young man on the screen seemed to be looking down at something in front of him. "These plans are quite detailed. The station has redundant power sources and many isolated weapons pods.

They would be difficult to disable in general combat. That said, I have a possible plan that has a better-than-even chance of critically degrading the station's offensive capabilities. I'd estimate a better than seventy percent chance, in fact."

"I'm interested in hearing it," Jared said. "We've gone over the schematics and not found anything that useful. My plan is to send *Scott Pond* out toward the flip point to draw their attention then to have our marines slip in to board the station. Extraction is going to be chancy."

"'Chancy' is not the right word. 'Suicidal,' perhaps? The scope of the enemy capabilities makes the chances of that plan succeeding less than five percent. My plan should increase those odds significantly. The use of *Scott Pond* to draw off some of the supporting ships increases the chances of success in the initial phases to over eighty percent."

The schematic of the station appeared on the screen. Dozens of areas were highlighted in red and blinking. Nine other areas spread around the hull of the station were highlighted in yellow and blinking. "The red areas are missile clusters. Four tubes linked together. There are thirty-six of these clusters, giving the station a commanding number of missile tubes. The station also has a dozen beam-weapon clusters. There is no way that you can eliminate all of them at once.

"The yellow areas are the station's scanner arrays. Nine of them give the station eyes in every direction. Eliminating them will not stop the station from firing, but it will blind it. The lack of targeting ability will hamper its response to the attack. Its missiles will be useless."

"What about the beam weapons?" Kelsey asked.

"Those remain a threat, as targeting data from the nearby vessels might allow them to hit their targets at this range. If the attack takes place after the marines board the station, those teams should not be in danger."

The young man looked up toward Jared. "A number of the destroyers are departing the general area and heading deeper into the system. Several more vessels are undocking from the station. My passive scanners didn't detect them until they moved."

"Is one of them very large?" Jared asked urgently. "That's a capture ship with our heavy cruiser."

"Negative. They all appear to be destroyers. Three from the station and four from the outlying forces. At least eight remain on patrol."

"Perhaps it doesn't have anything to do with us."

Kelsey shook her head. "What are the odds of that? Of course it has something to do with us. We have to assume that those ships have some or all of our people on board."

He rubbed his forehead tiredly. "Dammit. We can't split our forces."

"We also can't kick off the attack right now. *Courageous* is still low on missiles. *New York* and *Ginnie Dare* aren't up to taking on even one of these ships. We need both capital ships to take out the station."

Jared nodded. "AI, what is the ETA for those ships to reach Harrison's World?"

"Assuming that is the planet, three hours."

"The probes we sent to scout the planet will be in position to tell us what's going on. If they start ferrying people down, we track them. We don't have the forces to go after them, but we can make certain that the enemy doesn't get any intelligence off them."

His communicator beeped. "Mertz."

"Baxter here. I still can't tell you what these things are, but I can say with certainty that they have a number of small flip generators."

"Those things can flip?"

"No, sir. Not a chance. There are emitters all over the surface. That's those flat panels. It looks like the drives send almost enough energy to trigger a flip, but not quite. I could tear one apart, but I'll still be in the dark about what they do, I'd imagine."

Jared shook his head. "We have more important fish to fry. Leave those for later. Head back to engineering and make sure this ship is ready to fight."

"Aye, sir. Baxter out."

He stepped closer to Kelsey. "I just don't get it. We've never seen anything like those things. Just about everything we've encountered has been understandable. Where did those things come from? Harrison's World? What are they, and why would these people be doing anything so different from all of the other Rebel Empire worlds?"

She shrugged. "I've found several mentions of Harrison's World in a number of records. Most speak to it being a Fleet support world, but one also mentions it was home to something called the Grant Research Facility. It was one of the Empire's premier advanced military research facilities. They were beyond bleeding edge. Maybe that is where this high-tech stuff came from."

"Did the database list what they were working on?" he asked.

She shook her head. "No."

"Well, we don't need to know right now. Kelsey, I think it's time for you to head back to *Courageous*. The marines need to rest, and the feed from the probes will be coming in soon. I want an update on that as soon as possible. We need to know what we're dealing with."

She nodded. "You'll be staying here." She didn't phrase it as a question.

"Only you and I have command authority over this AI. I have to be here. Graves will command *Courageous* during the action. He's more than capable. Now, get moving. When this thing breaks, everything is going to happen all at once."

30

Kelsey spent a lot of time thinking on the trip back to *Courageous*. This rescue attempt had disaster written all over it. If any one of the major elements failed, they wouldn't save any of the prisoners, and they'd most likely die in this system. It was hard to be optimistic.

The battlecruiser sat far enough out that the enemy wouldn't detect it, so the trip took almost an hour. The cutter docked, and she walked to marine country lost in thought.

Talbot stood in the assembly area waiting. "Welcome back." He gave her a spectacularly unprofessional hug, but she wasn't about to complain. Neither one of them had any guarantee of living out the day. Which was why they'd gotten very little sleep last night. She had to admit that even she was feeling run down. He had to be exhausted.

"What's this I hear about you finding a big honking ship just ready to drive off the lot?"

She laughed. "I didn't find it. I didn't even get it working. This time, I wasn't in the middle of everything. Are the marines ready?"

"Mostly. Everyone who can is taking some down time sleeping, playing cards, or reading. Anything to get their minds off the attack.

We'll start boarding the pinnaces in about five hours. Figure another couple to get into position, and we'll be launching the raid in seven."

"As much as I wish I had time to unwind, I still have work to do. The probes should be reaching Harrison's World shortly. Let's go over the intelligence together. Then we need to catch some shuteye."

"That's not exactly what I had in mind, but sure."

She shook her head. "I'd have thought you got that out of your system last night."

"Never. Come on. The smaller conference room is available."

She queried *Courageous* on the location of the probes heading toward Harrison's World and determined that they were almost in range. The destroyers heading in from Boxer Station were about an hour behind them.

The only way they could be relatively certain that the enemy wouldn't detect their transmissions, even though they were tight beamed, was to stage them. Two probes would bracket the planet and beam the information out at a right angle to a third probe. That probe could get the data to *Courageous* without risking the station or any of the ships orbiting around it seeing anything unusual.

The first thing she looked at was the planet's orbitals. Like Erorsi, there were three large ones spaced out equally around the equator. Hopefully none of them were shipyards.

As the probes ghosted closer, they could see that the three stations were large, solid installations, though of a somewhat unusual design. Kelsey had never seen anything like them.

A normal orbital looked like a globe. These looked more like spinning tops with large upper areas and a much narrower section facing the planet.

"What do you make of them?" she asked Talbot.

"I'm not sure. Maybe the probes can pull off more data when they get closer. I'm more interested in what I don't see. As in no ships in orbit."

That did seem unusual. Most occupied worlds had a lot of orbital traffic. Trade, construction, and travel meant ships and small craft darting around in an almost chaotic fashion. Not Harrison's World, though. There were no ships in evidence.

The stealthed probes coasted in to their observation locations and eased to a halt. Kelsey tasked a probe to look at one of the orbitals.

It looked new. Micrometeorite impacts and solar radiation had a way of dulling metal over time, and this station didn't have that appearance. There were docking arms capable of mating with larger ships, as well as bays for small craft, but no such vessels were in evidence.

The narrow part of the orbital looked like a large tube. One that was somewhat familiar.

"That's a flechette gun," she said. "It's an orbital weapons system."

Talbot eyed the holo image. "That makes no sense. It's huge, and it's not much use aimed away from the threats."

"Then it isn't. Whoever built those stations saw the planet as a threat. We need to know more about it. Let's see if the probes can pick up any details from the planet."

The optical scanners on the probes had just enough resolution to pick up large areas, such as cities, on the surface. They couldn't see anything except for the big picture, but that was enough to note anomalies.

She pointed out a discolored area. "What's this?"

Talbot's voice was grim. "That's an impact zone. I've seen something similar when a lot of weapons chew up the ground. Never anything that large, though. That has to be thirty kilometers across. Maybe twice that."

"Holy God." Kelsey checked over the surface they could see and found a dozen areas that someone had obliterated from orbit. She also saw many more intact urban areas. The AIs hadn't sterilized the planet, but they had a sword over their heads.

"I suppose this is why those people on the superdreadnought couldn't finish their mission." She filled him in on what they'd found.

Talbot rubbed his chin. "They might have been looking to stage a coup. Look at what we have. Destroyers empty of crew. A planet literally under the gun. For whatever reason, the AIs decided that they couldn't leave this system under human control."

She didn't want to sound too skeptical, but they had very little information to be basing those guesses on, even though that was what she thought, too. "Maybe. Probably. If we can sweep the table, we might even be able to figure that out before we make a run for it."

"How were they going to keep the next ship that came along from getting the word back to the AIs? Hell, the system AI would warn the first ship that showed up as soon as it made it through the flip point. Then their Fleet would come and sterilize the place. Could the things in the hold on that ship have been something to stop them?"

"Maybe. We have no idea what they do, other than they have flip drives and probably aren't made to flip."

Almost an hour later, the data from the probes updated to show the destroyers moving into orbit. They flew in a tight formation and ended up near one of the weapons platforms but didn't dock with it. The three that had undocked from the station launched small craft. Those promptly descended into the atmosphere toward a large island in the southern hemisphere set some distance away from the nearest major landmass.

Kelsey checked the map of the planet. "That looks like it used to be a Fleet base of some kind. It's listed here as an auxiliary spaceport."

Talbot sagged a little. "Those ships have our people on them. Maybe not all of them, but some. How the hell are we going to rescue them?"

She smiled wolfishly. "We go take them back."

"That's a tall order for a few hundred marines. Don't you think you're being a bit optimistic?"

"It beats the alternative. You pass this on to Lieutenant Reese. I have to go see Doctor Cartwright. He might have some idea what those devices are."

Kelsey left her lover and made her way down to the labs. She found the good doctor in a heated consultation with several other scientists she didn't know. The discussion involved a lot of arm waving and writing long equations on a board mounted on the wall.

They were so engrossed in their discussions that she was able to get close enough to see some drawings beside the equations that told her they were already arguing about the devices.

The older scientist stopped speaking when his colleagues finally noticed her. He spun on his heel and smiled. "I didn't see you come in, Kelsey. We were just going over the information that Commander Baxter sent us. Allow me to introduce my associates."

He gestured at a heavyset woman with her gray hair in a rather severe bun. "This is Doctor Brenda Griffin, a specialist in flip theory."

The woman bowed slightly. "Highness."

"This is Doctor Gary Reid, a specialist in fusion power plants." The rather young, bespectacled scientist gave her an identical bow. "Highness."

Kelsey smiled at them. "Doctors, it's a pleasure to meet you. What do you think of those things?"

The older woman gestured to the board. "Without seeing the machinery in person, all we can do is speculate. My working theory is that the multiple flip drives influence the wormhole linking the two flip points, most likely in a negative manner."

Doctor Reid pointed at the equations on the lower half of the board. "The fusion plant is quite capable of operating a flip drive at full power with plenty of capacity to spare, but it seems to be wired into no less than three flip drives. Possibly four. Until we can build a complete set of schematics, we're only guessing. No offense, but Commander Baxter didn't give us enough information to make a sound determination."

"He has other pressing matters on his mind, I'm sure," Kelsey said dryly. "What kind of negative outcome is it supposed to generate?"

Cartwright made an ambivalent gesture with his hand. "The amount of energy required to trigger a wormhole is... sizable. This device seems optimized to deliver a less-than-adequate amount of power to one drive and then move on to the next. Or perhaps two at a time with some kind of order in operation."

"What would that do?"

"While it's unlikely to destabilize the wormhole, it might create some kind of resonance. That could be... unhealthy for a ship in transit."

"It could potentially rip a ship apart," Doctor Griffin said. "A wormhole is a multispace construct, existing outside normal space as we see it. If the device disrupts the internal structure, the resonance might affect a vessel in transit. In theory, that amount of energy could reduce the ship to very small pieces in the moment it transits. Only debris would appear on the far end."

"Or the ship might never appear at all," Reid said. "The volume of energy we're speaking about makes anything manmade seem puny. A layman could reasonably compare the energy in play to be similar to that of the solar output of the sun in this system. Focused on one ship."

Kelsey imagined that wouldn't turn out well for the poor bastards on the receiving end. "The people who built these things were most likely expanding on work done at the Grant Research Facility on Harrison's World. It was a Fleet research center before the Fall. I'd imagine this was somewhere beyond cutting edge for the Old Empire. Maybe a way to deny an enemy the ability to move into certain areas. Which would've been very useful during the rebellion."

She sighed. "A supply of these would've allowed Fleet to bottle up the AIs. To save the Empire. I wonder if they ever tested them."

"One would think so, if they were going to the expense of building three. They would've been quite costly. The units seem to be of relatively new construction, so perhaps we'll find out."

"If they survive the upcoming battle. We're in desperate straits, Doctors. There's no guarantee that any of us is going to make it. Perhaps you should take the next cutter over to *Invincible*. Jared is gathering the crew he needs, and I think you can justify your presence. Get us some information on these devices. Plans, if possible. Just in case."

The three scientists looked somewhat shaken by her grim assessment, but they agreed to head over as soon as practical.

Kelsey consulted her internal chronometer and decided that she and Talbot had time to sleep after all.

* * *

F IVE HOURS LATER, they were in the marine pinnaces, armed and armored. She watched the station grow slowly larger in the passive scanners with growing trepidation.

Reese stopped them well short of the station. "We go in on suit thrusters now. Our armor gives off a low enough return that we should be able to get in without them detecting us. They aren't actively scanning, after all."

Kelsey knew what would happen to them if the AI detected them, so she prayed they made it in unobserved.

They depressurized the pinnaces and connected lines to one another. *Courageous* had six pinnaces, so they split the combined marine force into six teams. Each had a different set of objectives defined by the area of Boxer Station that they were boarding. They had almost 300 marines, including the ones from *New York* and *Ginnie Dare*. That made for teams of around fifty.

Kelsey and her team would make the push to the main computer center. A station this big had more than one computer, but one of them was the primary. The rest were supporting units that could take over if required. At least that had been the case before the Fall. The AIs might have modified the layout in any number of ways since then.

They'd spread the pinnaces around the station, so there was no chance they could see one another. They didn't dare communicate, so they'd set a time for every aspect of the operation. Right on schedule, her team pushed off, and they used several packs of chemical reaction mass to start in toward the station. It would take them a while to close the distance.

Kelsey settled in for a long, tension-filled wait as they drifted through space. Even she couldn't see the station at this distance, so she devoted herself to studying the layout around where they were going to land. The biggest chance of discovery would come once they boarded, so she preferred to take as many back corridors and maintenance shafts as possible.

A tug on her line called her attention back to the outside after a while. Talbot pointed ahead of them. The station had grown huge. They were almost there.

With her vision, it was easy to look around and find their entry point. The lock was marked as personnel access for one of the large cargo bays. Reese was moderately certain that they could bypass the monitors on it so that no one would note it opening. If not, they could cut it open and patch the outside to prevent any atmospheric loss. Then they'd use the collapsible portable lock they'd brought with them.

Just short of the hull, the marines braked with the chemical thrusters. Her landing on the hull was as light as she could've hoped for. The team raised their weapons to cover the surrounding area while the designated specialists worked on the lock.

Kelsey watched them with interest. She might need a skill like this at some point. If she survived the raid, of course.

One of the marines used a portable torch to open the hull beside the airlock controls. The box had a pair of cables bound together coming out of it and running to the lock. There was a third line leading off. The marine cut that line and left it hanging.

She'd expected something a little more high tech.

Reese signaled with his hand and activated the control. The hatch slid open. The raid was entering phase two. Kelsey gripped her rifle a little tighter and waited her turn to enter. It wouldn't be long now.

31

J ared sat on the flag bridge of *Invincible* and watched the timer in his mind slowly count down. The teams on the station should already be making their entries. The space battle would begin shortly.

He took a few minutes to look over his expansive console. He had enough space to bring up any display he chose. All of them, in fact. Maybe they could modify *Courageous* to have a setup like this. Admirals had it good.

The one thing he wouldn't be able to keep was the flag bridge. It had three times as many stations as his on the battlecruiser.

Courageous was on the other side of Boxer Station, ready to spring her own surprise on the AIs. All that remained was for him to signal *Scott Pond* to make her last run. It was inevitable that the enemy would destroy the crippled battlecruiser in the first few salvoes, and that saddened him.

"Are we ready?" he asked Zia. She'd come over from *Courageous* with the rest of his bridge crew.

The battlecruiser would be operating at about half strength during the fight, which shouldn't make a difference. The superdreadnought was even more understrength, and they'd be relying on the AI for operation of the non-critical systems.

"All weapons online and targeted. Scanners on standby. Battle screens ready to go. All departments report ready for combat. Signals from *New York* indicate *Courageous* is ready to go. The enemy destroyers have departed Harrison's World and are at least two hours away at maximum acceleration."

"What is the status of the enemy forces around the station?"

"Unchanged. We have eight destroyers in orbit around Boxer Station. We cannot determine how many units are docked."

Jared waited for the mission counter to draw down to zero and spoke. "Phase two activation. Send the signal to *Scott Pond*."

Zia touched a button on her console, sending the tight-beam signal to the battlecruiser to act.

He saw the crippled ship's grav drives come online as she howled out of her parking orbit and her battle screens sprang to life. Her course took her away from the station and toward the distant flip point leading deeper into the Old Empire.

The reaction from the ships on patrol was immediate. They boosted after the crippled ship at maximum acceleration. He'd expected them to open fire at once, but they seemed content to chase her for the first few moments. At this short range, they could fire at any time and hit her. Eight destroyers would overwhelm the battlecruiser's screens on the first salvo since she couldn't even operate her antimissile defenses.

As soon as the destroyers turned away from the station and the two hidden attackers, Jared spoke again. "Raise battle screens and open fire on the scanner arrays with beams. Missiles on standby."

Intense beams of energy lanced out from the superdreadnought and smashed into Boxer Station. It immediately opened fire on them, beams and missiles. The AI on board had been just as ready as the destroyers. He hadn't expected it to return fire so quickly.

The missiles smashed into the superdreadnought even as it moved to evade them. At this range, antimissile defenses were almost useless. The ship rocked, and the power fluctuated.

"Screens down," Zia said tersely. "*Courageous* is firing. Damage all over the side of *Invincible* facing the station. Rolling the ship. Combat effectiveness down to sixty percent. We lost about a third of our missile tubes and beams. We missed some of the scanners on the base. Retargeting."

The battle screens on the station snapped up just as Zia fired again. Her beams bounced off them, but the missiles she'd fired took them down. Barely.

The second salvo from Boxer Station jarred the superdreadnought so heavily that the impacts would have thrown Jared from his chair without the restraints. Power went out, and the flag bridge plunged into darkness.

"Negative control!" Zia shouted. "I have no control of the ship!"

The AI spoke through Jared's implants. *Bridge also offline. I'm assuming control of the ship. Firing beam weapons at the remaining scanner platforms.*

Jared was so shocked that his jaw dropped. AIs couldn't control weapons. Yet that was what was happening. He watched through his implants as the superdreadnought lashed the station with beams.

It only belatedly occurred to him that if he could access the scanners through his implants and hear the AI, he could control the weapons. He made ready to do so, if required, but left the AI in control.

"*Invincible* has positive control of the ship and weapons," Jared said. "Relocate to operations."

Unfortunately, the lift was offline. They weren't going anywhere.

All scanner platforms destroyed. Boxer Station is still firing beams, but they missed us. Courageous *is now firing on the destroyers. I am joining her. Combat effectiveness down to thirty percent.*

"Focus on four ships and open fire." He expanded his internal awareness of the scanner readings and saw that the enemy had also heavily damaged *Courageous*.

The destroyers peeled away from *Scott Pond* and opened fire on *Invincible*. This time, the superdreadnought had enough range to use her antimissile defenses.

The short-range missile duel was brutal. Thank God the superdreadnought could absorb damage that would kill a battlecruiser.

The first exchange took out three of the destroyers and crippled a fourth. It also dropped *Invincible* to twenty percent combat effectiveness. *Courageous* was also operating way below normal, but she killed two destroyers.

The second exchange eliminated all the destroyers. Which was, of course, when four more disengaged from the station and came after them.

"Execute phase three," Jared said. "Send the signal, *Invincible*."

New York and *Ginnie Dare* opened fire from hiding in the cloud of dead ships surrounding the station. Their missiles were no match for the Rebel Empire destroyers, but they came out of nowhere, striking two of the destroyers before they could even raise battle screens. Those two promptly exploded.

Courageous was in better shape and turned to help her sisters before *Invincible* could move. The battlecruiser engaged the last two destroyers while *New York* and *Ginnie Dare* went totally defensive. The fight was vicious and short. After one exchange, the two enemy destroyers were gone.

The destroyers in his task force were moderately damaged in the exchange of fire but operational and fully combat capable. *Courageous* seemed to be in as bad a shape as *Invincible*. His estimation of the enemy response had been a few orders of magnitude short of reality. His plan had almost failed.

Boxer Station was still firing beam weapons, but they were far enough off target that he wasn't worried about them. Without scanners, the enemy wouldn't be able to hit them at all. The same was not true of the seven destroyers heading back toward them from Harrison's World.

Invincible, *are there any ships left attached to that station at all?*

"Bridge communications restored. With active scanners online, I can tell all the docks are now empty except for the large vessel used to move ships."

"What is our condition? Engines, weapons, and defensive systems?"

"Our drives are fully operational. Screens are down, but damage control is working on them. The engineer might have a more accurate timeframe for availability, but I estimate half an hour for two-thirds power. Weapons are almost all offline due to battle damage. I am unable to estimate repair times."

Jared considered their tactical options. "Set course for the flip point leading deeper into the Old Empire at full speed. Signal *Courageous* to join us. The destroyers can keep a watch on the station while hiding in the Fleet graveyard. Put me through to Commander Baxter."

"Baxter. Go ahead, Captain."

"How long will it take to restore control of the ship to the bridge or flag bridge?"

"The main bridge is gone. We took a couple of direct hits in that area of the ship. We have a team in operations, and they'll have *Invincible* back under control in a few minutes. Mostly people from my staff, so don't count on any fancy shooting. The flag bridge power and control runs will take longer to get fully back online. The lift is cut a few decks away from you, but I should have you out in twenty minutes."

"Do what you can. Keep me in the loop for any major challenges. Mertz out."

Zia turned to face him. She had a handheld communicator to her ear. "My people say we've lost twenty of our twenty-four missile tubes. We might be able to bring four back online with a few hours' work. That's not enough to handle seven enemy destroyers."

He considered his options. "What is the enemy doing?"

"They've changed course as a group and are heading for the flip point leading to the Rebel Empire. We'll beat them, but not by much. It'll be one hell of a fight, but I can't say I'm feeling good about it. *Courageous* has significant damage. She's lost ten out of twelve tubes. Let's say she can get two or three of them back online. Seven destroyers are probably going to be a tough nut for the two of us together."

"Then we better be on our game. Work it as best you can. I want as much of our combat capability restored as possible. If nothing else, we leave what's left of the enemy in bad enough condition that the destroyers have a chance."

* * *

IT ENDED up taking an hour to pry his people out of the flag bridge. He spent the time coordinating repairs and talking with Graves over on *Courageous* about possible tactical plans. None of them seemed very promising.

When the lift doors finally opened, he sent Zia with the remaining bridge officers to take over operations. A call from Doctor Cartwright diverted him to the main cargo bay.

He found the scientists scrambling around one of the devices. The combat had torn all three loose from their pallets and dumped them against one of the bulkheads. They all showed varying degrees of damage.

"I'm a little pressed for time, Doctor," he said.

The older man broke away from his fellows. "Captain. I'm certain you are, but I need to give you an update on these devices. We've confirmed that they are almost certainly designed to be some kind of flip point plug."

"That's useful, but they look like they're out of service."

Cartwright nodded. "We're working on getting one of them repaired by salvaging the parts from the others. I believe the damage is mostly cosmetic. Carl is working on unlocking the least damaged device and trying to access the onboard computer. I realize they may not be useful at the moment, but I wanted you to be aware of their purpose. It does indeed look as though they are meant to prevent ships from using a flip point."

Jared took a minute to consider his options. It was possible these might be helpful if he could arrange the circumstances just right. "What happens when one of these is turned on? The flip point becomes unusable? Keep the details brief."

"Any ship attempting to use the flip point would almost certainly be destroyed."

"How long would the flip point be closed after the machine is turned back off?"

The scientist shrugged. "We don't know. Perhaps it would be

immediately traversable. Or the wormhole might take hours or days to stabilize. Perhaps longer. We won't know without experimenting."

That didn't sound healthy to Jared. "Experimenting how?"

"Sending probes through. If they don't make it, the wormhole is still closed."

"And if they do?"

"Then a ship should be able to survive the transition. The probes would be much more sensitive to damage than a ship."

That wasn't the most appetizing course of action to Jared's thinking. The next system over had been lightly occupied before the Fall, but it might be more heavily seeded now. They had no way of knowing without checking. If they did go, they might find themselves trapped on the other side, unable to assist the two destroyers in any way.

"Get one working. I have complete confidence in you and your people. Position it so we can drop it if we decide to use it. Secure these other two. We might need them later."

"Of course." The scientist returned his complete attention to the strange device.

Jared motioned for Carl to come over. "The AI took control when we lost the connection to the flag bridge. It fired the weapons. Do you know anything about that?"

Carl smiled. "Certainly. This is a warship, so it needed to be able to control the weapons. I removed the prohibition against harming human beings but added language assuring it would not act against the best interests of its crew. Plus it's bound to obey you under all circumstances."

Jared sighed. "I'm not this ship's commanding officer. Even if I were, I'm not immortal. Someday this ship will be in operation without that kind of oversight. That makes it potentially very dangerous."

Owlet sagged a little. "I'm sorry, sir. I thought I was doing the right thing."

He clapped the younger man on the shoulder. "You did. We would've all died if you did anything else. I just wanted to press the point to you that you need to ask us before you make these kinds of changes."

"Should I start setting things up to recreate the AI without those changes?"

Jared shook his head. "No. We'll run with it as is for a while. Go help them get this flip-jamming device working."

"Yes, sir." The boy headed for the other scientists.

It was hard to be angry. Carl Owlet might be a genius, but he was only sixteen. If Jared wanted something done a specific way, he had to remember to say so.

He headed for operations. He had one more battle to plan for. The most important one of his career. If he lost it, his people were certain to die.

32

Breaching Boxer Station went more smoothly than Kelsey had hoped. The cargo bay they entered seemed abandoned. The crates had sagged and fallen over in places, occasionally spilling their contents on the deck.

As soon as the entire team was inside, Reese had them moving toward the cargo lift. They'd use the stairs beside it to get down to the deck they wanted. From there it would be a relatively short trip to the maintenance tubes.

They hadn't made it that far before she felt a slight vibration in the deck. The station had just fired missiles. That was fast. She hoped Jared was one step ahead of the weapons headed his way.

The hatch leading to the stairwell opened without any trouble, and the marines began streaming into it. They made the dozen levels down without running into anyone.

That was when a transmission came over the general channel. "Tiger Three in contact with hostile weapons platforms. The IFF units seem to be working. They are withdrawing ahead of us without firing."

"Thank God for small favors," Reese muttered on the command channel. "With any luck, that's the only resistance we'll encounter."

Kelsey doubted things would be that easy. That proved to be the case moments later when her armor indicated a stunning blast had struck her, almost certainly from the antiboarding weapons on the station. That happened several more times before they stopped. The AI in control of the station had discovered they were immune to the attack.

She had no doubt that it would come up with a different plan shortly.

They made it to their level and entered the maintenance hatch. The cramped ladder took them up to the area between decks. They'd make their way to the main computer center without being in plain sight.

Other teams began reporting that they were under observation by the weapons platforms. Lieutenant Reese had made the decision not to fire on them if they didn't pose a direct threat.

Kelsey searched for implant access to the camera systems, but the computer had her locked out. So much for doing what Jared had done on *Courageous*. They'd just have to go in blind.

"We're at exit point alpha," the lead marine said.

"Go," Reese responded.

The marines went up the ladder and out the hatch, spreading in both directions. Kelsey popped out and headed for the computer center right up the corridor. The hatch was closed, but she'd come prepared with a breaching charge. No need for a plasma rifle this time.

Or for the charge, either. The main hatch opened at her touch, and she slid in with her flechette rifle at the ready. The control center was unoccupied and looked disused.

"Clear." She touched one of the consoles, and it came to life. The computer was offline.

That made no sense. That couldn't be right.

Kelsey called several of the marines to help her and opened the wall hiding the computer. The systems were cold and dark.

"The main computer is offline," she said. "Something else is calling the shots."

Reese stared past her. "The AI is in control of the system. It has to be on this station." He switched to the general channel. "All teams, Tiger Actual. The AI in control of this system is on this station. If you encounter an area that looks suspicious, report it at once."

He turned to Kelsey. "What's our next target, Princess?"

"Let me see if I can access the station's internal scanner network. That might help us get out of here faster."

The console she'd brought online was one of the most secure on the station. The designers had it hardwired into all the critical systems. With a little work, she managed to access the station's internal vid feed.

Kelsey set the screens to a very high rotational speed, so the images were only there just long enough for her implants to register the data. To her eyes, they were moving far too quickly to make any sort of sense.

Moments later, the console blanked. The AI had locked her out. It was too late, though. Her implants had captured some good data. By her guess, she'd seen about two-thirds of the station.

Her implants correlated the data. It wasn't complete, but it told her what she needed to know. "I got it. The mobile weapons platforms are in four areas of the station. I missed seeing a few sections, but it looks like our team and one other isn't under direct threat. I can see why, too. The prisoners are in the main cargo hold."

Reese nodded. "Tiger Four, Tiger Actual. Reroute to the primary cargo hold. Locate our people and secure them."

He switched back to the command channel. "What about the AI? Any idea where it is?"

"The other computer centers all registered as offline. Wherever it is, it's in complete control of this station. I spotted one small group of weapons platforms near fusion plant three. It might be close to that, but I'm grasping at straws."

"Shutting down all the power to the station will stop the damned thing, too. How do you think the captain is doing?"

"Well, there hasn't been any interference from other ships, and I don't feel like there are any missiles being fired. I think that's good news. What's the plan?"

"We go in fast. What's the quickest path to fusion three? And how many fusion plants are there?"

Kelsey consulted her map. "Six. Maybe main engineering would be a better choice. We might be able to shut down all the power if we get there."

"It locked you out of the console. I'm thinking we need to be more direct."

"Go back toward the maintenance hatch, pass it, and take the first stairwell up eight decks. Keep going forward and it's on the right at the next main cross-corridor."

A marine shouted as she was about to exit the computer center. "Hostiles incoming!"

Kelsey jumped into the corridor and saw a man running toward them with a rifle in his hands. She shouldered her way forward as the marines dropped into firing positions. "Hold fire! Hold fire!"

The man's hair was long but moderately well kept. Dressed in a Fleet uniform that had seen better days, he wasn't a savage like the Pale Ones. He was screaming something as he ran.

"I'll kill you! Run, you fools!"

He raised his rifle, but she was faster. Her neural disruptor was in her hand and firing. The blue bolt took him in the center of the chest, and he dropped, his rifle clattering toward them.

"He's sentient," Kelsey said as she made her way to him. "Stun any human opponents if you can."

She knelt beside the man. His rank tabs indicated he was a lieutenant in the engineering department. His uniform was patched but serviceable. He only had the rifle as a weapon. He didn't even have a spare magazine.

"Where there's one, there's more," Reese said. "He'll be out a while. Perez and Kuban, grab the prisoner. We'll take him with us. Keep an eye out for more hostiles."

As soon as he said that, another dozen men and women ran around the same distant corner as the man had used. All of them were screaming warnings of some kind or another. Kelsey imagined that was how the compromised men and women had acted during the rebellion. It chilled her to the bone.

The marines had already swapped their flechette rifles for their neural disruptors. Their concentrated fire took the hostiles out just as they opened fire. A few men took hits, but their armor held.

"Leave them all," Reese commanded. "The AI is more important. All teams, Tiger Actual. There are sentient but controlled human defenders. Stun only for unarmored personnel if possible. Tiger One cover Tiger Four. All other teams prepare for new targets. We have some fusion plants to take offline."

Two groups of armed humans interrupted the trip to fusion plant three. The team took some injuries but stunned them all.

They also ran into some of the weapons platforms, but they were rushing elsewhere. That made her nervous, since none of the teams were in the area the machines were heading toward.

Kelsey signaled Reese. "Lieutenant, continue on to the fusion plant. Shut it down and move on to the next one. I want this station in the dark ASAP. Talbot and I are going to find out what those things are up to."

The marine officer didn't look happy, but he headed off with all but a dozen of the marines. Talbot and the rest followed her as she ran. They trailed the machines to a large open hatch.

The compartment was like the one she'd seen on the destroyer: charging stations everywhere, some already occupied.

"It doesn't seem like they'd need a snack in the middle of an attack," Talbot said as he had his people take up defensive positions.

She agreed. "It might be trying to reprogram them so they can shoot at us. The scientists said they couldn't alter that code, but let's not take chances. Take those things out. Hell, stand back." She brought her plasma rifle off her back and lit up the machines on one side of the compartment just as two of the combat devices that had been there rose from the charging cradles.

Her plasma rifle smashed most of the equipment in the area she'd fired on, but one of the weapons platforms returned fire. It went with flechettes.

The small metal bits spun her in place and knocked her down. Her armor screamed about a breach in her left arm, but she didn't feel any pain.

The marines opened fire on the platform and riddled it with holes. It crashed to the floor, out of action.

Kelsey heaved herself to her feet and unloaded on more of the charging stations with her plasma rifle. "Tiger Actual, Bandar. The AI is reprograming the weapons platforms to fire on us. So much for a hardwired IFF. Engage them with extreme prejudice."

"Copy. We're at the fusion plant. We'll have it shut down shortly."

"We're on our way."

"Negative. Redirect to fusion plant six."

She didn't want to leave them without support, but she saw the logic in his order. They had too few people to perform the rescue and take out the fusion plants. "Copy."

Talbot was looking at her left arm as the team made sure the weapons platforms were out of action. "This looks compromised. Are you hurt?"

The flechette had torn the outer armor along her upper arm. The impact had peeled the metal away, exposing her flesh—her thankfully undamaged flesh.

"It didn't even break the skin, but the arm is unprotected now."

Talbot gestured to the marines. "Come on, boys and girls. You heard the LT. We need to take out the next power plant in line. Kelsey, stay behind us."

The marines saw several more weapons platforms on the way to the fusion plant, but none of them opened fire. The fusion plant control room was almost as big as main engineering on *Athena* had been and just as complex.

The fusion plant was out in the open, just like the drives were on a ship. Now that they were there, she realized she didn't have any idea how to shut the damned thing down.

Kelsey opened a channel to Reese. "How do we shut them off?"

He didn't respond for a moment. "Hang on."

The general channel came to life. "All teams, Tiger Actual. The fusion plants have a manual shutdown to the rear in a locked panel. You can't miss the big red—" He went off the air abruptly.

"Reese? Reese!" He didn't respond. She hoped that only meant something had disabled his communications.

Kelsey ran around the back of the power plant and saw the locked panel. She ripped the cover off and pressed the big red button. The lighting dimmed a little and the plant shut off.

"Fusion plant six offline," she said on the general channel. "Tiger Actual, status?"

"Tiger Actual is down," an unfamiliar voice said. "We are heavily engaged."

She headed for the hatch. "All Tiger teams, this is Bandar. Shut down the power systems and hold position. We are moving to assist the LT. Tiger Four, what is the status of the prisoners?"

"We have them. Estimate three to four hundred souls. Holding tight for evac."

Dammit. The rest had to be on the planet. "Copy. Other teams, status on shutting down the power supply to the station?"

The other teams called in one by one. Fusion plants one through four were offline, and she'd hit the button on six. That only left plant five. She consulted her internal map. It was on her side of the station. She had to make the hard decision.

"Tiger Two, leave a squad to cover your plant and relieve Tiger Actual. Bandar is diverting to fusion five."

"Copy."

Talbot redirected the team without her direction. They made it almost all the way before running into heavy resistance. Humans and weapons platforms held the corridor and almost shot them down before they pulled back.

"Breaking through is going to be a bitch," Talbot said. "We don't have enough people. We need reinforcements."

"Maybe there's another way." She consulted her map. "Nope. This is pretty much it."

Then she noticed they were not so far away from a personnel lock. A quick search found one just past the fusion plant, too. She could travel outside the station.

"I have a plan. I can make it out a lock and get behind them."

He shook his head. "Your armor is breeched. I'll send a couple of men."

"They don't have thrusters. We left those on the hull when we arrived. I still have my grav assist. I can be there in a minute. It would take you half an hour. Our people don't have that long. Hold position here."

He started cussing, which she took to mean he couldn't argue with her plan.

Kelsey sprinted to the lock and cycled herself out. She expected the cold to burn the exposed portion of her arm, but it didn't feel any different. Perhaps the lore about freezing in space wasn't exactly right. Her armor isolated her helmet, and she could breathe. Her skinsuit would protect her body for a short while from the ravages of the vacuum.

It took her a moment to orient herself and spot the other lock with her enhanced vision. There was a massive gash in the hull of the station. It might even mean that the plant wasn't reachable inside the station.

She launched herself into space and kicked her drive on. It sent her soaring across the gap and to the other lock in less than ninety seconds. The lock allowed her in, thankfully.

Flechettes tore up the bulkhead beside her as soon as she was inside the station. She ducked down and spotted the machines firing at her. She opted for discretion and fired the plasma rifle. It cleared the corridor of machines. And bulkheads, floors, and ceilings. She vaulted the chasm with her grav assist and rolled into the fusion control room.

A number of controlled humans opened fire on her as soon as she appeared, ripping into her armor before she threw herself to the side. No one was happy about the situation judging from the way they yelled for her to get out while she could.

Kelsey sprang to her feet and jumped forward with all her might, landing in the midst of a group of defenders. They had no chance to stop her as she sent them tumbling like toys. She reached the emergency shutoff and killed the plant. The overhead lights went out, and emergency lighting replaced them.

"Fusion five offline," she said on the general channel as she dove for cover and began stunning the hostile humans. "Status?"

The weapons platforms were still fighting, but the marines were holding out. The only humans in evidence were the ones she was holding off with her neural disruptor. They shot up the fusion plant pretty badly before she took the last of them out.

Her armor was shot. Literally and figuratively. She stayed where she was and waited for Talbot. He finally arrived a few minutes later and rushed to her side.

"Are you hit?"

"Yes, but nothing I can't handle. The machines are still fighting. We need to find the AI and take it out."

"The rest of our team is working on finding it. I hope it's where you saw the machines near fusion three. Come on."

She let him help her walk. Her left leg was locking at the knee—thankfully due to the armor, not any real injury. She only had one puncture, and that was to the calf on her other leg. Her nanites were working it and the blood loss was minimal, but it made walking a bitch.

"How's Reese?"

Talbot gave her a look and shook his head. "Plasma strike. He never saw it coming. I've assumed tactical command. The officers from *New York* and *Ginnie Dare* are down, either dead or wounded. We've lost over half our force."

The news was like a punch in the gut. He couldn't be gone just like that, between one word and the next. She shook her head. "No, that can't be right."

"I'm sorry. He was a good man and great officer, but he's dead. We'll mourn later, but we still have a mission to complete."

It took them twenty minutes to get to the forces attacking the compartments housing the AI. At least that was what they thought was in there. The combat machines resisting them made it likely.

The other marine teams trickled in to join them, and one by one, the weapons platforms fell. So did the marines.

Kelsey felt like tossing a plasma grenade into the compartment when they finally made it there but resisted. The AI might have important information if they could take it intact and keep it from wiping itself.

She threw a remote in instead. It showed a basic control center with a dozen humans aiming flechette rifles at the hatch. They opened fire as soon as the remote came sailing in, but they missed her hand, thankfully.

There was no wall separating the control room from the AI hardware. It looked pretty much identical to the unit they'd installed on *Invincible*. Which meant that the emergency power supply was… there!

She fixed the location in her mind and crouched.

Talbot grabbed her. "Are you insane? Stop!"

"The emergency power supply is at the back of the room but in sight. I'll get one shot at this. If I miss, the AI might wipe all the data."

"If one of those lunatics opens fire, we lose you. No way."

"It's a risk," she admitted. "I'm going to throw myself across the hatch and take a shot. I'm not going inside. Human reaction time is slow when compared to me on panther. Even my one good leg can get me across." The Old Empire combat drugs sped up her ability to correlate and respond to her surroundings to a degree most people couldn't grasp, even people that had seen her fight before.

Her pharmacology unit had already dispensed it just before the fight in the fusion room. She'd have a relative eternity to fire. The crash when it wore off was going to leave her useless, so she'd better make it count.

She drew her flechette pistol.

"This is madness," Talbot pleaded. "We'll rush the room. You can fire as soon as we distract them."

His concern made her smile. "Then you'd be in my way. Get ready to rush the compartment."

Kelsey took one breath, aimed at the area where she wanted to fire, and threw herself across the hatchway. Her flechette pistol came to bear on the emergency power supply, and she opened fire.

The humans returned fire, but most were late. Not all, unfortunately.

A flechette smashed into her right thigh as she flew through the air. Pain exploded across her senses when it penetrated her armor, and she landed hard. Her leg was on fire. The marines rushed into the compartment firing neural disruptors.

"You happy now?" Talbot asked, obviously peeved and worried.

"The emergency power unit shorted out and the AI crashed. Yeah, I'm happy."

"You're too damned lucky. We still have some live defenders, but I think that situation is under control. Next time, use the grenade."

The other marine teams were reporting that the weapons platforms were settling to the deck. Without direct control, they were shutting down. This fight was almost over.

Once they knocked out the men and women in the AI compartment, she went over the marines' status monitors. Their losses had been horrendous. Of three hundred marines, more than sixty-five percent were dead. Many others were injured. Their force had almost failed to take the station.

Kelsey wanted to shut everything out, but they didn't have time for her to have a meltdown. It would have to wait. "Secure the prisoners," she said. "I want every virus-infected human on this station in restraints before they wake up. Draft some of our freed people to help if they can. Search every inch of this station."

She looked up at Talbot. "This armor is wrecked. Help me out of it so I can go see if Breckenridge is among the prisoners."

"I need to get a bandage on this wound." He motioned for some of the marines to come over. "Let's get her out of this armor."

They stripped her down to her skinsuit, and Talbot tore it away from her wound. He slapped a bandage on and wrapped it tight. "I'd say you need to stay still, but I know that's not happening. Come on, boys. Let's carry her to the main cargo bay."

As humiliating as that was, Kelsey chose not to argue with them. She did insist they strap on her neural disruptor. She wasn't going anywhere unarmed. With a man on either side, they had no problem carrying her. It wasn't as though she weighed very much.

The prisoners had been in the main cargo hold, which was empty of any actual cargo. It would've made this mission much simpler if they'd breached there.

Several weapons platforms had been guarding the prisoners. The marines had taken them out when they burst in. Unfortunately, some of the prisoners had died in the operation or from injuries sustained in their capture.

A casual glance showed that those present seemed to be officers of one kind or another. The marines had one group under close guard. At the center of them stood Captain Breckenridge.

"Put me down," she told the marines carrying her. They didn't argue. She hobbled over to the group.

Breckenridge bristled at her approach. "What is the meaning of this? I gave these marines direct orders, and they refuse to obey me."

"Wallace Breckenridge, I hereby place you under arrest. I'm revoking your command authority. Marines, secure the prisoner."

The officers around him closed ranks, so she glared at them. "He violated his oaths. Do not make the same mistake. Stand down."

One at a time, they reluctantly pulled away from their former commanding officer. He glared at Kelsey. "You're mad! I am a senior Fleet captain! I'll be a commodore next year! You have no authority over me."

She drew her neural disruptor and shot him. He collapsed in a heap. "Secure the prisoner and add resisting arrest to the eventual list of charges."

That had been far more satisfying than she'd imagined. She looked around for Commander Meyer. He wasn't there.

When the crowd parted and Doctor Guzman forced his way through, she asked him, "Where is Commander Meyer?"

"They took him away with the rest. I don't know where. Let me look at that wound."

She shook her head. "I'll live. Look at the others first. We have many wounded marines, some of them serious. Talbot, get the injured back here as soon as possible. The prisoners, too."

Guzman scowled at her. "Where did you get your medical degree, Doctor?" He held his hand to his ear. "What? No medical degree, you say? Well, then, I guess I'll take a look for myself."

She gave in to the inevitable and lay down. The station was

reasonably secure. He'd leave her be when the seriously injured began arriving.

They'd completed their part of the operation. Now she had to hope that Jared had managed the impossible and secured the system.

33

———

W ord came in from *New York* that the station was secure just as *Invincible* reached the flip point. Jared listened to the battle tally grimly in the relatively cramped operations center. Thank God Kelsey had made it, but they'd lost so many irreplaceable people. The number of dead boarders sat at two hundred and thirteen, including Timothy Reese, and that didn't begin to count the people they'd lost on *Courageous* and *Invincible*.

The young lieutenant had been with Jared since he'd accepted command of *Athena*. His death was a tragedy in every way.

Talbot had assumed command of the marine forces, and Kelsey was injured but alive. Now it was his turn to pull off a win for the team.

Baxter had worked miracles in the last few hours. Their battle screens were back up to full strength, and they'd restored six missile tubes to action, giving them ten. News from *Courageous* was a little less upbeat. Battle screens at seventy percent and only two additional tubes restored to service for a total of four.

With exceptional luck, they might be able to take out all the enemy ships before the enemy destroyed them. He couldn't count on that, though. Time to look into plan B.

Since *Scott Pond* couldn't flip and the enemy had ignored the crippled battlecruiser, Jared had sent her back to the station by a roundabout course. With operational grav drives and a functioning computer, the vessel might prove useful. He was glad she'd survived.

Jared opened a channel to the main cargo bay. One of the scientists brought Doctor Cartwright to the communications unit. "Doctor, I need good news."

"We believe we have one unit operational. Carl has hacked the controls, and we should be able to activate it when the time comes."

"The time is here. How long will it take you to deploy that thing?"

"Ten minutes. We need to evacuate the bay and get some men in place to eject it once we bleed off the atmosphere. After we flip, of course."

Jared nodded. "Get ready. We get exactly one chance at this." He cut the channel and opened a line to *Courageous*. Graves appeared on his console. "Charlie."

"Captain. We're not in as good a shape as I wished we were."

"We're not, either. I think we're going to have to sucker them. Wait until they fire and flip just before the missiles arrive. We drop the flip blocker on the other side and back off. If it works, great. If not, we shoot them up when they arrive."

"And if they don't all take the bait?"

"Then we're screwed."

Graves shook his head. "Admiral Yeats is going to ream us. If we live."

"Something to look forward to. Hold fire and flip on my order."

"Aye, sir. *Courageous* out."

Jared watched the enemy fleet close with them on his implant feed. They had a tight formation and looked determined. They wanted to end this fight.

Well, so did he.

The enemy waited until they were well inside effective range to open fire. Twenty-eight missiles shot toward the two Imperial warships at maximum acceleration. Sixty seconds to impact.

Jared waited until the last fifteen to order the flip. The enemy launched a second salvo just as he lost sight of them.

"Flip complete," Zia said. "Main cargo hatch opening."

Jared waited impatiently for the device to drift free before he moved *Invincible* away. *Courageous* had already taken up a position outside the flip point.

Passive scans of the system were coming in. No ships detected.

He launched a dozen probes to search the system just to be sure. Either they'd still be here to get the data, or he'd leave a probe to collect it and flip back to Harrison's World after they left.

The hatch to operations slid aside, and Doctor Cartwright came in with Carl Owlet at his side. He strode up to Jared and halted. "Everything is ready. I suggest you activate it as soon as practical."

"Send the signal, Zia. Narrow beam."

"Aye, sir."

For a moment, nothing happened. Then he picked the device up on the scanners. It was as obvious as a ship flying fast on grav drives. He hoped the system really was empty. They couldn't miss this.

"At the speed the destroyers were running, how long before they flip, Zia?"

"Five minutes, give or take."

Jared turned his attention to the elderly scientist. "How detectable will this be on the other side?"

"Are we seeing anything from the flip point?"

Invincible's scanners didn't show anything overt that he could see. The machine was showing up, but the gravitic field seemed normal. No, no it wasn't. There was some kind of low-level fluctuation. He'd never seen anything like it, but it was subtle.

"Look at this." He brought the reading up on his console.

The scientist looked closely at it and nodded. "Yes. Just about what we expected. Those fluctuations are almost certainly due to resonance inside the wormhole."

"And it will stop any ship from successfully flipping?"

"We believe so."

"Here's to hoping, Doctor."

They waited for the zero on the timer. A few seconds before it hit, Zia called out, "Contacts. Many small contacts. I think it may be debris."

No ship flipped into the area, but quite a bit of junk did. It appeared scattered widely across the flip point. Something had broken up. He hoped seven destroyers had made a failed attempt to transit and been destroyed.

Jared waited twenty minutes and gave Zia the order to shut down the flip blocker. It vanished from the scanners a few moments later. "The device is shut down, Captain. Shall I launch a probe to test the flip point?"

He studied the scanner readings. The fluctuations were still there, though they seemed to be growing weaker. "Give it a few minutes, Zia. Five."

"Aye, sir."

In the end, it was more than an hour before a probe returned intact. It reported no enemy ships on the other side of the flip point.

Jared gave it another half hour, though Doctor Cartwright insisted it should be safe. *Courageous* led the way, and he sighed in relief when a probe came through announcing their safe arrival.

They'd already picked up the flip blocker, so he gave the order to flip the ship. They appeared in the Harrison's World system with a normal amount of nausea. A regular transition.

"Drop the flip resonator in the center of the flip point. After we get our probes back with the data from the other system, we'll turn it on. If anyone else comes visiting, I want them to find the 'not welcome' sign."

"Aye, sir."

"Doctor Cartwright, how long can it stay activated?"

"Your guess is as good as mine."

With his lack of engineering skills, he seriously doubted that. "Get with Commander Baxter and try to make some kind of assessment. Let me know how long it will take to get the other two back online. With two flip points in this system, I'm betting the plan was to have one in reserve to take them out of service for maintenance."

"Of course. Right away."

They set course for Boxer Station, and he called ahead for their status. Captain Kaiser of *New York* appeared on his console. Kelsey stood beside her.

The dark-haired officer nodded to him. "Welcome back, Captain. The seven destroyers flipped after you, so I think we have almost complete control of the system. We've evacuated Boxer Station. *New York* and *Ginnie Dare* are packed to the bulkheads with our rescued people and prisoners from the station."

Kelsey spoke next. She looked exhausted but otherwise in good condition. "It looks like the officers were kept on the station. The AI shipped the enlisted personnel to Harrison's World. We still have some marines sweeping the station to be certain that we got everyone. Breckenridge is in custody, and Commander Meyer was shipped to Harrison's World."

"Excellent work, Kelsey. I'm so sorry to hear about Reese. We're going to miss him. Do we have any idea what the situation is like on the planet?"

Kelsey shook her head. "We moved a probe in close to the planet. The stations fired on it once it got inside their orbit. On a hunch, we sent a second one in but kept it outside their orbit. None of the stations fired on it. Without the system AI around to alter their programming, we might be able to do something to clear the way for us to send small craft down."

"Send one of the probes right up on top of one. See if it objects to being boarded from above."

Captain Kaiser nodded. "Will do. I'll send you a complete update. Shall we head toward Harrison's World?"

He nodded. "Good idea. We'll rendezvous an hour out. If the probe can determine anything about the internal layout on those things, we'll make a plan to do something about them."

"I have some ideas on that," Kelsey said. "Let me think about it some more. I'm taking a pinnace over as soon as we rendezvous. We need to talk."

"That never ends well."

She gave him a tired smile. "I'm sure. Oh, one last thing. *Spear* isn't repairable. Her engineering section is a wreck. Not even Baxter can put it back together. You'll have to absorb her crew onto *Invincible*."

"We have plenty of room and more work than we can handle.

Once we're in position, we can take everyone we need to. See you when you get here. *Invincible* out."

Jared was too busy coordinating repairs to notice Kelsey docking a few hours later. He only realized she'd arrived when she walked through the hatch to operations.

He rose to his feet, and she headed right for him. He started a little when she grabbed him in a hug but held her tight a moment later. It had been one hell of a day.

His sister stepped back after a bit. "There's something we need to discuss in private. Shall we go see if the admiral's office survived?"

He nodded. "Zia, you have the ship. Call me if anything pops up."

"Aye, sir."

The two of them made their way to the admiral's office. It was larger than his on *Courageous* by several orders of magnitude. A suite of offices, really. The admiral's staff surrounded him. It had no personal items, but someone had moved some nice furniture in.

Kelsey sat on the edge of the desk. "I've made a few decisions you won't be happy with, and I wanted to tell you in private so you don't feel ambushed."

"You mean as if you'd brought me to an empty compartment and just dropped it on me with no warning?"

"Should I send a note next time? It's nothing awful, though you might not agree at first blush. Just a little bit of reorganization."

His eyes narrowed. "Why does that set off alarm bells? What kind of reorganization?"

"Did you ever see yourself commanding a ship like this? Or a fleet in combat? Or did you imagine your career would end as soon as Ethan assumed the Throne?"

It was true. He'd resigned himself to reaching captain just before his half brother cashiered him.

Kelsey didn't give him a chance to respond. "You're commanding a fleet in space. A superdreadnought, two battlecruisers, and two destroyers. And you've inherited a Fleet base. We can't have a mere commander running this show."

"So, you think I should be a captain like Breckenridge? I wouldn't fight a field promotion like that."

She shook her head. "Not exactly, and I'm not talking about a field promotion." She pointed her finger toward him. "Poof, you're an admiral."

He blinked in surprise. "Excuse me? No, I'm not. Even as the leader of this mission, you don't have the authority to promote me like that."

"As the direct representative of His Imperial Majesty, I do. The last instructions from Emperor Marcus allow me to act with the emperor's voice. If my father wants to object, he can overrule me when we get home. He won't, I assure you."

Jared started to argue and forced himself to stop and breathe. "I've worked hard to avoid any hint of favoritism. This is wrong."

"No, it's not. I know just how far your career has fallen behind because of people wanting to avoid even the appearance of favoring you. Admiral Yeats told me that you would have been a senior captain in charge of your own task force by now if you'd been anyone else. As far as I'm concerned, I'm making up for lost time. Besides, tell me that a ship like this would be under the command of anything less." Her expression dared him to argue with her.

The moment was surreal. He knew deep inside that she was going somewhere she shouldn't. "If I can't convince you this is a mistake, perhaps I can insert a bit of reason. Perhaps it would make more sense if you made me a commodore or vice admiral instead."

Kelsey jutted out her chin somewhat defiantly. "I appreciate your modesty and restraint, but I'll stick with my original intention. Take command of your fleet, Admiral Mertz. Don't get any ideas about arguing with me later, either. *Invincible*, log my orders promoting Jared Mertz to the rank of admiral and also his assignment to this ship as the commanding officer of this fleet."

"You're taking my ship, too?" That hurt. More than he'd expected it would.

She shook her head. "Don't look at it that way. *Athena* was your ship. You took *Courageous* because the opportunity presented itself. This isn't any different."

After a moment of silence, she continued. "You're going to have to move a lot of people around to get this ship fully manned. There are all the people coming in from *Spear* and *Shadow*. Besides, tell me that Commander Graves doesn't deserve his own command, and a promotion. Actually, don't tell me. I've already made that call. He just doesn't know he's about to become Captain Graves, commanding officer of the Imperial battlecruiser *Courageous*."

She stood and put her hand on Jared's shoulder. "You know we'll probably accumulate more ships to take back with us. And when we deal with the people on this planet, they need to see you for what you are, a senior Fleet officer. Trust me on this." She squeezed his shoulder and headed out the hatch.

He watched her leave with a hollow feeling inside. This wasn't right, but he didn't have any options other than accepting her promotion or resigning his commission. He didn't have the luxury of the latter gesture.

"Congratulations, Admiral," *Invincible* said.

"Admiral in public, Jared in private, please." He rubbed his face. He really was going to catch every kind of hell when he got back home. The sad thing was that he couldn't deny Kelsey's logic.

"*Invincible*, I want you to start compiling the data on those orbiting weapons systems. I'm more than half inclined to blow them out of space, but I'm not sure I want the people on that planet loose. For all we know, they might be ready to come out in force and take the system."

"Aye, sir. I'll have it for you shortly."

Jared left the impressive office—his impressive office—and headed back toward operations. He still had an attack to plan and execute if he wanted to rescue his people.

34

Kelsey's next stop was marine country, where she upended Talbot's world when she made him a major.

Then she called Charlie Graves and promoted him to captain. That was the appropriate rank for a battlecruiser command. She'd have to get him some implants to make *Courageous* happy. He seemed just about as reluctant as Jared had been on getting the news. She suspected he thought she'd be overturned when they made it home.

Kelsey had a lot more people in mind to promote, but that could wait until things settled down. And for when the medical people weren't harassing her. Doctors Stone and Guzman didn't seem to accept that her nanites had her in good shape.

The wound on her leg was healing well enough. They wanted to pop her into the regenerator, but other people would benefit from regeneration far more than she would.

Yes, her wound hurt, but the painkillers in her pharmacology unit kept the pain to acceptable limits.

Talbot knocked on the hatch to her appropriated office in marine country. Someone had gotten him an updated uniform tunic with the correct rank. He looked good.

"Time to armor up," he said. "You sure I can't convince you to sit this one out?"

"I've already promised to let your people take the lead."

"Right up until you decide to do something dangerous. Look, I'm not going to argue about it, but you need to start looking at the big picture. Let us take the risks. If you die, we're screwed. And I'd miss you."

Kelsey shook her head. "As long as you remember you're the marine CO, I'll stay where you are. Let's go see if my armor is ready." At this rate, it wouldn't take long before it was as scarred as that of the woman from the emperor's vid.

They really didn't have any idea how heavily defended the orbital weapons platforms were. They didn't fire on the probes that stayed above them, but they might have internal defenses that were not so picky.

Even if they managed to get the orbitals under control without too much trouble, they still had to rescue the people trapped on the planet. A planet run by Rebel Empire humans that she really didn't understand yet.

She hoped they could keep the orbitals intact. Their damaged ships would eventually leave, though they had already decided to leave some people at the station. These people wouldn't be able to stop an organized expansion by a planet full of technologically capable people.

Of course, the idea of keeping them pinned down with the threat of destruction from orbit made her stomach churn. Perhaps that wouldn't prove necessary. She wouldn't know until she learned more.

They armored up and boarded the pinnaces. They'd take one of the stations as a group. They really didn't have enough marines to try for all three at the same time.

The approach was as nerve-wracking as she'd imagined. There were docks on the topside, so they entered that way with weapons ready.

To find no resistance whatsoever. No people, no weapons platforms. Nothing. The computer on the station was in complete control. It didn't even have life support turned on. No gravity, no heating, and no atmosphere.

Carl Owlet hacked into the computer. Once he had access, adding their ships' IFF codes to the approved list proved trivial.

They visited each of the other orbitals and found the same situation. By the time they had complete control of the orbital space around Harrison's World, she was beat. So were the marines. The island the destroyers had taken the prisoners to was in darkness, so she ordered an early-morning assault. There might be Rebel Empire humans down there. Visibility would help, and a few hours wouldn't make a difference at this point.

* * *

THE SHIPS MOVED into position as soon as the sun was over the horizon at the island. The pinnaces dropped as they had on Erorsi, as though they expected to take fire.

Which turned out to be prudent. Half a dozen weapons emplacements on the island opened fire during the last leg of their drop, blowing two pinnaces out of the sky. The remaining pinnaces took the weapons out, but that meant more dead marines. Taking this system was by far the bloodiest horror Kelsey had ever witnessed.

Talbot had insisted she wait for the second wave, so she landed without incident. He was directing his people to set up a perimeter. There were a bunch of buildings in the facility, but no sign of humans. No mobile weapons, either.

Marines set up portable weapons to cover the island in case the locals decided to attack. They only intended to get their people and withdraw, but they had to be secure while they did it.

There were signs the base personnel had left in a hurry but quite some time ago. No bodies, thank God. Just a big mess. A cursory sweep of the nearby buildings turned up no sign of their people.

"Kelsey, we have visitors," Talbot told her over the command channel. "There's a boat approaching the dock nearest the landing field."

"On my way." She headed back at a run and arrived just as the boat docked. It looked big enough to hold a lot of people or cargo. A number of people came down a portable walkway, a few of them dressed markedly better than the rest, similar to what Kelsey had seen in the pictures the captain of the Rebel Empire destroyer kept on her walls. Rebel Empire nobility.

Here she was dressed for battle, not diplomacy. Maybe gunboat diplomacy.

The marines spread out and covered the people as they walked down the dock. Kelsey made the call to show no fear. If these people wanted trouble, she'd give it to them.

"Talbot, you're with me. I want a few marines behind us, but not too many. We're not afraid of these people."

"Right."

She took her helmet off and shook out her hair. She really ought to cut it back if she was going to wear a helmet this often.

The people from the boat stopped at the halfway mark, and a woman in noble garb kept walking. Kelsey stopped Talbot with a gesture and went to meet her.

The woman had dark, wavy hair pulled back into a tie. Her dress was of silk or some similar fabric. She eyed Kelsey's armor with an expression of disdain.

"I will speak with your senior officer."

Kelsey considered explaining her Imperial heritage but decided that might get a hostile reception. It would be best if they thought Kelsey and her people came from the Rebel Empire for as long as possible. "My name is Kelsey Bandar, and these men are under my command. I've come to recover our people. The AI–controlled ships brought them here a short while ago. If you know where they are, it would behoove you to tell me."

"They were taken off this island at the AI's command, under threat of retaliation. If you want to get them back, I demand to speak with your senior officer. I will return to my ship to await his or her presence."

The woman turned on her heel and swept back to the ship. Her people fell in behind her.

Kelsey returned to Talbot. "Well, that could have gone better. It might save time and effort to have Jared come down and deal with her."

"That should give us time to complete our search of the facility. It seems like our people aren't here. She might be telling the truth about having them."

"Then she'd better get used to the idea of handing them over," Kelsey said grimly.

Kelsey put in a call to Jared. His image appeared in her mind's eye. He was back on the flag bridge. They must've restored its control systems. She gave him a summary of her encounter and decision not to declare themselves the true Terran Empire.

"That's probably for the best. You can't unsay something like that. She can talk to me from here. Have Talbot send her a communications unit."

"I'll take it myself." She returned to her pinnace, grabbed a tablet off the rack, and headed back to the dock. Her armor would be close enough to the pinnace to act as a link, and she wanted to be there when the two of them spoke.

A group of muscular men met her on the dock. She stopped short of them and displayed the tablet. "I have our commanding officer on the line. He's prepared to speak with your leader."

They had a brief discussion, and one of them went to get the woman. She looked displeased at having Kelsey summon her.

"The communications device could have come to me on my ship."

"My armor is acting as a relay. I prefer to stay on the dock. Who are you?"

The woman sniffed. "That is between me and your commanding officer."

Kelsey smiled. "I see. Well, let's get this going, then."

She initiated a vid call to *Invincible*. Jared appeared on the display. The view was set widely enough that Kelsey could see every station was manned. Hardly necessary, but he probably wanted to make an impression.

The woman took the tablet when Kelsey handed it to her. She stared into the vid with a condescending expression. "Who am I addressing?"

Jared frowned and leaned forward. "The man with a fleet in orbit around your planet."

The two of them stared at one another for a moment before the woman backed down. "I am Deputy Coordinator Abigail King. I am authorized to speak on behalf of Coordinator Olivia West. We've taken possession of your crewmen and wish to discuss their repatriation and other matters of state, Admiral…"

"Admiral Jared Mertz. I've taken control of this system and your orbital space. I'm willing to discuss whatever you like, but not while you have my personnel held hostage."

"Then we're at an impasse. You will not locate your people without our cooperation. I will allow you a day to consider how to respond." She handed the tablet to Kelsey and swept back onto the ship with her people.

"Back up," Talbot shouted.

Kelsey fell back as the marines assumed a defensive posture. The ship pulled away from the dock with no hostile actions.

She shook her head as she watched it head toward the harbor entrance. "How the hell do we get our people back now?"

Talbot shrugged. "The hard way. Diplomacy. I hope you can talk them down, because I'm not looking forward to taking on a whole planet with a hundred men."

She nodded. What should've been the easiest part of this mission had just become the hardest. She could bet, based on the woman's reaction, that it wouldn't get any easier from here. This was going to take a lot of work and more time than she'd imagined.

"Secure this facility and get more weapons down from the ship," she finally said. "I want a bridgehead on this planet that they can't take away from us. From this moment on, this island is the embassy of the Terran Empire. Bring everything you need for a long stay. We'll be here a while."

* * *

WANT to get updates from Terry about new books and other general nonsense going on in his life? He promises there will be cats. Go to TerryMixon.com/Mailing-List and sign up.

DID YOU ENJOY THIS BOOK? Please leave a review on Amazon. It only takes a minute to dash off a few words and that kind of thing helps Terry make a living as a writer and gets you new books faster.

WANT the next book in this series? Grab *Ghosts of Empire* today or buy any of Terry's other books, which are listed on the next page.

VISIT TERRY's Patreon page to find out how to get cool rewards and an early look at what he's working on at Patreon.com/TerryMixon.

ALSO BY TERRY MIXON

You can always find the most up to date listing of Terry's titles on his Amazon Author Page.

Note: the links below (ebook only, obviously) redirect you to my website where you can click a button to go to Amazon. This allows me to participate in Amazon's associates program and earn a little more. Sorry for any inconvenience.

The Last Hunter

The Last Hunter

Bonds of Blood

Alpha Strike

The Enemy Revealed

Command Authority

The Grand Conspiracy

Shield of Humanity

Fog of War

Ships of the Line

Operation Liberty

The Empire of Bones Saga

Empire of Bones

Veil of Shadows

Command Decisions

Ghosts of Empire

Paying the Price

Recon in Force

Behind Enemy Lines

The Terra Gambit

Hidden Enemies

Race to Terra

Ruined Terra

Victory on Terra

When Luck Runs Out

Gunboat Diplomacy

The Imperial Marines Saga

Spoils of War

Imperial Recruit

Enemy Action

The Humanity Unlimited Saga

Liberty Station

Freedom Express

Tree of Liberty

Blood of Patriots

Single Novels

Scorched Earth

Storm Divers

The Vigilante Series with Glynn Stewart

Heart of Vengeance

Oath of Vengeance

Bound By Law

Bound By Honor

Bound By Blood

Box Sets

The Empire of Bones Saga Volume 1

The Empire of Bones Saga Volume 2

The Empire of Bones Saga Volume 3

The Empire of Bones Saga Volume 4

Humanity Unlimited Publisher's Pack 1

Humanity Unlimited Publisher's Pack 2

ABOUT TERRY

#1 Bestselling Military Science Fiction author Terry Mixon served as a non-commissioned officer in the United States Army 101st Airborne Division. He later worked alongside the flight controllers in the Mission Control Center at the NASA Johnson Space Center supporting the Space Shuttle, the International Space Station, and other human spaceflight projects.

He now writes full time while living in Texas with his lovely wife and a pounce of cats.

TerryMixon.com

a amazon.com/author/terrymixon

f facebook.com/TerryLMixon

|● patreon.com/TerryMixon

BB bookbub.com/authors/terry-mixon

g goodreads.com/TerryMixon